# Studious

## LESLIE MCADAM

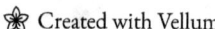

## About this book

After a disastrous high school game of spin the bottle, I gave up trying to get a boyfriend and spent my time studying instead. Now I'm twenty-four, and I'm not only a virgin, I haven't even been kissed.

When I meet Danny, a handsome legal hotshot, he catches my eye. Right before I trip on flat ground. *Ugh.*

He's got a massive ... reputation. He's the most popular guy in the club, a total playboy with a new conquest every night. There's no way he'd be interested in me.

But one night after I imbibe too much, he winds up taking care of me. And when I ask for his help with my travesty of a social life, he agrees to teach me how to be less awkward with men ... if I let him document my progress so he can win a bet with his best friend.

Even though he's just my love tutor and I'm just his apprentice, this starts to feel like more.

Too bad it can't be anything but a high-level seminar in how to seduce someone else.

*Studious is a sweet and sexy contemporary opposites-attract m/m romance about a suave attorney who's scared to love and the shy, nerdy bookkeeper he's teaching how to be a player. Cue makeover montage and a smoldering first kiss. These heroes most definitely are not falling in love. (Okay, heartwarming HEA guaranteed.)*

# Author's note

Alden's mother has cancer and makes a full recovery, with a good prognosis throughout the book. My mother-in-law was not so lucky. Please indulge me in this fantasy of a happy ever after and know that his mom is written in loving memory of Kay McAdam (1941–2022).

## Prologue—Alden

I exit Mason's mom's royal blue BMW X3 and stand on the sidewalk outside the large Mid-Wilshire home, trying to hide my shaking hands.

I can do this.

"I can't do this," I whisper into Mason's ear as I eye the mass of chattering kids sipping Cokes and loitering on the front porch. It's early October. Hip-hop music blares through the open door, and I wince at the sound of raucous laughter as if it's directed at me—even though I know it's likely not. Old habits die hard.

He slaps me on the shoulder. "Yes, you can. It'll be fun!" He shuts the car door behind me and waves at his mom, who drives off. While I've never thought of Mrs. Gray as anything other than warm and welcoming, as I watch her taillights head down the pretty, tree-lined street, I'm feeling rather abandoned, and my urge to run after her zooms to stratospheric levels.

I shouldn't have let Mason talk me into coming to the party today. He's my polar opposite and has no problem making friends. I have no idea why he latched on to me way back when we were eight, but he did. Basically, I'm friends with no one but him. I don't mean just at this party, I mean in real life.

It's fine. I don't want any other friends. Okay, maybe I do, but I've never felt comfortable around people I don't know. I always clam up or say the wrong thing.

And my loneliness is more acute now that we're in a new school. While a few kids went to the same private middle school as us, for the most part they're strangers—although I recognize some of the honors kids.

"This is going to be awful," I mutter. I have trouble peopling under the best of circumstances. Taking me out of my comfort zone is a recipe for absolute disaster. "No one's going to want to talk to me, and I barely know anyone. I don't belong here."

"Kayla invited everyone," he says.

"I bet she didn't mean me. I should just leave. I'll call my mom and have her pick me up."

Mason grabs me by the scruff of the neck and pushes me toward the house.

"Ow," I complain, although he wasn't that rough. Not really.

"All you need is confidence. Which you'll never get if you don't put yourself out there. It's not like you've never been to a birthday party. I went to yours last month."

"You were the only guest besides my grandparents," I huff. "And middle school wasn't like this," I say, gesturing at two kids making out by the hibiscus bush. Where are Kayla's parents? Maybe they don't care. I know it's not cool, but I'm not ready for a wild party. I'd have enough trouble with a normal one.

I'm used to the people in my grade being older than me, because I started kindergarten early, but I feel really young at times like this. Kind of like when the girls started wearing bras and makeup and the guys started growing facial hair. Meanwhile, I stayed ... me. Younger than everyone else, and small for my age on top of that.

"You're building it up in your mind. Come be social."

"What if I don't want to do anything social? What if my goal in life is to be Supreme Hermit of the World?"

He grins. "You said that in capitals, didn't you? You, my friend, are shy and introverted, but not a hermit. I wouldn't be forcing you if I didn't think it was a good idea. Stay for this party, and I won't make you go to any more."

His words make hope bloom in my chest. "You mean that?"

Mason nods. "Yeah. Unless you end up actually liking it, or there's some really good reason for a different party—like, oh, it's mine—I won't make you go to any other party with me. Even if I'd want you to."

My best friend is braver than I am. He's more ... *everything* than I am. But he's right. I should figure out how to be more social.

"I know this is hard for you, but chances are you'll like *someone*." His voice takes on a gently teasing tone. "I bet Sean is here." Sean's my crush.

I shove Mason. *What's good for the goose ...* "I bet Ben is here, if Kayla invited *everyone*." Mason's ears pink, but it's just for a moment. Ben's *his* crush.

"Come on!" He grabs my hand and strides confidently toward the house.

Mason is bi, but he's not my boyfriend or anything. We don't like each other that way. His hand feels like friendly comfort.

Guess there's no turning back now. I take a deep breath and follow Mason up the walk into the party, squeezing past groups of chattering kids everywhere. Leaning against the porch columns, sitting on furniture, standing on the lawn. Mason drops my hand and greets a girl in a crop top and high-waisted shorts, giving her a hug. After they say hi, he excuses himself quickly, gesturing to me, and we make our way to the heart of the throbbing party.

When we get inside the modern mansion, it's worse. Since Kayla invited the entire ninth-grade class, it's like we're in the crowded, locker-lined hallways of our private high school, but there are no uniforms to equalize us. I stare down at my T-shirt of a cat with laser eyes riding a llama unicorn. I'd thought it was funny, but now I'm scared that I'm completely out of place, given how many trendy outfits and school sports jerseys I'm seeing. I don't see anyone wearing intentionally geeky or ironic clothes. Oh well.

"Want something to drink?" Mason asks.

I shrug. "Okay."

No one's drinking alcohol or anything like that, but the whole vibe feels more grown up than I'm comfortable with, given the couples making out and not an adult to be seen. Oh, wait. It looks like maybe Kayla's parents are kicking back in a TV room off to the side while the party goes on around them. Their presence makes me feel a little better that this isn't going to get too out of control. I relax slightly.

We walk into the large, open kitchen where there's sodas and pizza and bowls of chips and snacks. On a side table sits a big sheet cake, too, from a nice bakery. Mason looks at it longingly. "Valley Bakery! I love that place. I'd like to work there someday."

"Don't you want to own your own place?" I ask.

He waves at someone across the room. "Have to start somewhere. And you? What do you wanna do after high school?"

"Maybe something with math." I understand math. There's a right answer every time. I don't have to guess or interpret anything.

"Figures. I could've guessed that. C'mon." Mason tugs me to a bar where soda bottles, cups, and ice are set up so we can make our own Italian sodas. I let him make me a vanilla cream soda, and we wind through the party, him waving at a few kids we know. But they're overshadowed by the ones I don't know. The kind who never speak to me.

"What do I do?" I whisper. "At a party, I mean."

"You talk to people." Seeing the panic on my face, he says, "Or you listen to other people talk. I don't know if they're going to play any games." He cranes his neck. "Hmm."

"I just walk up to someone I barely know and say ... what? 'How'd you do on that Spanish test?' Like any of these people

4

care." I set down my drink and rub my hands over my face. "I'm sorry. I'm a disaster. A disaster gay. That's me."

"Your issues have nothing to do with you being gay. Everyone's cool with it. Find some guy to talk to. Or whoever. Just have fun."

"Have fun," I huff. "I'd have more fun playing *Angry Birds*."

"Okay, grouch." He gives me an exaggerated pout. "Let's go outside by the pool. You'll feel better with some fresh air and more space."

I nod and follow. Even though he's pushing me, he's taking care of me, and I appreciate it. I know he'll always have my back.

We skirt a group of kids who often say mean things in class and go to the large backyard. I feel like I escaped a firing line.

Here, I guess it's better. I'm not stepping over anyone's feet, but I also don't see any friendly smiles. Everything in me wants to turn around and leave and never come back. But Mason's right. I should at least try to be a normal, social human being. I smile at the closest kid, and I get a smile back. Baby steps.

It's a sunny, clear Southern California day, but there's a cool breeze so no one's swimming. The guy I think is cute, Sean Moses, is standing in a group off to the side, one hand behind his back, laughing at something another kid said. Mason and I are headed to an area with unoccupied chairs when we hear a loud voice.

"Everyone, gather round!" The birthday girl, Kayla, is standing on a low patio table, waving at everyone. "Time for some fun!"

"What are we doing?" a popular girl named Sofia asks, chewing gum and looking up from her phone.

"Spin the bottle."

Sofia grins, and a few other kids look smug, but my stomach clenches. I've heard it's some kind of kissing game, but I don't know the rules and I don't know how to play and I don't—

"It's going to be okay," Mason assures me, sensing my distress. "All that happens is you spin the bottle and kiss whoever the bottle points to."

"B-but it would be my first kiss." I glance around in a panic. "I don't know if I want anyone here to be my first kiss."

"You're making it out to be too big a deal," he says coolly. He's kissed two girls and one guy, so he's got way more experience than me.

I take a deep breath, but dread is still tightening my throat. I look for an exit. Maybe I should call my mom after all.

But then Sean sidles up and asks, "What's going on?"

"Spin the bottle. You in?" Kayla murmurs.

He gives her his popular-boy smile. "Sure."

Mason elbows me meaningfully.

I whisper, "But how would I even know if it would land on him? What if it lands on someone I don't want to kiss?"

"You don't have to kiss them on the lips. You can just kiss their cheek or whatever."

"If I do that, will people think I'm a wuss?"

He glances around. "Maybe."

I follow his gaze and silently inventory who wouldn't be too judgy. I see no one. I'm not sure I'd choose to hang out with anyone here except for Mason. When you go to school with kids whose parents are in the industry, it can be a drag. Everyone's trying to one-up each other—who they know, what movies they've been in, how much money they have to blow on clothes or whatever. I have no interest in any of that. My idea of fun is bingeing the latest cult sci-fi show or going to a Dodger game—or maybe watching a car race. Otherwise, let me at some algebra.

I do want to be kissed, though. Or more than kissed. I just always wanted my first to be special. Maybe I'm a romantic at heart.

And maybe I need to get over it.

"Fine," I huff. "I'll do this. Can I at least watch a round first?"

He nods. "I think you can skip your turn, too."

The patio furniture is shoved aside, and everyone moves so we're sitting on the concrete next to the pool in a tight, lopsided oval. I end up sitting crisscross between Mason and a girl in my history class. A few kids ignore the game and sit on the coping, dipping their bare feet in the water. I'm tempted to join them.

Kayla hops down off the table and produces a Diet Dr Pepper bottle—the twenty-ounce plastic kind, still full—and spins it around on the concrete, everyone whooping and cheering, which grates on my nerves. The bottle turns just fine, but it seems like she really had to twist it to get it going. I'm also concerned it's going to explode.

The cap lands so it's pointing at Mason, who squeaks but hides it by thumping his chest a few times. Kayla saunters toward him. He stands up and steps between the girls in front of us, entering the circle. He glances around at everyone watching him, tilts his chin up, and lets Kayla smack a quick kiss kind of near his lips. Everyone whoops.

"Your turn," she says, tapping a finger on Mason's chest. "But this bottle sucks. Someone have an empty one?"

A kid guzzles down the last of a Sprite and hands the bottle to Mason. He grins and spins the bottle. With no liquid inside, it goes and goes and goes—and it eventually lands on Ben, who stands up faster than Mason did for Kayla.

Now I'm starting to see why people play this game. It's an excuse to get experience. I calm down a little.

Mason bounds over and kisses him, and it's not quite the quick peck Kayla dropped on him. There are louder hoots and hollers than there were with Kayla's kiss.

When they're done, Kayla says, "Okay, Ben. Your turn."

After a lingering look at Mason, Ben spins the bottle, and the game continues to play out, the bottle never pointing at me. So now I'm getting worried that I'm never going to get to participate in a game I didn't want to play to begin with.

When it's Sofia's turn, the bottle lands on another girl. I'm pretty sure both of them are straight, but they do a quick peck without hesitating. For Hollywood types, kissing's no big deal.

It's a big deal to me.

I start to zone out, wondering if I should text my mom to come get me.

Then all of a sudden the crowd quiets. The bottle's pointing at Sean. A girl kisses him, and I can't help the tightness in my chest. I wish it were me doing that. Oh well. It's not my day.

Who's the bottle going to choose for him? I hold my breath, watching the spinning green plastic until the bottle stops and it's ...

Pointing at me. I blink.

"M-me?" I stutter, looking frantically at Mason. For help.

Is this really happening?

"I guess it's your turn," Sean says in a low voice. He glances at his friends, who are howling with laughter. He picks himself up from where he was crouching by the bottle and saunters over to me.

My heart speeds up. Am I going to kiss him? Is he going to kiss me? Am I going to get my first kiss right now, in front of half my class? From my crush?

I uncross my legs and go to stand up, but in trying to avoid bumping into anyone, I stumble two steps back. Except there's nothing behind me but a swimming pool.

Windmilling my arms wildly, I try to straighten up, but it's no use.

Everything happens in slow motion. Mason's expression morphs to horror, and he lunges for me, yelling, "Alden!"—but he misses my hand.

I fall backward, ass over teakettle, into the pool, making an awful splash.

The cool salt water is a shock to my senses, and my shoes and clothes weigh me down. There are shouts and laughter and concern as hands reach out to help me out of the pool. I ignore them, trying to shove myself up with both arms on the pool edge, except I'm not really all that strong, so I end up ungracefully swinging one leg, then the other, until I'm sprawled on the pool deck on my belly, a bedraggled, wet cat.

Even though it's not cold, my teeth are chattering, and tears sting my eyes.

I've never been more embarrassed in my life. Heat singes my cheeks. I kneel, then stand, and Kayla disappears into the house, saying that she's going to grab me some towels. My clothes stick to my skin, and my white shirt is see-through. My phone's a hard rectangle in my pocket, likely ruined.

"Oh my God," Mason says, "are you okay?" He swings an arm over my shoulder and helps me walk, dripping with every step.

I shrug, knowing that if I say anything I'll start crying and be called a baby.

"I'll call your mom," he says, pulling out his phone.

"Thanks," I whisper.

But as we go into the house, I look over my shoulder at Sean and see an amused expression on his face. His friends push him, and one of them says, "Good thing you got out of kissing that nerd."

"Right?" Sean says, smirking. "Close one."

And that's too much for me. Throwing Mason's arm from my shoulder, I take off, running to the street.

# Prologue—Danny

I grin at myself in the full-length mirror, twisting to inspect all angles, my hands smoothing my cummerbund. Even though I'm wearing rented clothes and stiff, glossy black shoes, everything fits well. My ass is *fine*. The barber did a great fade, and I managed a close shave for once in my life. I look sharp.

As a final check, I pat down my jacket pockets to make sure I've remembered tonight's necessities. Cell phone. Wallet. Jewelry box, which makes my heart squeeze. And condoms and lube packets, which make other parts of my body tingle. I'm ready. I pick up the boutonniere in its plastic clamshell and head out.

When I walk into the kitchen, my mom sets down the glass she's drying with an old flour-sack towel and holds out her arms. "Mijo, you look so handsome."

"Don't pinch my cheek." I duck—even though she's a foot shorter than me—and evade her outstretched fingers.

She gives me a fake pout. "But it's just so pinchable."

My mouth opens in mock surprise. "Mom, you said a bad word."

Mom puts her hand on her hip, still gripping the towel, shaking her finger. "I did not say pinche. I said pinchable."

I grin down at her. "*Now*, you said pinche."

"Hmm." She goes up on tiptoes and gives me a kiss on the cheek, then immediately wipes away the lipstick. "My boy has grown. Let me take your picture." She sets down the towel and fishes her phone out of her pocket, holding it up to frame the shot.

"Can't it wait till Brian gets here?"

"No. I want one just of you." Her expression is insistent. "In the future, you may be with another boy ..."

"That's not likely to happen," I scoff.

Mom presses her lips together and shrugs. "Perhaps. I still want a picture of my son in a tuxedo. All dressed up and going to prom."

I lift my chin as she snaps a photo of me standing in front of the stainless steel fridge. She peers at the digital image. "Can't you ever smile?"

"Nope."

"Too cool for your mom. Fine." She sighs. "If only your father could see you. You're the exact image of him when I met him." She looks down as her hands fuss with my lapels, but I'm sure unshed tears fill her eyes.

My parents were high school sweethearts. Every once in a while I'll catch her looking at me with a wistful expression. But Dad's been gone so long I don't know if my few memories—him throwing me a ball, chasing behind me as I pedal a tricycle—are truly of him ... or if they're things I made up after seeing the photos so many times.

The low rumble of an engine interrupts my moment of melancholy.

I head to the door, my heart thumping. I've never been in a limo before, but Brian and I decided to go all out to celebrate fourteen months of dating. We were going to share with some other kids, but they bailed. I ended up having to pay for the whole thing, but I don't really care. Why else am I bagging groceries if not to spoil the man I love?

It's almost sunset. The sleek black stretch Cadillac idles at the curb. It's a rare sight in my South LA neighborhood, and it's drawn half the block outside to gossip. My mom waves at the Garcias next door and the Jacksons across the street.

The driver opens the door to reveal my boyfriend sitting in the back seat, looking very small in the large space. He emerges and greets my mother first, because he was raised that way. I know him down to his freckles.

"Brian," she cries, throwing up her arms to give him a hug. "Come take pictures, guapo."

When he finally extricates himself from her, I kiss him lightly. "Hey. Happy birthday!"

Brian's smile seems off to me, but maybe he's not comfortable in his tuxedo. The dark fabric contrasts with his ginger hair. He studies me up and down. "Thanks. You look great."

"Thanks, babe."

My mom wipes a tear from her eyes. "Come gather together, boys. Let me take your picture."

I pin Brian's flower to his lapel, and he gives me one in return. We stand by the car, arm in arm, while my mom fusses over us, taking photo after photo.

Finally, I look at my phone. "We gotta get going, or we're going to be late for our dinner reservation."

She wrings her hands. "Call if you need something. I'll see you in the morning."

Honestly, I can't believe my mom didn't object to our getting a hotel room, but maybe she's being realistic and thinks we'll be safer if we stay put.

Mom gives me another kiss, then wipes the lipstick off my cheek *again*. Brian says goodbye, and we climb into the back seat of the limo.

"This is cool." I touch every control, watching the different windows and the partition go up and down.

"Yeah." He settles in, and the driver takes off.

Passing by the familiar houses of my neighborhood in such a fancy vehicle, I feel removed from my roots. But I also feel like I'm taking that first step toward becoming the person I want to be. I have ambitions, and I'm gonna go far. I'm not good enough at baseball, even though I love it, to go pro, so I'm using my brains. College, law school. Limos will be no big deal by the time I'm twenty-five, because I'll be rolling in the cheddah.

"So," Brian says, once we're on our way to the restaurant we booked for dinner. "How are you?"

I blink at him. "How am *I*? How are *you*?"

"I'm good." Brian fiddles with his hands and studies his feet.

"Do you want to know what I got you? I mean, besides my body?"

Brian laughs, but it sounds strained. "Um, you didn't have to get me anything."

"What do you mean, 'You didn't have to get me anything'? Of course I did. You're my boyfriend. We're in love. I get you presents. That's the way this works."

He nods. "Okay, okay."

I pull the wrapped box out of my pocket. "Here, birthday boy."

Brian takes the package and studies it. "What did you do?"

"Just a little something." The ring cost a full week's pay, but it was worth it.

"Should I open it now?"

"You can open it whenever you want."

Fingering the wrapping paper, he nods. "I think I'll wait a bit." He slides it into his pocket. "Thank you, though."

We drive in silence, and I'm trying to come up with the nerve to ask him what the hell his problem is. Because it's never been like this between us before. It's always been easy.

When I imagine my future, he's part of it. He's the one there with me buying a house. Or having kids. Or traveling the world.

Whether he wants to do all of that or none of it, I'm here for him, and I always will be. Maybe he's just a bit down because of his birthday, officially becoming an adult, leaving the kid world behind. I know when I turned eighteen, after I bought a lottery ticket, I felt off—like I'd passed the point of no return, except I kinda wanted to leave open the option of returning.

I reach out to hold his hand. "Looking forward to tonight?"

He stares down at our joined fingers. "Yeah."

Scooting away from him, I square my shoulders and let out a breath. "D'ya mind please telling me what's up with you?"

"Hmm? Nothing."

"Yeah, that's not gonna fly."

Brian scrubs his face and sighs. "I guess I've been thinking about how everything's going to change after this year."

I shrug. "We'll figure it out." He's going to college in Texas. I'm staying here and going to UCLA.

"Uh-huh." He won't look at me, and an uneasy feeling comes over me.

Lifting up our hands, I kiss the back of his. "Why are you such an Eeyore tonight?"

Brian doesn't answer me, and that delay makes my stomach twist up like a barber pole.

"Hey." My voice gentles. "Talk to me. You can tell me anything."

"It's just …" And now that I study him, his eyes are brimming with tears. "I don't want to do this anymore." My skin gets this horrible prickly sensation. Is he for real? He's not doing what I think he's doing.

"This? What do you mean by 'this'?"

"You know. This. Us."

He *is* doing what I think he's doing. He's fucking breaking up with me on prom night. He couldn't even wait until tomorrow or the end of the school year? What the hell?

I manage one word: "What?"

"I don't want to go out with you."

"B-b-but …" I take a shuddering breath. "But we're in love."

He pulls his shoulders back and looks me straight in the eye, his next words gutting me. "I'm sorry, Danny. I'm not in love with you anymore."

My lip juts out—a childhood habit I haven't been able to break—at the same time anger ignites inside me, heating my cheeks. "Are you serious?"

He nods miserably. "I don't want to go to prom. I'll pay you for my half of the limo. And the room. And whatever else. I just don't think I should go with you. I mean," and now he's really getting into it, "we're going away to separate states. We should be free to date other people."

"But if we're in love, we don't *want* to date other people. We're enough for each other."

Brian's face is devastated, but his words are resolute. "I guess you aren't enough for me."

My stomach bottoms out. *Fuck*. I scoot away from him like he's poisonous. Maybe he is. How can he be so cool about this? I don't know if I'm numb or pissed or sad—or all three.

Confused. That's what I am. Very confused, because this isn't the way tonight was supposed to go. At all.

He fidgets some more. "Do you want to drop me off at home?"

I nod, and he tells the driver, who seems perplexed. *You and me both, buddy*. We pass the next ten minutes in total silence.

When we get to Brian's house, it's dark out, and the driver opens the door and stands respectfully off to the side, giving us some space.

Brian slides out of the car, teary and regretful. "Just … I'm sorry. I couldn't go through with it, knowing I didn't love you."

But I do—did?—love him. Can I fall out of love that fast?

Was it really love at all?

"Okay," I say, my throat raw. "Well, I guess I'll see you

around." I'm too stunned to say more than that. If I knew what I was feeling, I'd let him have it. I think I'm in shock.

"Yeah. See you."

He hands the driver some crumpled-up bills and shuts the door. When the driver gets back in, he lowers the screen. "Do you still want to go to the restaurant, sir?"

I stare at my clenched fists. What do I want to do? I don't want to eat by myself, and there's no way I can show up to prom without a date. Everyone will know we broke up. I can't face anyone from school right now. I'm feeling too exposed.

But I also have a limousine all to myself, a hotel room booked, and supplies in my pocket. I'm teeter-tottering between anger and tears, and anger wins. "Do you know any eighteen-and-over gay clubs?"

The driver smiles. "Yes. Perks of this job. I know where everything is."

"Take me to the closest one."

"Right away, sir." He puts the limo in gear.

I'm going to turn tonight into the best night of my life. Brian's going to regret dumping me, and I'm gonna live so large he can't ignore me if he tries.

I sit in the back seat of a stretch limousine, dressed up like I've never been dressed up before, my heart torn out, with a single, dominant purpose developing.

The limo pulls up to a club called One. The driver lets me out, and I approach the front door. I show my ID to the huge mountain of a bouncer, and he lets me in after drawing a large black X on my hand.

No big deal. I don't have to drink. I just want to lose my fucking virginity tonight to someone. *Anyone.*

I make my way through the dark room. While it's early in the evening, music pulses, and men grind on the dance floor.

The place seems like it has lots of rooms, some upstairs, some in maybe an underground level, judging by another set of stairs. You could get lost in here.

Not sure what to do—and feeling more alone than I've ever felt in my life—I belly up to the smooth counter of the bar. The bartender, a heavily tattooed bear, eyes me up and down.

"What'll it be, baby gay?"

"Just a Coke, please." I'm not even going to try to order alcohol, and I'm going to be polite, because this isn't my scene.

Not yet. *It will be*, I vow.

With a nozzle, he fills a highball glass, then plunks it down before me on top of a heavy paper coaster with a stylized "One" on it.

"How much?" I yell into his ear as he leans over.

"On the house."

Well, okay. I leave him a tip anyway and take my drink, sipping deeply. It's watered down, more seltzer than syrup, and there's too much ice. Holding it at least makes me feel like I have something to do.

Turning away, I put an elbow on the bar and study the room as if I've been here before. Trying to be like Harrison Ford or James Bond, instantly cool in any situation. Casual, like this is just me, nothing noteworthy at all.

Except, you know, I'm fucking rocking this tux.

But truth? That's all bravado. In reality, my insides are turning to mush while my dick's at a semi what with all those hot guys gyrating a few feet away. I've never seen anything like it. I've never been to a Pride parade. I've only seen this many gay men in one place in my dreams.

And I'm gonna take full advantage.

Even though I'm a mess. I'm shoving thoughts of Brian, who ripped my heart out, to the side. Brian who?

I'm pissed off, sad, and feeling reckless. I toss back the soda—some of it going down the wrong pipe, so I splutter a bit—and make my way onto the dance floor.

I *can* dance, after all.

My hips move, and before I know it, I'm in the middle of a group of guys in tight T-shirts and jeans, dancing to a sped-up club mix of last summer's big hit by the Paradise. I'm sweating, and my tuxedo jacket becomes heavy and uncomfortable, but I don't want to take it off. The stiff shoes pinch my aching feet, and the crap in my pockets weighs me down.

Soft lips and a bristly chin rub against my ear. "Hey, handsome. Did you escape from a wedding?"

Two hands are on my waist. I turn around and grin. The guy's good-looking and slightly older than me. Maybe early twenties. Shorter than me. He smells like strawberries. I make a quick decision: he'll do. "Nope. This is how I always dress."

"Liar," he shouts.

Still dancing, I shrug and lean into him. "Maybe. Maybe not."

By the next song, we're kissing. He tastes like the strawberry I smelled, but also mint. It's nothing like kissing Brian.

And he's gonna be the best thing I could do to forget I got dumped on prom night.

I can feel club boy's hardening cock when our zippers touch, and I reach down to grab his ass. Soon we're grinding and making out hardcore to hoots and hollers from the dancers around us.

I don't know his name. I don't want to know it. All I want is to get past how much it hurts that Brian doesn't love me enough to stay with me when we go to college ... or even dance with me at prom.

Club boy's helping me forget. After teasing me through another few songs, he says in my ear, "Want to go down the hall?"

I nod. I don't know what's "down the hall," but I'm ready for anything. I want to be inside him, if possible, but I'll take what I can get.

I'm horny, desperate, and angry. I want to feel better. I want to feel less alone. I want to feel like someone wants me.

I don't want to count on anyone ever again.

Taking my hand, the guy tugs me to an area where guys lurk in the shadows making out. And more.

Fuck yes. *This* is what I want.

Only there's no room. We both cast around, but ...

"Where do you want to go, hot stuff?" the guy asks.

A solution comes to me. "I have a limo."

He grins and follows me to where my driver is waiting. I ask him to just drive for a while and raise the privacy screen.

Eighteen minutes later, strawberry-mint and I slump into the leather upholstery, our sated dicks flopping against sticky skin.

Oh, *hell* yes. Sex is awesome. What was I thinking, waiting for Brian? Waiting for *love*? What a joke.

I'm going to fuck my way through Los Angeles. Try and stop me.

# CHAPTER 1

*Alden*

*present day, ten years later*

P
I let myself out of the Lyft and trip on ... flat pavement. Oh, man. *Nerts*. Good thing I catch myself before I do a face-plant. After I regain my balance, I glance around to see how many people saw that. Apparently none. Not even the driver, since when I go to give him a little wave, he's already sped off.

With a few clicks on my phone, I give him five stars—because he didn't say a word to me, which is worth a perfect score—and leave him a tip. I slip my phone into my pocket, brush my damp hands on my slacks, and head into the Santa Monica restaurant located just across the street from the ocean.

Inside, it's packed. People are waiting everywhere, and between the music and chatter, the noise level is higher than the sounds of traffic and waves outside. Thankfully, the restaurant has a "Please wait to be seated" sign up—I need that kind of step-by-step guidance—so I head for the host stand. The guy at the podium is wearing black sweatpants that must be designer, since they have a weird cut—a dropped crotch but tight around his shins—along with a dress shirt and white leather running shoes studded with silver spikes. None of those garments look like they've ever been

worn for exercise. He's about my age, but way cooler than I'll
ever be.

I'm in baggy khakis and a ringer tee that says, "Curse your
sudden but inevitable betrayal." Scratching the back of my neck, I
realize I probably should've worn something else, but the shirt
makes me happy, and I'm about as out of my comfort zone as I get.
I needed something familiar—like a blankie. Plus, I didn't get the
memo that this was a trendy place.

"Do you have a reservation?" host boy says in a bored tone.

"Yes. At least I think so." While I'll never be good at social
interactions, at least I can kind of talk to strangers now, unlike
when I was a kid.

He yawns. "Name?"

I clear my throat. "Alden Meyer."

He frowns and checks his iPad, then looks up and grins over
my shoulder at someone, giving them a chin lift. Focusing back on
me, an overly patient expression clicking back into place, he asks,
"Could it be under another name?"

"Probably. I didn't make the reservation." I know I'm testing
his patience, but it's not intentional. I'm just not good at talking
with other people. *Numbers. Give me numbers any day of the week.
I understand those.* "I'm meeting a guy named Sumner Banning."

Sliding his fingers over the screen, he locates our table and gives
me a tight smile. "Ah, yes. Let me show you to your seat. He's
already here."

I follow the host through the crowded restaurant, my hands
trembling the closer I get to my destination. "Here we are," he says
with a flourish, gesturing at a booth where a beefy man in a pink
polo is waiting. My date, whom I've never met.

And I have no idea what I'm expected to do. Shake his hand?
Say hi? Just sit down? Run away?

Thankfully, he saves me. "Are you Alden?" the beefy guy asks
with a skeptical expression, sliding out of the booth and looming
over me.

"Yeh-yes." I offer my hand.

"Sumner." He clasps my hand and shakes it firmly. I hope he doesn't notice how clammy my palm is, but I'm pretty sure he can't miss it. His paw dwarfs mine. I hold it until he pulls it back and sits down. Should I wait for him to invite me to sit? I stand for a moment, until the host does a little cough behind me.

"Is it okay?" I gesture at the place opposite Sumner.

"Of course."

When I'm settled, the host picks up the menu already on the table and places it in my hands. "Enjoy your meal."

I look up at the host. "You, too." I wince. "I mean, uh, you have a good day, too." He restrains an eye roll before he leaves to help more competent folks.

Hopeless. I'm Hopeless with a capital H. I just get so nervous that, despite this not being my first date, despite everything I've done over the years to try and get over being awkward, I forget ... *everything*.

While I want to bury myself in studying the menu for the foreseeable future—setting aside the fact that my anxiety has killed my appetite—I look at my date and aim for a smile, although it might be a grimace. It's hard to know what my face does without my permission.

Sumner has thick, shiny, golden blond hair, cut short, and hazel-green eyes. He smiles back at me. His teeth are very white, and his biceps bulge under his tight sleeves.

I'm so out of my league. I don't know why I ever thought this would be a good idea.

Well, the truth is I *didn't* think it was a good idea, but his great-aunt and my grandmother are friends, and I daren't say no to my gran. She thought this date would make me come out of my shell or something. She thought wrong.

"I don't bite, you know," Sumner says, interrupting my spiral.

"Wha-what?"

"You look nervous. I don't bite. Not unless it's called for." He gives me a wolfish grin that makes me feel all kinds of embarrassed, because I'm pretty sure it's just a line.

Unless he has a thing for geeky guys with unruly hair, this date is a lost cause. Dead on arrival.

I gulp. "Okay. Good to know." I start reading the menu, but I have no idea what to do. While obviously I've ordered in restaurants before, I normally go to ones I know, and I always order the same thing so I don't have the pressure of having to choose. Because what if I choose wrong?

Here, though, I have no idea what's right. The words are in English, but that's not helping me at all. Will I like air bread filled with Fiscalini cheddar espuma? Or hibiscus pectin marmalade?

Help.

I straighten my shoulders. I can do this. "Um. What's good here?" I ask.

"Everything." He grins again, but his face falls when he sees that mine hasn't changed expression. Because that was no help at all.

"Okay," I whisper, and go back to reading the menu. I hadn't realized I needed to study before going out to lunch. Would it be tacky for me to pull out my phone and google the choices?

Finally, I see chicken soup with matzo balls—even though this isn't a kosher restaurant—that looks safe.

And I realize I've gone long moments without saying a word to Sumner.

"You all right?" he asks, tilting his head and studying me. He's very attractive, but it's the plastic, perfect kind of good-looking. The kind that's not at all like my nerdy mess.

"Yeah. I'm just not very good at this."

"Good at what? Ordering in restaurants? Eating?"

"Humaning."

He gives me a sympathetic smile. "I'm sorry I make you nervous."

"It's not you," I hasten to say. "Or it's not only you. I'm really ... I have ... I'm awkward."

"Relax. It's not that big of a deal. It's only a date."

I nod. His words don't soothe me in the slightest. Why do people always say that things that feel like a big deal to me aren't? It's not like they can see inside my brain. Just because perhaps objectively they aren't a big deal doesn't mean I'm not a mess inside.

He tries again. "So, tell me about yourself, Alden."

I'm saved by the waiter, who chooses this moment to refill our water glasses and take our order. Once I've told him my choice—which, in retrospect, was an awful selection, because the chances of me spilling soup all over myself are extraordinarily high—I realize Sumner's still waiting for an answer.

Shyness plus social anxiety plus awkwardness for me equals a dull date for him. I know it's like pulling teeth to get me to talk, but I don't know how to be any different. "There's not much to tell. I'm starting a new job on Monday."

He seems relieved that I responded at all. "Really? That's interesting. Where?"

"At Weston & Ramirez. It's a law firm."

Sumner adopts a thoughtful expression. "I've heard of it. They do LGBTQ advocacy."

"How did you know?" I ask, surprised. My gran didn't say anything about Sumner working in the legal field. I don't know what he does. He looks like he gives tennis lessons.

Maybe that's the point. I'm supposed to talk with him and find out.

"Oh, it's in the news sometimes because Sam Stone works there. And his boyfriend is—"

"Julian Hill." I nod. Sam's the governor's grandson. Julian's the biggest rock star on the planet. "I'm pretty excited to be there."

I'm nervous about it, too, but not as nervous as being on a date. At my new job, it's going to be just me and a computer, and I get along very well with computers. They don't talk back, they're logical, and they don't ask me questions I can't answer.

"You look a little young to be a lawyer, unless you're a prodigy."

"I'm not a lawyer." I sip my water and then realize he's waiting for me to explain. "Oh, I'm a bookkeeper."

"Are you a CPA?"

"No."

I wish I were good at this. I wish I had the gift of gab. I wish I could attract men easily and find the love of my life. Or at least not be so awful at social interactions.

But I *am* awful at them, and I can't attract anyone, and I fail hard at maneuvering the territory of polite company. It's not that I don't try. I'm just ... unsure of what I should say. And then, by the time I've worried about saying the wrong thing, I've said nothing and made everything worse. Sumner must be thinking how boring I am, and the sooner I get out of this date, the happier everyone will be.

Bless him, he keeps trying. "Is there a reason why you're not a CPA?"

"Sort of." I realize he's waiting for me to expound on that. "I like working with the nitty-gritty day-to-day numbers rather than the big-picture financials of an organization. I like details. Little things."

He nods like he's tired of asking me questions. I'm tired of him asking me questions. I'm tired of all of this, and I wish it were easier, but it isn't.

We're quiet, both of us looking around the room without saying anything. When our food comes, it's a relief to have something to focus on, but I'm too nervous to eat more than a few spoonfuls.

After a while, he gestures at my shirt with his fork. "What does your shirt mean?"

I pick at it. "It's a *Firefly* reference."

"*Firefly*?" He cocks his head.

"TV show from the early 2000s. It got canceled midseason, but it had some pretty great moments. And then there was a movie ..." I suppose now is not the time to get into an in-depth discussion about the finer points of the plot or any controversy surrounding people associated with the show. Or my feelings about when creators ruin things I love by behaving badly, making me feel guilty—or at least conflicted—for still loving them. Like I'll ever be able to hash all that out with anyone who understands.

"Ah," he says.

If this date were a test, I'd not only be failing it, I'd be failing with such a low score I'd never be able to pass the class even if I aced everything from here on out.

It dawns on me that I haven't asked him anything at all. "What do you do, Sumner?"

He narrows his eyes. "You don't have to ask. I can tell you're not into me. It's okay. Not every date is a winner."

Ouch. "Sorry. New people make me nervous. You make me nervous because you're way out of my league. I'm sorry my gran put you up to this."

"It's okay. Just because this"—he gestures between us—"isn't going anywhere doesn't mean the right guy isn't out there for you. And you *are* doing me a favor. Now that we've had a meal and it didn't work out, I can get my great-aunt off my case and move on with my life."

"Cool," I say, glad to know this date will have some benefit, no matter how small. But I can't wait to call my Lyft and go back home. Apparently, neither can he.

\* \* \*

After my humdinger of a lunch date, I open the door to my house as quietly as I can, but my mom still calls out in her thin voice, "Alden?"

27

It makes my heart hurt. I set down my phone on the hall table, but it falls to the floor, so I pick it up again. I go to her bedroom and bend to kiss her cheek. "Hey, Mom. How are you?"

She smiles. "Pretty good today. How did your date go?"

"It was fine," I hedge.

Mom gives me a look. It's amazing how fierce she is, despite cancer ravaging her insides. The prognosis is positive, and I'm so grateful for that. Her counts are good, and the tumors are shrinking. But seeing her this way—thin, in a wig, and nauseated—is awful. Chemo can go take a long walk off a short pier.

"The date was *okay*," I correct. "Actually, it was pretty bad. I was my usual awkward self, and by the end, we agreed that we would never ever see each other again or speak of it to another person."

"It couldn't have been that bad."

"It was worse. I get around strangers, and I can't even say my own name."

"And yet around me you're as chatty as a windup doll."

"Well, it's easy with you. I know you, and you don't expect me to be someone I'm not."

"Honey, no one else expects that, either."

"It's still easier to stick with people I know. Family. Mason. It's hard to get to know someone else."

"You can do it." She sighs. "I just want you to be happy."

"What if I'm happy as I am?"

I'm not. I want more friends, although Mason's great. I'd love to not be so awkward with men. I'd like to have *some* experience in the bedroom, since I have, oh, none at all.

But it's not like wishes come true.

Mom gestures that she wants to sit up, and I help adjust her hospital bed and prop her up with pillows. Her surprisingly strong fingers grip my biceps. "Alden, listen to me. The first thing you need to know is that you're perfect exactly the way you are. Don't let anyone tell you that you need to change."

"Yeah, I know—"

"But the second thing is, don't be afraid to change if it helps you become who you're meant to be."

I open my mouth to protest, but nothing comes out. So I swallow and nod.

I want to change pretty damned badly. After all, I'm twenty-four years old, and I've never even been kissed.

## CHAPTER 2

## *Danny*

I'd like to say this is the first time I've forgotten the name of a guy whose dick is in my mouth, but it isn't.

Don't get me wrong. I'm smart, and if something matters to me, I remember it. But this guy's name doesn't matter —sorry to be that asshole.

Like I do a few times a week, tonight I went to One, met a guy, and went back to his place. It's nothing special. He's just another in the pantheon of nameless, faceless fucks I've had over the years.

At some point, they all started blending together. But I gave my heart to someone once, only to have it ripped out. I've never done it again.

And I never will.

That said, a guy has needs, and I'm very good at getting them met. I'm famous for satisfying my partners, too. I'm well aware of my rep—I'm the best in bed, and every guy in that club wants me. Exactly how I like it.

So, yeah, remembering names isn't exactly on my priority list. Still, now I'm distracted, and I pull off the guy with a pop, blinking hard, treating this situation like a memory game.

Eddie? Elio? Something with an E, I think.

"Dude," he whines from where he's straddling my shoulders, attempting to feed his dick into my mouth again.

I jerk my head back. "Give me a sec," I mutter. I study his face for clues, but I'm finding no names in my mental inventory. Brain's delivering an error message.

Oh well. It's not important. I'm never going to see him again. I don't do repeats, and even if I did, he wouldn't be particularly tempting. He's hot, but I don't really like his voice. I also don't like his apartment that much. Or wherever we are.

I need to finish sucking him off and get out of here. My jaw is aching a bit, and I could use a break.

That makes me stiffen, and not in a good way.

I. The king of one-night stands and hookups. Am *bored*.

*What's happening here?*

Time to focus. I take his cock deep, letting it hit the back of my throat, and I do this undulating sucking motion I know feels good when someone does it to me.

Bingo. He groans and tugs my hair, and I hope he'll come fast.

He does, releasing with a yell, and it's not all that sexy. He collapses on the bed next to me. I stroke myself off, then lie back on the bed, panting.

I got the job done. Another notch on the bedpost, so to speak.

"Thanks, man," Evan/Ethan says.

I roll onto my side and give him my most charming grin. "No problem." I spy a box of tissues on a bedside table and take some to wipe up. Then I fish around for my clothes.

He clears his throat. "So, I was wondering."

Those four words may be my least favorite in the English language.

Looking over my shoulder as I put on my pants, I raise an eyebrow. "Yes?"

"Any chance you'd want to break your rule? I'd like to see you again."

I shake my head, trying to look regretful, and grab my shirt. "One night only. Remember?"

He sighs and scrubs his face, then flops back on the bed. "Yeah, that's what you said. But it was so good. Didn't you feel it?"

"Yeah, dude." Everett? Eric? "But I'm not in the headspace for repeats these days." Or for any kind of strings. Ever.

All strings do is choke you. And not in a kinky way.

I shove my feet into my shoes, check that I have my phone and wallet and keys, and give him a little salute. He's naked on the bed, watching me go.

I wish I felt something, but I don't.

And that not-feeling? That's what really gets me down. I should be on a high after coming, and instead, I'm just kind of tired—physically and mentally. I need a new challenge.

Once I'm home, I pour myself a glass of water as my cat wraps herself around my feet. She's a scrawny, homely thing, but she adopted me, so I had to keep her. Even though she's not much to look at, she's got the best personality.

She could be mistaken for a common black cat, but if you look at her fur in the sunlight, she's actually a tabby with dark brown stripes alternating with the black.

"Hey there, Mamacita," I coo, picking her up. She acts more like a dog than a cat. She's sociable, comes when I call, likes to hang out. She's fucking awesome.

Carrying her draped across my forearm, I putter around the house, setting out her food and letting her down to eat. She bounds over to her bowl and takes a few delicate bites.

My phone buzzes, even though it's after midnight.

**Charlie**: You get home okay?

I grin. He's my best friend and snarky as hell, but he worries, which is sweet.

**Danny**: Yeah. You?

**Charlie**: Struck out at One so I came home and couldn't sleep. I'm working on a new shelf for the garage.

Charlie and I are both partners at Weston & Ramirez, a small firm that's full of go-getters. They brought us on after Charlie and I won a huge award in a discrimination case we started working on during law school clinic. The contingency fees from that case paid off my student loans, with some left over for the down payment on my house. While we could've hung out our own shingle, I like the camaraderie and lack of pretension at W&R and have been happy there for the past year or so.

In the off hours, Charlie and his brother Camden do a lot of woodworking—Camden's a licensed contractor. Charlie builds stuff as a way of letting off steam, but his real talent is making these time-lapse videos of their projects, which he posts on social media. He has like nine million followers.

**Danny**: Figures.

**Charlie**: You just wish you had my skillz

**Danny**: I got my own skillz.

**Charlie**: Wasn't talking about being a man whore

**Danny**: Don't be sexist.

**Charlie**: Okay. Then you're just a plain whore.

**Danny**: Anddd don't slut shame

**Charlie**: SIGH. I'm not doing that. You know how much I love me some men.

He's as much of a playboy as I am. I'm sure he could've found someone to go home with tonight if he really tried.

**Danny**: Same.

**Danny**: You making a video of how you took an Ikea cabinet and made it into a koi pond?

**Charlie**: Don't make fun.

**Charlie**: You're just jealous of my reach.

**Danny**: Hardly.

**Danny**: Social media is for hacks.

**Charlie**: You say that because you have no followers.

**Danny**: I haven't tried. If I put myself out there, I bet I could get double your followers in half the time.

**Charlie**: Oh yeah? Eighteen million followers in six months?

Why am I even considering this? I couldn't care less about being an influencer. My real-life friends follow me on social media —and vice versa—but I don't hashtag a damned thing.

**Danny**: Easy.

**Danny**: I just don't feel like ticking and/or tocking.

**Danny**: Don't want my data mined.

**Charlie**: What about Ad/VICE?

Ad/VICE is a new social media platform designed for people to dispense advice and advertise their products, and its bent is ... NSFW—hence the VICE—although there are plenty of regular accounts. At least so I'm told. I'm not on it.

But between the unsatisfying evening and Charlie's implicit dare, my mind's starting to spin.

What am I doing with my life?

I'm ten years out of high school, and I've already achieved all the goals I set for myself. I have an equity partnership in a thriving boutique firm that furthers social justice causes. I make the money I want. I help my mom. I drive my dream car. My house is killer, although I haven't had time to decorate it much. While some of the cases I handle are challenging, I'm feeling like I've ... plateaued.

*Is* what I need to be a social media icon? Do I want to take over Ad/VICE?

This is the kind of shit my tired, not drunk but not entirely sober self comes up with. A social media follower challenge.

Great.

**Danny**: I'm in.

I hit send and immediately regret it. Because how the hell am I going to get that many followers in six months? I have to do something that will go viral.

**Charlie**: Prepare to lose your bet.

**Danny**: Not on your life.

**Danny**: What are we betting, anyway?

**Charlie**: Your car?

**Danny**: No.

**Charlie**: Your cat?

**Danny**: You're an asshole.

**Charlie**: You lose, you have to come on my socials and tell everyone how you failed.

**Danny**: I'm not going to fail, but okay. Deal. And if I win?

**Charlie**: Shoutout from me.

**Danny**: You wouldn't do that just as a friend?

**Charlie**: Fuck no. I have sponsors.

**Danny**: Fine.

I shut off the lights and go to bed. As always, Mamacita curls up in the bend of my knees as I lie on my side. I'm sure I can come up with some way to make myself go viral. Tomorrow.

\* \* \*

On Monday morning, I'm in court. This is only a preliminary hearing, but of course I've dressed in my usual bespoke suit and custom shoes. I'm feeling good but trying not to grin.

When I win—which is often—I do my best to maintain appropriate courtroom decorum. Meaning I don't say, "Take that, motherfucker!" in front of the judge. Instead, I say, "Thank you, Your Honor," and close my laptop, sliding it into my briefcase.

As we stand up to leave, I reach over and shake the opposing counsel's hand. Amelia Crowley and I face off against each other regularly, since I advocate for LGBTQIA+ employees and her firm often represents employers. "Well done," she says, with a gleam in her eye. "I'll get you next time."

I smile and shrug. "Maybe."

I'm representing Johnny Haskell, who's better known as Velvet the Cowboy. He's not here today, because this is just a spat about discovery. Still, a reporter was sitting in the back of the courtroom taking notes. This is a messy case, and it's starting to get publicity, because it's not every day a porn star sues for sexual harassment.

I haven't watched any of his scenes since I've been on the case, because that would be awkward, but I've seen some of them before.

Sooo, yeah. My job's a little different than if I were representing some faceless company. I love being a lawyer. It's all I ever wanted to do. But I'm really glad I chose to work at Weston & Ramirez rather than some firm where I'd be defending jackass executives every day.

As I step out of the courthouse into the bright midmorning sunshine, someone takes my photo. I'm sure it's the press. On my way to my car, I call Johnny.

He picks up immediately. "How'd it go?" he asks, a nervous squeak in his voice. You'd never know this is a dude who's fucked more men than me—and on camera, no less. He's the shyest man when he's not in character as a dom.

I grin. "We won this round."

"Yes. *God*. Thank you, Danny."

"No problem. And let's not get ahead of ourselves. We still have a lot to do before trial. Or maybe they'll do the right thing and settle. Their attorney is pretty savvy, but she can only do what her clients want her to. For now, don't worry about it. I have it under control."

"Cool. Are you going to send me a bill anytime soon?"

"Yeah. There's been a delay because we lost our bookkeeper. I think the new one started today—I dunno, I haven't been in the office yet this morning. But thanks for staying on top of that."

"I just want to make sure you get compensated. I appreciate your work."

I walk through the parking lot and say goodbye, then get in my sports car, headed to the office.

Still wondering how I'm going to get the followers to win my bet with Charlie.

# CHAPTER 3

## *Alden*

The elevator pings, and the doors open to the fourteenth floor reception area of this Century City office tower. Or, really, the thirteenth, but this is one of those buildings where the planners thought superstition was more important than accuracy.

As a bookkeeper, I disapprove of skipping numbers or pretending they don't exist. It makes it seem like the architect or engineer can't count, which is not encouraging when you're fourteen—or thirteen—floors off the ground.

Nerves make my stomach churn. I hope I'll like it here. I *want* to like it here.

I adjust my tie and, doing my best to look confident, stride toward the receptionist behind the front desk. He's a slim man with a bleached platinum coif and shiny lip gloss, wearing an expensive-looking light blue polo that fits like it was designed specifically for him. He runs out to meet me before I get halfway into the room, though.

"Are you Alden? Our new bookkeeper?" he asks eagerly.

My stomach unknots a bit. "Yeah, er, yes. I am. He's me. That's me."

"I'm Shelby. We're so glad you're here! Let me show you around." The grin he gives me puts me much more at ease. It's amazing what a warm welcome can do.

Shelby goes to walk me down a hall, but Noah Weston, one of the owners—and the managing partner—appears, holding a cup of coffee. "Alden! Welcome. Did you have any trouble getting here?" He reaches out a hand and gives me a charming smile.

Noah has blond hair and blue eyes and is quite a bit taller than I am. His suit is almost the exact same shade of gray as mine, although his looks a lot more expensive. He's young to be one of the guys with his name on the wall. I would seriously doubt that he's past his midthirties.

"Yes, thank you." He and Shelby both furrow their brows. I cringe. "I mean it was easy. Thanks. I'm looking forward to getting started."

"We need you," Noah says. "Our last bookkeeper had to move out of town for family reasons—and even before then, she was overloaded. Once you get a handle on things, I want you to let us know if we need more than one person doing the work. We don't want to set you up for failure."

I rub my hands together, and I'm sure my eyes are bright. This, this I can do. I can organize my way out of anything. Just don't make me talk. "Put me in, Coach. I love cleaning up messes."

Noah grins. "Awesome. It's all yours. Let me show you where your office is." With a finger wave, Shelby goes back to the reception desk, and I follow Noah down the hall.

"We've expanded to take up this entire floor," he says. "Hard to believe we've grown so big in five years." He sounds proud—and he has reason to be. The rooms are sleek but comfortable, with posters commemorating various LGBTQIA+ historical events, mostly since Stonewall. He shows me where the break room—stocked with snacks and soft drinks, in addition to coffee and tea—is and introduces me to every employee we pass: attorneys, legal assistants, other staff.

We stop at a closed door, and Noah opens it to show a small office chock full of papers on every surface. He gestures. "Yeah. So. We need some help."

"Yesssss," I say. "This is gonna be so much fun."

Noah's phone buzzes in his pocket, and he gets a pained but amused look on his face.

When he doesn't reach for it, I say, "You can get that."

"It'll wait. I know who it is. And if I get it now, I'll have to explain way too much."

I nod, not understanding. "Okay."

Shelby pops his head in and hands me a slip of paper. "Here's your username and password."

"Thanks."

"Demi, our office manager, told me she'll be able to meet with you at nine thirty. She's meeting with August right now."

"Is that where he is?" Noah asks.

Shelby nods and gets a funny look on his face. I'll have to ask about that later.

"Well, officially, welcome," Noah says. "Will you be able to get started on your own until Demi is free? If not, it's fine if you just grab some coffee or something until then."

I make a noise to the effect that I'm sure I can keep busy. Judging by the piles of printouts all around me, that won't be a problem.

"Did you bring a lunch?" Noah asks.

"No. I was planning on finding something close."

"Well, join us. A lot of us usually go out to eat together. There are a lot of great places in the basement mall. I can come by or—"

"I'll grab you," Shelby says.

"Sure," I say. "Thanks."

Noah gives me another friendly smile. "We'll see you down there."

I'm really liking how there's apparently no segregation between the attorneys and the staff here. Noah's treating me and

Shelby like we're just part of the team, even though we don't have the same degree and training that he does. It's refreshing.

"Good to know." I settle into the chair and turn on the computer. "I can't wait to get started."

"I'll stop by when it's time for lunch," Shelby says.

I smile and tap my fingers on the keyboard. I already love this job.

* * *

I'd like to say that, when I first see him, a flurry of songbirds fly in. Or trumpets sound. Or something happens to mark the moment. But in reality, this really cute guy walks down the hallway past my office, and he catches my eye.

Cute's the wrong word.

He's smoking hot.

You know how there are some people you can't take your eyes off of? Something about him draws me in, and it's a struggle to look away. (Or act like a normal human being—not that I'm too good at doing that anyhow.)

Over the years, I've become quite a connoisseur of men, especially well-dressed men. Since I'm too awkward to touch them or even talk to them, I look plenty. There's something I can't resist about a man in a suit, and he's wearing a nice one: dark gray, with a light blue shirt and a dark-blue-and-gray tie.

It's a flash—eye contact—and then he's gone, walking briskly, like a man on a mission.

I forget to breathe, and I drop my stack of Post-its on the floor.

But it wasn't his face or his height or his clothing that made my heart pound. How can I explain attraction? This is LA. I see beautiful people every day, and I'm not attracted to all of them.

With this guy, though ... After glimpsing him for a few seconds, I want to know everything about him. What's his name, for starters, and what does his voice sound like? What does he eat for breakfast and what does he think about sci-fi and does he have any pets? Instantly, I'm back in high school and tongue-tied.

Who am I kidding? I'm twenty-four and *still* tongue-tied. I wouldn't know what to do with a man if he spun me around and planted a kiss on my lips.

Since, you know, I've never been kissed.

And I'm going to be working with this guy? Oh jeez. This is gonna be trouble. I'll have to stay away so I don't embarrass myself any more than usual.

I do a little shake and focus back on familiarizing myself with the firm's accounting software.

When Shelby comes to collect me for lunch and we walk out to the elevators together, I try to think of a way to ask about the man without being too overt, but he saves me the trouble.

"Danny?" he calls, as we walk by Hot Guy's office, "join us for lunch?"

I trip on a flat area of carpet but manage not to fall.

*Danny* is standing and leaning over his desk, clicking something on his computer. When he looks up, those dark eyes scan us.

*Help me.* He's just so yummy.

"Can't. Sorry," he says. His voice is rich. "I'm headed to court again this afternoon."

Shelby smiles. "Well, you should meet our new hire, at least. Danny, this is Alden Meyer, the new bookkeeper. Alden, Danny Villaseñor, one of our partners."

Danny leaves the mouse, straightens, and crosses the office to shake my hand. He looms over me, very imposing and very, very handsome. He smells amazing—some kind of aftershave, but it's subtle, not overwhelming. Just, like, a clean man who's well-groomed.

I'm lucky I don't trip over the floor again. Or my own tongue.

He gives me a broad smile. "Nice to meet you, Alden." I clutch his hand, then realize I'm being weird, so I release it quickly.

"S-s-same," I stutter.

"We'll have to do lunch some other time," he promises. "But now I have to get ready for my next hearing."

"Cool," I say faintly.

Shelby tugs on my sleeve. "C'mon. Let's go get something to eat. I'm starving."

I'd like to nibble on Danny, but I suppose a sandwich will have to do.

\* \* \*

Shelby plops down next to me in the lunch spot downstairs and tilts his head. "So, what do you think so far?"

"Everyone's really nice. I'm sure I'll like the work." The other founder of the firm, August Ramirez, is sitting with Noah at the table next to us, but the place is noisy, so we can't really hear their conversation. As Noah said earlier, a lot of the firm's attorneys, as well as quite a few paralegals and office staff, are eating together. Many names to remember. I'm grateful to have Shelby to talk to, because he's so bubbly and nonthreatening.

He sips his soda through a paper straw. "Uh-huh. And what about Danny?"

I startle and knock over my Coke. Thankfully, there's a lid on it, so only a few drops spill. Shelby grabs some brown paper napkins and helps me put everything to rights. "What about him?"

"I saw the way you looked at him."

My cheeks heat. "Well, um. He's good-looking."

He gets a faraway look and sighs. "That he is. My advice, though, is don't go for him. He has a new guy every night."

"How do you know that?"

Shelby suddenly goes very stern. He sits up straight and catches my eyes, squaring his shoulders. "This isn't anything secret: Danny's totally up front about his social life, plus most of us see each other at the club anyway. I wouldn't have mentioned it otherwise. But I don't want to make you uncomfortable. We can talk about something else."

"Oh. I get it. It's okay. This isn't harassment. I'm curious."

"You sure? I don't want to step over any lines."

"I'm fine."

"Then ..." He resumes his chatty pose. "I can tell you he's a healthy boy with a healthy appetite. At least I figure it's healthy. He's never invited me into his bed, but I've seen him work the bar. I've seen him lip-lock a guy and take him home in no time flat."

I sigh. "I wish I could do that."

"Why can't you?" He puts both his hands on the table and leans toward me. "Don't tell me you can't get a date."

"I can't." I redden. "Well, I've been on dates, but I never get to a second one."

"Really?" Shelby seems genuinely shocked. "But you're adorable." He gestures to my entire body. "You have this geeky vibe."

"Exactly. People don't like geeks."

"Oh, sure they do. Or at least some do. Just like they like twinks. Not everyone, of course. We all have our favorite flavor— the types that do it for us. But those who love twinks?" He grins. "They *love* me. And many, many people will be into you, you adorable techie. I promise."

"I wish I had your confidence."

"Why don't you?"

"Because reasons," I say, knowing that's not a very good answer. I'm not eager to explain my inexperience to my coworker, though I expect he'll figure it out soon enough.

"Hmm. Okay, if you're not feeling the love the way you deserve to, I can see wanting to step things up a bit. But is being a ... a *rake* really the answer? Surely there's a happy medium."

"I'd settle for an indifferent beginning. Maybe I can't be one, but I'd like to know what it's like to be *with* one."

"Being with one isn't all that. While the players may make you feel good, it's only for that moment. I want to be the center of someone's world for their entire life." He bites his fingers. "Although I won't say no to, well, *you know*, in the meanwhile."

"I wouldn't know," I mutter.

His eyes widen. "Not at all? Really?"

I nod. "No experience. I barely attract anyone—and if I do, I end up being so awkward and weird that they're gone before we get past the introductions. What's your secret?"

"Mostly I just bat my eyes and act helpless, and these big, strong men come to my rescue," he says. I can picture Shelby sucking on a lollipop or something, sticking his hip out, and having three guys fighting over him.

"Isn't that a little manipulative?"

"Probably. Ask me if I care."

That makes me grin.

"My problem is, the ones I like are usually straight or unavailable. But it's a burden I'll have to bear. I'm sure with a little help, you'll get all the boys. Or whoever you're into," he adds hastily. "I mean, you were making cartoon eyes at Danny, but I don't want to assume."

"No, you're right. I'm gay." I sigh. "I just wish it were more than theoretical."

"You should get Danny to teach you."

I laugh. "That sounds like a terrible idea."

"Well, I'm sure he could give you some tips." He shoots me a concerned look. "But even if you do get some help, don't go having a personality transplant. I think you're fine just the way you are."

"I don't want to be fine," I mutter under my breath. "I wanna get laid."

# CHAPTER 4

*Danny*

M y cell phone rings, and my mom's number shows on the display.

"Hola," I say, leaning back in my office chair and clicking out of an email.

"Mijo. ¿Cómo estás?"

"I'm fine. Busy. Work is good."

She clucks her tongue. "You work too much."

"I play, too, Mom." I bite my lip, grinning at her exasperated sigh.

"You're at the age where you should be settling down," she insists.

I huff out a laugh. "Not any time soon."

"Well, you should at least be dating people you want to introduce to me."

"I haven't met anyone in that category. If that changes, I'll let you know."

The person I met most recently is our new bookkeeper, Alden, who I spoke with briefly when he started on Monday. I've seen him around this week, but I haven't talked with him again. He's short and super cute, in a nerdy way, with those big light brown eyes and unruly dark brown hair. He looks like he's playing dress-up in his suits and ties, although I think there's a lithe body under the ill-fitting clothes.

Something about him makes me want to protect him from everything bad in this world. He just looks so innocent, and from the first time I saw him, I felt this tug at my heart that I haven't felt in ... ever. Years, certainly. But I'm not gonna pick a flower from my own garden—not gonna fuck anyone from work. Still, there's nothing wrong with a bit of flirting.

As if reading my thoughts, Mom says, "I worry about you. Being the town flirt is okay when you're in your twenties, but you're getting older and need stability in your life. A companion."

"There's no way I'm settling down now. I'm still at the age to sow my wild oats."

"You've been sowing wild oats for so many years. You don't need to do that anymore. You need some meat."

"Mom!" I say. "Cripes. Don't be so crass."

"I'm not crass. I'm only telling the truth. And I just want you to be happy. That's all a mother wants."

I roll my eyes, but secretly I'm glad. She could've been very judgmental about me being gay, since she was raised pretty conservatively. But she isn't, at all. It's like she knew that was who I was all along and accepted me. She never tried to tell me to be something I'm not. And while she can be a little manipulative, it's only in this way—wanting to see me happy.

I *am* happy ... right?

"I'm fine. Don't worry about me."

"When am I going to see you next, mijo?"

"Want me to come by this weekend?" I pause. "Friday is happy hour at the office. What about Saturday afternoon? Will that work? I could help you install that new bookshelf."

I can hear the smile in her voice. "That would be wonderful. I'll make your favorite."

"Al pastor?"

"Claro que sí."

"Yum. I can't wait. Thanks. But I'm not bringing anyone with me."

"Whatever you say," she says.

We exchange affectionate goodbyes, and I think about how weird my life is. I'm winning big cases, driving a flashy car, fucking a different hot man every week—if not more often. And apparently now aiming for views on Ad/VICE. This is exactly the life I imagined when I was dumped on prom night and vowed to live my best life as revenge.

But sometimes I just want my cat and my mom.

* * *

There's a knock on my door, and I glance up to see our new bookkeeper. He looks nervous.

"Um, hey," he says. "I'm Alden."

"I know," I say, smiling. "We met the other day. How's your first week been so far?"

His cheeks flush for some reason. "Umm—" he starts, but then the intercom buzzes. It's Shelby.

"Hang on?" I ask Alden, and he nods. "Go ahead," I say to Shelby.

"Mr. Villaseñor ..." Shelby can be so proper, but it's all an act. "There's someone here to see you. Earl Gorges."

Earl? I don't know an Earl.

Unless it's the dude from the other night? *Fuck. No.*

Alden frowns. Guess I said that out loud—or maybe my expression spoke for me. "What's wrong?" he asks.

"Hang on." I grimace and put Shelby on mute. "I think this visitor might be here for the wrong reason." Alden justifiably looks confused, since that's not any real explanation. I continue, "I think it's some guy I hooked up with, but I don't want to see him again."

"Oh." He turns to look down the hall, then whispers, "Do you want me to go shoo him away?"

I almost laugh, because it's precious, him wanting to ... defend me? "Nah, I can take care of my own messes." *I think.* "Shelby," I say, unmuting the intercom, "it's okay to send him down."

Alden's wearing a dubious expression, and I don't blame him. Who has their hookups follow them to the office?

A moment later, Earl barges in, carrying a Vons grocery bag that appears to have a belt in it. I let out a sigh of relief. For a moment, I'd thought he might be bringing me flowers or something equally mushy and romantic. No, thanks.

He gives Alden only a passing glance, which pisses me off. Alden's a person. This guy should show some respect. We'll ignore my hypocrisy, since I couldn't even remember Earl's name while we were actually in bed. But he focuses on me and says, "You left this." He holds out the plastic bag.

I accept it and set it down on my desk, then cock my head. "How did you know where to find me? I never told you my last name."

"You're a legend. Everyone knows who you are."

"Well, thanks." I hope he'll get the hint and leave, but I can almost predict his next words.

Yep, here they come: "But it was so good."

"I'm sorry. I don't do more than one night." Which I told him.

Alden's watching us with the sort of fascination usually reserved for *60 Minutes*—it's not something you were planning on watching, but you got sucked in, and you won't want to tell your friends because it's not at all cool, but it's kind of absorbing anyway. I *am* interesting, but this is embarrassing. Or it will be, if I don't turn this encounter around.

"Look," I say. "Thanks for the compliment, but it's not going to happen again."

"Actually," Alden says, "he's with me." He scoots over to my side of the desk and stands next to me.

I force myself to maintain my best courtroom demeanor—no unplanned reactions, ever. But inside, I'm grinning. Thanks, Alden, you've made my day.

"Then what were you doing with me the other night?" Earl sounds indignant—it seems like it's on Alden's behalf, which is both surprising and cute—and his eyes are wide as he looks at Alden. "Does he cheat on you?" he demands. I'm grateful Earl seems to have not picked up on how my "one night" rule applies in this context. I decide to roll with it.

I get up and put my arm around Alden's shoulder, kissing the top of his head. He smells like shampoo. "Nah, we're new. When you find the one, you know he's forever."

"He's decided to hang up his belt for the last time," Alden says, sliding an arm around my waist and giving me a squeeze. "Now that we're together." He looks up at me and smiles, and it hits me somewhere weird. It's a sweet smile, and his eyes sparkle with intelligence and good humor.

Earl's face drops, and I'm almost sorry I'm hurting him. Almost. He knew the rules. "Okay, well. It was worth a shot." He shoves his hands into his pockets and makes his way out, escorted by Shelby, who magically appears, leaving Alden in my office. Hastily, I take my arm off him and look down, resisting the urge to run my fingers through his messy hair. "Sorry you had to see that. Thanks for your quick thinking."

"It's okay," he says. "I've never done anything like that before. That kind of situation is new to me."

"Not for me, although usually they don't show up at work," I mutter.

Alden's still standing next to me, and I can feel the heat from his body. Now that I sorta hugged him, I'm aware of his compact form underneath those clothes. *Which I should definitely ignore.* "You didn't come in here to rescue me. How can I help you?"

"Oh, yeah," he says, setting a file down before me. "Do you mind taking a look at this prebill before we finalize and send it to the client? Noah asked if this entry was an error." He points, and I notice his long, slender fingers. "It looks fine to me, but it might be a duplicate of this other one?"

Alden isn't the typical guy I pick up who knows the score. Nevertheless, I find him very intriguing.

# CHAPTER 5

# *Alden*

I float back to my office and settle into my chair, touching my hair where Danny kissed it. All I can think is, *I had my arm around Danny Villaseñor.* Like it was natural. Like I was meant to fit there.

Today's the best day of my life.

I blink. Okay, I need to calm my wishing-I-had-a-guy self down. I have a crush on a man who, by definition, isn't one I should have a crush on, because it can't go anywhere. He doesn't give guys more than one night. And even if I got lucky on one night, I'd have to see him the next day, and that would be as awkward as that one time—okay, *multiple* times—I waved at someone only to realize they were greeting the person behind me.

I need to distract myself. I enter search terms on my computer for a report, but it's going to take a moment to compile, so I pull out my phone. Before I know what I'm doing, I enter "Danny Villaseñor"—oops—and find his social media. I look at his profile picture. He's such a hottie.

The icon's still spinning as my computer gathers the data, so I click around a bit. He's got a smaller social media following than I expected, actually, although it's more than I have. To be fair, I have no following, because my accounts are private, I don't post anything, and my only social media friends are people I know IRL. That's not really a recipe to go viral, so obviously I care not about social media success.

In the public photos and the ones Danny's tagged in, he looks really, really, really good. Damn crush. I put my phone away without adding him as a friend or following him anywhere.

My report is ready, and I go back to work, but I smell his lingering cologne and feel the phantom weight of his arm around me all morning.

* * *

After lunch, I hear footsteps, then Danny talking with another attorney, who I think is named Charlie. They pause near my office, likely making copies at the copy machine next door. Even though Noah told me they want the firm to be paperless, there's still a lot of work that needs to be done with original signatures.

"Damn, dude," Charlie says. "He really came into the office? Talk about a hookup gone bad."

Danny sighs. "Some guys don't want to believe the rules apply to them."

"How many guys have you been through?"

I don't hear Danny's answer—for all I know it's just a shit-eating grin—but Charlie's laugh is loud.

I look down at the papers I need to copy. I'm not being too obvious, am I?

Whatever. I stand up and grab my documents, then walk into the room. Charlie and Danny go silent and give each other meaningful looks.

"Hey," Danny says, smiling.

Charlie gives me a chin lift.

"Huh-hi," I stutter. "You don't have to stop talking on my account, sorry."

Danny smiles apologetically. "I hope our conversation didn't make you uncomfortable. Of course, since you were there when the guy barged in, you already had to hear more about my sex life than you should have to. Thanks again for the save." I nod. "Even so, it's not an appropriate topic for the office. Charlie and I are friends, and he forgets where we are sometimes."

"Throw me under the bus, why don't you?" Charlie mutters.

"It's okay," I say quickly, and I mean it. "I'm a nerd who lives with my mom. It's the closest I've gotten to a social life in ... ever," I mutter.

Charlie pats me on the shoulder. "Being social isn't all it's cracked up to be."

"I dunno. Going out and hooking up are pretty fun," Danny says, "so long as you never let hearts get involved. Get what you need. Give the other guy a good time. Move along. Simple."

Simple for him, maybe.

* * *

At four thirty on Friday, Shelby comes barreling into my office.

I've been wondering if I should stay late and get a jump on next week's work. In this rabbit warren of receipts they left me, there's quite a bit to organize. But my brain was built for tidying numbers. I love it.

And staying late could distract me from the fact that I'm going to be alone this weekend with no one but my mom for company. Like every weekend.

Don't get me wrong—she's great. But I wish I had my own place, especially now that she's responding to chemo and I'm starting to make decent money.

"Come on!" Shelby says, reaching over the desk and tugging on my arm. Then he freezes and we both stare down at his hand. He pulls back. "Sorry. I just get excited. I'm not coming on to you, I swear."

I huff out a laugh. "Thanks a lot."

"Remember, I only go for guys who are unavailable."

"And since I'm gay and single—"

"Precisely. Not my type."

That makes me laugh harder. "Okay, no worries. So ... come where?"

"Firm happy hour! Every Friday. Didn't they tell you that in your interview?"

"Oh, that's right." I don't really drink, and it feels slightly strange to mix work and alcohol. Even in college, I focused more on studying than partying.

Yes, people like me exist. This may also have something to do with why I've never been kissed.

But I want to be a team player—and besides, I actually do like my job and want to get to know the people who work here better.

"I don't drink that much."

"That's no problem—just have whatever you want. They get the good stuff, and there are craft sodas and seltzers too. If you want to try it, we have it. But no one's going to peer-pressure you into drinking if you'd rather not."

"Well ... I do want to try something new. I took this job because I wasn't feeling so welcome at my old firm."

"You're welcome here. Come on."

"Let me shut things down. Where do I meet you?"

"Just in the break room. We don't bother going far. The point of getting together is, the owners didn't want there to be a separation between attorneys and staff. They wanted us all to be a team, and they figure a moment on Fridays when everyone can chat is a good way to do it."

"Wow. Okay. See you there."

A few minutes later, I walk into the crowded space. While I've met just about everyone, they—unsurprisingly, I suppose—seem looser at happy hour. Shoes are off, ties are undone, sleeves are rolled up, and long hair's piled in messy buns. A tall woman hands me a glass of red wine. I know I could have a Diet Coke or one of the funky fruit-flavored sodas, but that seems like such an Alden thing to do, and I want to be someone else. Someone more interesting. "Uh, thanks," I say, trying to remember the woman's name.

"You're welcome, Alden. And it's Reyna," she says.

"Thanks for the reminder," I mutter. "It's hard to keep track when I've met so many people this week." I take a sip and manage to not make a face. It's not the first alcohol I've ever had, but I don't make a habit of drinking wine except at Passover, and this tastes nothing like kiddush wine. I guess I'm not a fan. It does warm my cheeks a bit.

"You'll learn the names soon enough." She gives me a huge smile. "If you forget someone, just ask. Everyone's pretty mellow. Except Charlie. He's an asshole." She must read the shock on my face, because she laughs. "He's my brother. I'm allowed to make fun of him."

"Ah." Before I can say more, Shelby whirls by, hooks my arm in his, and tugs me away. I wave goodbye to Reyna, and Shelby involves me in a conversation with Noah, August, Sam, and a guy named Owen about where they're each going for vacation this summer. Sisters named Lavender and Miel join us, as does another attorney named Briony.

I don't see Danny, so maybe he's still in his office. I keep looking for him while trying not to be obvious. I'm pretty sure I'm not doing a very good job of being sly.

I feel like I'm in high school and the hot guy on the football team has a locker by mine. How long can I hang out in hopes of having him say hi before I feel like a dork? All day and into the early evening, apparently.

Shelby whispers in my ear, "Noah and August have been best friends since the dawn of time. They grew up next door, went all through school together, including law school, and started this firm together."

I grin. "That's so cool."

"It's an open secret that they should be *together* together. Everyone knows it except them—or, more accurately, everyone knows it except August."

August is a tall, confident man with a precisely tailored suit and an even more precise fade haircut. The look on Noah's face as he watches August gesture and talk tells me that Shelby may be on to something. "How long has this been going on?"

"Their whole lives, I think."

"Oh my God," I whisper. "Do you think they'll ever, you know ..."

"Get their heads out of their asses? One can only hope. There's an office pool on it—let me know if you want in." Shelby grins mischievously and calls out, "Hey, Noah. I wanted to know, does Weston & Ramirez have a no-fraternizing policy?"

Noah chokes on his wine. "Um, no. I don't think we do." August thumps Noah's back and grins, slinging an arm around him. I don't miss the pained look Noah gives him—not as if he's in physical pain, but a flash of longing.

"Oh my God, will they just kiss already," Shelby mutters under his breath.

"Should we?" August asks, and it takes me a moment to realize he's not responding to Shelby's suggestion but to his earlier policy question.

Having recovered from his dangerous sip, Noah shakes his head. "I suppose we could do what some places do—if people who work together start dating, we could have them sign a love contract."

Shelby laughs. "A love contract?"

Someone refills my wine, and I nod my thanks.

"Basically insulating the firm from a sexual harassment claim. It says that the relationship is consensual. But I think that's all we'd do."

"Is that an official HR position?" Shelby asks. Weston &

Ramirez isn't big enough for a separate HR department, so what the partners say goes.

August and Noah nod in unison.

"Good to know."

I keep listening to the chatter, and after a while, Shelby gestures at my glass. "Let me get you another drink."

"Sure," I say, and hiccup. How many have I had? More than two? Three? I can feel the wine going to my head, and my stomach is feeling a little lurch-y. The room's starting to go swirly, too.

I should probably cut it down. Cut it out? Put it down? What am I doing?

With the next glass, I get very friendly. I start telling everyone how happy I am to work here and how it's just the best place ever. Because it is.

Somehow I'm at the bottom of the glass again.

"Is this one a lightweight?" I hear an amused voice ask.

"Do we need to get him home?"

A really sexy, deep voice says, "I'll take care of him. Leave him to me."

And I don't remember anything else.

## CHAPTER 6
## *Danny*

I got to happy hour late, after one last client call, and my gaze immediately homed in on Alden, whose red cheeks and wild hair were a big change from his usual buttoned-up persona. I'm pretty sure he's not a drinker. I've been stuck in a conversation with Reyna about one of our cases—not ideal happy hour talk, but you get a bunch of lawyers together, it's gonna happen. Once I saw Alden was having some trouble, though, I figured my extensive experience with inebriated people might come in handy.

"I got him," I tell Shelby. "How much did he drink?"

"Not that much. I think he just isn't used to it. I can drive him home," Shelby says. "I wouldn't want him to be drunk in a Lyft by himself."

Alden lets out a light snore.

"No," I say. "Let me. Keep an eye on him while I close up my office."

Shelby nods.

When I come back, everyone's gone except Alden, who has his head down on the table, and Shelby, who's gently stroking his hair.

I get a flash of jealousy for some reason. Even though I know Shelby means nothing by the touch—he likes a different kind of guy—and even though I have absolutely no claim on Alden, nor do I want a claim on any guy. I still growl, "I got it."

Shelby gives me a weird look. "Well, aren't you the knight in shining armor."

I grimace. "Not really. I just know what it's like to be drunk in a club. Someone needs to take care of him." I ignore the fact that Shelby was the first one to offer to take care of Alden.

I reach down, about to sling Alden over my shoulder in a fire-fighter's lift, but I realize that might make him puke. So I pick him up bride-style and carry him to the elevator.

As we descend and make our way to my car, I get a few looks from other late-leaving workers. Even though it's nearly eight on a Friday evening, lots of people, especially attorneys, work long hours. "He's not feeling well," I whisper. I don't want to give away that he's drunk as a skunk, but I suspect I'm not fooling anyone.

I had one beer over an hour ago, so I know I'm fine to drive. No problem.

Well, there's one problem. I don't know where Alden lives.

I'm feeling the strain in my muscles as I reach the garage. I prop Alden up against the back door while I open my car.

Once I pour him in, I have to lean over to put on his seat belt. I realize that, under the alcohol, I like the way he smells.

After I get him situated, I fish in my trunk and find a Redweld —the folders we take to court. I dump out the contents and tuck the bucket file under his chin. It will at least collect the worst of it if he needs to ralph on the way home.

I get behind the wheel and let out a sigh.

I'm taking him to my place. I don't do that, but it's okay. He's not a hookup. Besides, he helped me fend off Earl, so I owe him one.

59

When I pull up in my driveway, I realize I'm in about the same situation I was in back at the office. I don't have a way of getting Alden out of the car other than picking him up. I shut off the engine and walk around to the side to get him.

He's passed out with a bit of drool coming out of the side of his mouth, but he's breathing normally. His hair flops in his eyes. He's totally adorable.

I reach over to unbuckle his seat belt, and he mumbles something. It sounds like, "Hottie." I chuckle, then gather him up again and carry him into the house.

I love my house. It's on a quiet, jacaranda-shaded street not too far from work, and it's perfect for me. What it isn't, is big. I don't need it to be, because I don't share it with anyone, nor do I want to. I don't have a guest room, because I don't ever have people stay over. I just have an office for the rare times I work from home. If I put Alden on the couch, he's likely to roll off and brain himself. So, my bed it is.

He's the first guy to sleep there other than me. This bedroom is my sanctuary, and I'm eager to come home to it every night —alone.

This is me being decent to a coworker, nothing more. As Mamacita rubs her face against my legs, I lay Alden carefully on my bedspread and tug off his shoes.

He's wearing striped socks, and for some reason that detail makes my heart thump. He's so quiet, and yet he has this little rebellion going on underneath.

Now what do I do? Do I take his pants off? He shouldn't sleep in that belt, at least. Or the tie. It could be uncomfortable or even dangerous. It's cute that he dresses up, though. Most people in the office do. We don't really have casual Fridays, because so many of us go to court, but Alden could be trying to impress us as well.

With cautious fingers, I unbuckle his belt and slide it through the loops on his trousers. I've never done this to an unconscious man before. I feel like I need to be extra careful with him.

I untie his tie and coil it, along with the belt, on the chair by the bed, then arrange his shoes under it. Fishing in his pockets, I find his cell and wallet and keys. His cell needs to be charged, so I plug it in, since we have the same kind.

As I pick it up, I notice a text from "Mom" asking where he is.

I think for a minute. Then I unlock the phone with his thumb and text back.

**Alden**: I stayed late at work, and now I'm spending the night at a coworker's house. His name is Danny. Here's his phone number and address.

I text my contact info.

**Alden**: Everything okay? I'll see you in the morning.

A response comes back immediately.

**Mom**: I'm so happy for you! I'm fine. I'll see you tomorrow. Xoxo Mom

I let out a sigh. I don't want anyone who loves him worrying about him. Also, should I take more of his clothes off?

"What do you think I should do about his clothes, Mamacita?" I whisper.

My cat meows, which likely means she's thinking what I'm thinking. Or she's hungry.

"You're right. He can't sleep in a suit. That's all there is to it." I'll help him into something of mine.

Holding my breath, I unbutton and unzip his pants, then chuckle at the rather hot CK underwear he has on underneath.

Who is this guy?

I'm walking a thin line, though, privacy- and consent-wise, so rather than spending any more time staring at Alden's skivvies, I pull some sweats out of my dresser and drag them up his legs. Then I tackle the upper half of his body, which is tricky since he's dead weight. I unbutton his shirt and slide it and his jacket off at the same time.

His bare chest is as adorable as the rest of him. Svelte, with brown-pink nipples. Again, I make myself move on without ogling.

I wrestle one of my T-shirts onto him, and he curls up on my pillow, locks of wavy hair falling into his eyes.

*Why don't you have anyone better than me to take care of you?*

Poor guy. Didn't they teach him how to party in ... whatever kind of school you attend to become a bookkeeper?

I don't know when he'll wake up or how he'll be feeling when he does, so I go and get a bottle of water, Advil, and an empty wastebasket. Just in case. I drape his clothes over the chair so they can air out a bit before he has to put them on again.

Without thinking too hard about what I'm doing, I brush his hair from his face, kiss his forehead, and turn off the light. I grab a couple of blankets out of my closet and drop my suit and dress shirt in the dry cleaning bag.

Then I look at the clock and realize it's still early. But I'm exhausted from a long week and from carrying Alden around like a bride. I pad out to the kitchen and feed Mamacita, then make a bed on the couch, turning on the television with the volume low—not that Alden's likely to notice anything short of the smoke alarms going off.

My phone sounds with a call from Charlie. "You at One yet?"

"Nah, you'll have to party without me tonight."

Silence. Then, "Are you serious? What the hell? You're never one to turn down going out."

I chuckle. "Yeah, I know. But I had something come up."

"Something? Or someone?"

"Kind of both. The new bookkeeper had a little too much happy hour and needed someone to babysit him while he slept it off." I hope I'm not giving away any secrets. But there were plenty of people there tonight who saw. And besides, Charlie's a good guy.

"Oops."

"Oops is right. And since I don't know where he lives, I brought him home with me."

"Uh ... you could've looked in his wallet."

I blink.

He laughs. "Didn't think of that one, did you."

"No," I admit. "I just wanted to get him somewhere safe."

"Well, then maybe it's a good thing you were there. Who knows what kind of trouble he would've gotten in."

"I know, right?" I scratch my belly. "Anyway, it's an early night for me. Catch up with you tomorrow night?"

"You got it."

We hang up, and I let myself drift off to the sounds of a car show, my cat curled up at my feet.

# CHAPTER 7

*Alden*

U m.

Where am I?

Judging by the light, it's late morning, and I'm in a huge bed that isn't mine. I don't know where I am. I don't know whose bed this is. My heart revs to a panic, and then I clutch the sheets and groan.

Oh, fuck. My head hurts so bad. I feel like there's cement in my blood. I'm both nauseated and not able to puke.

Rubbing my face with my hands, I sit up, wincing, and notice the bottle of water and another bottle of pain reliever on the bedside table and my clothes neatly hung over a nearby chair.

Then I clutch at my chest. I'm not wearing my own clothes. I'm wearing a T-shirt that is soft and thick and too large for me. What the hell?

Why does my mouth taste like a sewer? Actually, I think a sewer might taste better. I went on a field trip to a sewage treatment plant for an environmental studies class in college, and it gave me faith in humanity because of how much cleaner the treatment leaves the water.

Thinking is a challenge, but I eventually decide that hydration and pain relief are important. After a brief battle with the Advil cap, I swallow a few pills and about half the bottle of water. Then I swing my feet out of bed and almost step on a cat, who yowls at me.

"Hello?" I call. "Um ..."

I hear a low chuckle and smell sizzling bacon along with coffee. If I weren't so hungover—I'm assuming that's what this feeling is—food would be welcome. Right now, though, the thought makes my stomach lurch.

Still, I can't hide in some unknown person's bedroom forever. I venture into the hallway, where I spot a bathroom and make grateful use of the facilities before following the breakfast smells through a nicely furnished living room. As I enter the sunlit kitchen beyond, I look up and see the man of my dreams standing in front of the stove, wearing nothing but boxer shorts. I grip the nearest surface, a chair back, for balance. "Danny," I say hoarsely. "What? How?"

"Good morning, sleepyhead."

"How did I get here?"

Again, that quiet, sexy chuckle. "You had a bit too much to drink at the office happy hour last night, so I brought you here. I texted your mom, too, so she wouldn't be worried."

My head feels fuzzy. He ... texted my mom? What? I'm so confused. "Am I fired?"

He'd been raising a cup of coffee to his lips but stops. "No! Why would you say that?"

"Pretty sure I wasn't supposed to get so drunk at an office party that I can't even remember the end of it. I don't normally drink very much. I guess I overestimated my ability to keep up."

"You're fine. It was pretty much just you, me, and Shelby at the end, so not many people probably even noticed. Well, there were a few who saw me carry you out of the building, but they don't know you."

My cheeks heat up so fast it's like they're going to explode. "Oh, God," I whisper. "I'm so embarrassed."

He gives me this kind, genuine smile. I don't know if it makes me feel better or worse. "We've all been there, and I don't think anyone will judge you. I think maybe you needed to cut loose a little bit. That's all. It'll be forgotten."

But I'm not going to forget waking up here. Did he sleep in the same bed as me? The way the room was decorated, it didn't seem like a guest room. I look around and see a pillow and some blankets on his couch. I point at them. "Did I do that? Make you sleep on your couch?"

He nods, and when he sees me open my mouth to apologize, says, "Don't. It was no big deal. It's a very nice couch."

"Did you change my clothes?"

"I did, but I tried to not linger, if you know what I mean. You were pretty out of it, though, and I didn't think you could sleep comfortably in a suit and tie."

"I couldn't. Thank you." I try to figure out what I feel about him seeing me undressed. It certainly flusters me, because I wonder what he thought. I'm happy he got me out of my suit, though. His clothes feel oh so good. They're big, but they smell like him, and I don't want to take them off.

"Here," he says, rummaging in the refrigerator and then handing me a cold Gatorade. "Drink. Slowly. You need to get some fluids in you."

I nod and take a sip.

"How do you feel?"

I rub my free hand over my face. "I feel like someone put out a hit on me, but the hit man changed his mind halfway through and didn't finish the job."

He chuckles. "You're funny. Drink that while I finish making breakfast."

While I still feel like Satan's asshole, at least the liquid tastes good. I take a seat on a barstool and watch Danny cook.

This feels so intimate. I've never had a man cook for me before —not like this. I barely even slept over at friends' houses when I was a kid. I'm very inexperienced in *everything*.

"I'm just so sorry," I say again.

"Don't be. I think you need to get some food in that stomach after you get rehydrated. And greasy food often does the trick for a hangover. Hence, bacon and eggs. You're not allergic, right?"

"No allergies, although I don't eat bacon."

"Okay. More for me. Are you Jewish?"

"Yeah. I don't follow most of the rules or go to services more than a few times a year, but I grew up not eating pork or shellfish, and it kind of stuck."

"Fair enough. My mom still does fish on Fridays because we're Catholic." He finishes scrambling the eggs and then plates them along with grilled mushrooms (plus bacon for him) and toast. He puts the dishes on the table and adds a little bowl of fruit salad next to each.

I stare at the fluffy pile of eggs and the mushrooms and stack of toast jostling for space. You basically can't see the plate. "There's no way I can eat this much."

"Then don't. I won't be offended. I know you're not feeling great. Just eat what you can. It'll stabilize your blood sugar and make you feel better."

He sits across from me, still mostly naked.

Oh God.

I already knew he was pretty, but close up, he's devastating. Dark brown eyes beneath long lashes. A strong, square jaw and pouty lips. He has a dimple in his chin. He hasn't shaved yet, so his cheeks and throat are covered with stubble, and he's a little rumpled and a little sleepy-looking. His bare chest has a light layer of hair all over it, and he's not lean but not big, either. Just ... tasty.

I've never seen anyone sexier, and I'm very conscious of how my body is reacting to being near him. I concentrate on my plate so I don't stare, but I'm still hyperaware of his presence.

What's more, I revel in it. I'm enjoying having a man in my life —even for one morning. One to talk to and have a meal with. I don't feel so much like a loser.

I bet he has people over all the time. I bet he has no shortage of things to talk about with them, too, unlike me.

"Is this a common thing for you?" I ask.

He takes a bite of eggs. "Bringing a drunk guy home? No. I don't bring my hookups here."

I'm surprised. "Why not?"

"Because I always go to their place."

I hum, thinking about it. Would I be scared going to some strange man's house? I couldn't bring him to my mom's house.

But I have to start sometime. I'm never going to change if I don't try something new.

"You're good at getting guys in bed, aren't you?"

Danny shrugs, then grins. "Yeah."

"I wish I could do that. I wish I were different."

"How so? I like the way you are."

The warm feeling in my chest is just from drinking coffee, right? I ignore his question and straighten my shoulders, deciding I can be brave. After all, for some reason, I'm not inarticulate around Danny anymore. Maybe it's because it's morning and we're sitting here in our sleep clothes. Maybe it's because it feels like we're equal when he's made me breakfast and seen me at my worst. So I decide to go for it. "Can I ask you something?"

"Sure." His eyes are soft and interested.

"I kind of already knew that you were good at ... you know. Even before the whole thing with Earl. Shelby told me that you're the king of one-night stands."

He sputters.

"Sorry," I add hastily. "Not that we were ... talking about you." I cringe, since we were. "It's just that you came up in a discussion about One. And he thought you could help me. So I wanted to know if you could give me some tips."

"Tips? What do you need tips for?"

"Because I'm ... Well, look at me."

He rakes his eyes over me, and I shiver. I like having his attention on me. "I don't understand. You're a cute guy."

"I— What?" I shake my head, trying to make sense of his words. "Most people think I'm an awkward geek."

"Geeks aren't necessarily unattractive. You have great bone structure." He reaches out a finger and runs it down my cheekbone, which raises the hairs on the back of my neck. "And your eyes are gorgeous. And that tight body?" He blows out a breath. "Yeah, you're beautiful."

"Well, you're the first to say that."

Danny looks genuinely surprised. "Really? Do people not have eyes?"

I shrug.

"I mean, if I'm being honest, while your clothes are fine, they don't fit you well. It's all in the cut. And I dig your hair, but it could be tamed a bit."

"See," I say. "I don't know these things."

"Most stores have stylists who can help."

"I don't just need a stylist, though. I need a full-on glow-up."

"Meh. Glow-ups are overrated."

"Coming from someone who's already had one. Or was born that way."

He snorts. "I wasn't born this way." A dark look passes over his face. "I definitely became who I am."

I wonder what he means. What has he gone through? Whatever it was, he made himself irresistible.

"I wish I were more like you." Then my eyes widen. "Shit, I'm embarrassed to say it like that."

"It's okay. It's a compliment." He grins. "I can be complimentary, too. You look good in my space, wearing my shirt, with that sexy pillow mark on your cheek."

"I do?"

"Yes."

But he hasn't given me any tips. Maybe because I haven't asked him right.

"Can you help me?" I blurt out.

He blinks. "Help you how?"

"Help me be more like you."

Danny throws his head back and laughs. "Why on earth would you want to be more like me? Just be yourself. You seem like a pretty cool person."

"I'm too shy, and I don't know how to ask for what I want."

"You did it pretty well just now," he points out.

"That's because I'm desperate." I bite my lower lip and let out a sigh. "Never mind."

He holds up his hands. "Whoa, whoa. What is it that you want?"

"I'm really inexperienced," I say. "It's embarrassing. I see you all confident, and I wish I could have that kind of confidence."

"You have plenty of confidence. You're the absolute boss of spreadsheets."

"But I know nothing about what to do *between* the sheets."

Danny smiles. "Oh, is that all? You can get experience in the bedroom. That's easy."

"That's what I'm saying. It *isn't* easy. I don't even know where to start."

Now his face morphs to confusion. "What do you mean?"

I straighten my shoulders. Might as well confess everything. "I've never even kissed anyone. Like a real kiss, I mean."

He studies me. "You haven't kissed anyone?"

"Go ahead and say it," I mutter. "I'm the biggest nerd you've ever met."

"No. I think you may be the most genuine person I've ever met. You're not letting yourself be talked into something you don't want to do."

I falter. "But that's the point. I *do* want to."

"Would you want to kiss me?" Danny's question isn't teasing or an offer. It comes out as a genuine inquiry.

My huffed-out laugh is loud and fast. "Yes. I mean, no, that's not right."

I can't believe I'm talking about kissing with Danny while he's wearing only boxers and looking so kissable I could die from ... *something*. Desire or shame, not sure which. It could go either way.

Right now, it's looking like shame since I'm aghast that I managed to ask my crush for help.

Oh, shit.

This is going to implode. I'm going to lose my job and be blackballed from ever working again.

I take a deep breath. I've come this far, and I'm ashamed enough as it is to both be a virgin and be asking one of my new bosses for help. I'm not going to leave here without having done my best to plead my case. Except ...

"I'd like to kiss you, but I wouldn't want you to feel guilted into it," I say.

"Fair enough," Danny says. "But that isn't what I meant. I'm just trying to figure out where you're coming from. You want me to help you find someone else to kiss."

Now or never.

"Yes, and I want you to teach me how to kiss. And how to have sex."

Danny chokes on his coffee but recovers quickly. "Like, be a sex tutor?"

"Yes."

"Jesus. I need a moment." He puts his cup down and takes a deep breath. "Do you have any idea how enticing the idea of being someone's first is? At least to a guy like me?"

"So will you help me? Because the only dates I've been on have sucked. I'm not having any luck at all."

He rubs a hand over his face. "I'm trying to figure out what it is you're asking. What exactly do you want me to teach you, and how? Because I'm not fucking you," he adds quickly. "I mean, you're plenty fuckable. But I'm not the right one for you. You should save that for someone you care about."

"You don't have that kind of restriction."

"I don't do feelings or commitments. So the emotional part of sex doesn't matter to me."

"I don't want it to matter for me, either. I'm sick of this." I gesture at myself helplessly.

He's silent for a long moment. Then he shakes his head. "I'm sorry, but I think it's a bad idea. I can't do it."

Disappointment swells in my stomach, though I can't say I'm surprised. He's out of my league. My headache threatens to burst through the dulling from the pain pills. "I get it. No worries. I'm not your type. Fine."

"It has nothing to do with that. You're sexy, and I don't have a type. But you're too sweet and innocent to be trying to become a guy like me."

"Whatever," I mutter, and pick up my dishes. "Thanks for breakfast." I'm so embarrassed. I can't believe Danny had to see me drunk. I can't believe he took me home and put me to bed. And I can't believe I asked him to teach me how to seduce guys. If I could burn up from mortification, I would. "I'm sorry for asking."

"Hey, it's nothing. Don't worry. You're okay. We're good." He glances up at me. "It's just that you don't need my help with this. You're great exactly how you are."

I let out an exasperated huff. "Yeah, yeah. I know all that positive self-talk stuff. What I don't know is how to get a guy into bed. That's all I was asking." I redden. "I mean, you have this reputation of being a sex god. You can have any guy you want. And I want to be like that. I want to know what I'm doing."

"Trust me, you don't want to be a player."

"It seems to be working out pretty well for you," I argue.

He shrugs. "But you're not me."

"I don't want to be you," I mutter. "I just want to be a better version of me."

Danny opens his mouth to say something—presumably argue more—but then appears to change his mind. He gives me a tight smile. "Tell you what: I'll think about it. Give me some time, okay? Let's get your things."

Nodding, I set my dishes in the sink, then go down the hall to change into my clothes from yesterday. When I pick up my phone, which Danny helpfully charged overnight, I see the text thread where he talked with my mom. Reading it, I get a swoopy feeling in my belly. He let her know I was okay without betraying what a fool I'd made of myself. I'm not sure whether his kindness makes me feel better or worse.

I sit quietly in his fancy car as he drives me back to the office. We don't say anything the entire time until I need to tell him what level of the parking garage my car is on.

When we pull up next to my much more modest hatchback, I pause before opening the door, staring down at my knees. "I'm sorry I was such a lightweight and got drunk, and I'm grateful to you for taking care of me. I'm sorry I asked you for help with my love life—"

He holds up a hand to stop my chattering. "What if I have a proposition for you?"

"What kind of proposition?"

"What if I help you out, and in exchange, you let me talk about you on my socials. I tell your story. Like, I'm the love coach or sex tutor or whatever."

What the hell? "I don't want to be known on social media as a huge loser."

"You won't be. I wouldn't even name you. I'd just talk about your progress. And I'd run the videos by you first, of course." He gives me a mildly embarrassed look. "In a moment of ... I don't know what, I agreed to a bet with Charlie about going viral on Ad/VICE in six months. Documenting your progress from virgin to confident, accomplished stud could be something that people would want to watch. They'd be dying to know when you finally get dicked down." He grins. "I mean, I know I would be."

I tilt my head. Do I really want to have my story splashed all over the interwebs? Even if it's anonymous?

I guess, if no one knows it's me, I don't really care. And, honestly, even if they found out my name, what's the worst thing that could happen? It's not like I have friends other than Mason. So ... I'd be even more undateable? I'd get pity dates? I'd get roasted on the internet? I'd be embarrassed and publicly humiliated?

It can't be worse than fumbling my first kiss and never having anyone go after me again.

"If I agree to let you tell my story, you'll teach me how to be more confident? How to talk to guys ... and do more than talk?"

He nods, and I shiver, because the burning look he's giving me is making me *feel*. I want him, and it will hurt that he's going to be teaching me how to go after someone else.

But if that's where I'm destined to go, then that's that. And how bad could it be? If this is a way of helping him get what he needs, then it feels less like pity and more like an even trade. I'm helping him out while he's helping me out.

"Okay," I say. "I'll let you document me."

"You will?" He gets this surprised, but kind of pleased and kind of concerned look on his face that makes the potential embarrassment worth it. In any case, I don't really know that I can be more embarrassed with Danny. He's already seen me at my worst and is still being nice to me. He hasn't shunned me.

Danny feels safe.

I nod.

"Then I'll help you with your love life. Be your wingman or whatever. Give you advice." He gives me the sweetest grin. "I guess I didn't think I had much to offer. But if you want my advice, it's yours. And maybe it can help someone else, too. Maybe someone watching your story can get courage from it as well."

A knot that had settled deep in my stomach loosens at his words. "You mean that? This could help other people, not just me?"

"I do. Let me have your phone number."

I give it to him, and he immediately texts me a thumbs-up.

For some reason, that gives me a thrill. This uber-hot man has my number, which is something I always dreamed of. Of course, it's an artificial situation, but with my love life, I need to take what I can get.

I enter his name as Danny, even though I really want to enter it as "the most gorgeous guy I've ever seen in real life." But that would be fanboying a little too hard, so no.

"Is there something specific you want me to teach you?" he asks.

"Everything. I don't know how to talk to guys that I like. I have no idea how to pick up a guy in a bar. I don't know the first thing about kissing. Or anything else. I don't know how to do anything sexual at all. I'm just ... a loser."

My stomach knots up again. I hate saying this stuff out loud. You'd think I'd be smoother, now that I'm well into my twenties, but nope.

"No." Danny holds up a hand. "For starters, if I'm going to do this with you, I need positive self-talk. You do want to get an A in my Playboy 101 class, right?" The grin he gives me makes my insides weak.

Could Danny really help me? Flutters of excitement start to chip away at the heavy weight in my heart.

I smile back. "I always was a good student."

"Of course you were. What that means now is that you'll need to challenge yourself to do things differently than you have been. You're going to need to listen to me and try some things that you don't like. Like complimenting yourself. If you're not your greatest fan, no one else will be."

"Okay." I nod a few times, determinedly. "I can do that."

"I believe in you." Danny rubs his hands together. "I'm going to have a good time assigning you a lot of homework." His tone gets flirty, and he pushes my shoulder playfully. "Maybe you should get a notebook. Do I need to prepare a syllabus?"

But I answer him seriously. "Maybe so. I might do better if I know what to expect. Like, am I going to have to go to a bar and pick someone up immediately? Because that feels like a final exam without any studying. I don't think I can do that."

"I'll ease you in," he assures me.

"Thanks, Danny. I appreciate it."

He nods. "Feel better. I'll check in with you."

A part of me doesn't expect him to. People sometimes say nice things, but I'm not the kind of guy who actually gets what he wants.

But if I do? If he helps me?

This could be a game changer.

# CHAPTER 8
## Danny

I've done a lot of foolish things in my life. Fucked the pizza delivery guy after he came in for a tip. Ran into a hookup's roommate when I went in the bathroom to spit after a blowjob—while I was still hard, with come in my mouth—and ended up banging him, too. Slept with a guy who later said he was actually interested in my mom. But taking on a sex apprentice might be the most ill-advised, because what if I fuck this up? My excuse is that I need to do something dramatic to build my social media and win this ridiculous bet with Charlie. And who wouldn't want to see sweet Alden gain confidence and learn how to slay?

I have to admit that I really couldn't say no. Not when he leveled those eyes at me. He's this tempting, innocent package I can mold into whatever and whoever I want.

Except what and who I want him to be is ... himself, as is. He's interesting and adorable, and there's zero reason for him to need to change. Still, it couldn't hurt to get him some experience. Even though, for some reason, I'm not really liking the idea of sending him to get friendly with other guys.

I rub my face. Better get this thing started.

As soon as I get home from dropping him off, I download the Ad/VICE app and open a new account. While what I'm planning doesn't run counter to any ethical rules, it probably would be best for me to remain somewhat anonymous. So I'm now LoveTutor-Dan. I also hop on Amazon and order a tripod.

But I can do an intro without all the bells and whistles.

I turn on my phone camera and walk around my place, talking.

"I'm Danny, and I want to introduce you to my project. Please make sure to follow me as I give sex lessons to a friend of mine. He's a virgin. I'm definitely not." I grin. "He agreed that I could chart his progress. Feel free to ask questions—I'm sure you'll have plenty. But for now just know that this channel is going to feature me teaching my friend all the skills he needs to get whatever man he wants and be a success in the bedroom. What do you think my first lesson should be?" I wink, then click off the camera and save the video. Best to keep this short. I send the file to Alden. I don't want to post without his permission.

**Danny**: This okay?

I stare at my phone—something I never do. I never watch for a "read" receipt or three animated dots, because I'm never waiting for someone to text me back. They're waiting for me.

This is different, though. Alden's too pure for this world, and the fact that he sees something in me makes me want to treat him extra special. Makes me want to know what's going on under that mass of curly hair and inside that bookkeeper brain.

I wait. And I wait. And I wait.

Until, finally, the message shows up as "read," and then I wait for him to watch the video.

Why am I still pacing? Why am I getting short of breath? Do I have an undiagnosed medical condition?

At last, my phone buzzes with a text.

**Alden**: Sure.

I burst out laughing. He's got playing it cool down pat. Maybe I don't need to teach him anything other than self-confidence.

Mamacita wraps herself around my legs, and I pick her up and text Charlie.

**Danny**: Here's my new channel. Six months. Watch it grow.

After a moment, he replies.

**Charlie**: What the hell are you doing? Teaching some poor schmo how to catch a man?

**Danny**: Who better?

**Charlie**: Well, we shall see. Clock's ticking.

**Danny**: Get ready to lose.

**Charlie**: Nah. I'm going to be the one winning.

**Danny**: As you say, we shall see.

* * *

That afternoon, I walk into my mom's place, find her in the kitchen stirring a pot of delicious-smelling food, and give her a hug. "Hey," I say, and kiss her cheek.

She swats my arm. "Don't you 'Hey' me, mijo. What have you been doing?"

"Oh, you know. The usual."

Mom raises one eyebrow. I grin, but she knows me too well.

"Work is good. I have some interesting cases." I pause, then figure I'm going to end up telling her at some point anyway. "There's a new guy at work who's pretty innocent, and he's asked me to help him be more successful with the mens."

She bursts out laughing.

"Hey," I say, offended.

"I'm not saying you can't do it. I'm just wondering why someone would ask you. I'm your mother, and I know you aren't one for a steady boyfriend."

"That's not what he's looking for. He wants to be brave enough to ask a guy out. Other stuff, too."

"Oh, well, then. Just give him some confidence. Everyone needs to be themselves, that's all."

"That's basically what I said, but he didn't seem to think that was enough."

"Nobody thinks they're enough. Even los orgullosos—their pride hides insecurity. You need to help him understand that he's okay just the way he is." She cocks her head. "Are you going to Pygmalion him?"

"Pygmalion?"

"Dress him up? Show him off?"

"He could use some new clothes. Not," I add hurriedly, "because he dresses badly. But he doesn't look like he's proud of how he dresses. It seems like his clothes are only functional."

"So he needs some fun."

I nod. "And he has this great hair, but maybe I should take him to get it styled anyway. A knowledgeable hairstylist can work miracles."

"Just make sure you let him know that all you are doing is polishing who he is already, not giving him a personality transplant."

"I can't believe you're supporting this."

"Of course I support you. You're my son. You have my unconditional support in whatever you choose to do. Be a lawyer, be a hotshot, take on a student."

I grin. "I love you, Mom."

"I love you, too. Now, set the table."

I do as I'm told, and when we sit down to dinner, I ask, "What kind of lessons do you think I should plan, besides dressing him up?"

"Does he have problems talking with people?"

"Not that I know of. I find him easy to talk to. He doesn't seem nervous around me."

"Well, you're not that intimidating."

"Hey!"

She tilts her head. "Maybe have him practice talking with a stranger. Basic stuff. Does he even know what he wants? Half the process is knowing what you want and don't want, so you can recognize it when you come across it."

"You're talking about small, practice things, aren't you?" Alden's not going to go straight to blowjobs—and I don't want to be discussing sex with my mom, anyway. But she has some good ideas.

I pull out my phone and start taking notes.

I'm back at home when my phone buzzes later that evening. For a moment, my heart does this weird leap, but then I realize it's not Alden, but Charlie.

**Charlie**: Coming out?

Crap. I'd forgotten. And it's not like me to forget. I guess I just am not into it tonight.

**Danny**: Dunno.

**Charlie**: Who are you and what have you done with Daniel Villaseñor?

**Danny**: I'm fine, just a little tired.

**Charlie**: How old are you now?

**Danny**: Fuck off. Younger than you.

**Charlie**: Don't make me go all alooooone

**Danny**: How can you sound so whiny over text?

**Charlie**: Superpower?

**Danny**: For real, I'm not feeling it. Maybe next time?

**Charlie**: Of course.

Apart from last night, when I was dealing with a passed-out Alden, I can't remember a time I've turned Charlie down, but there's a first time for everything. Besides, he doesn't need a wingman. He does all right on his own.

\* \* \*

When I get to work Monday morning, I try not to be obvious that I'm keeping an eye out for Alden, even though I am. I'm about to go down to see him when I hear my name. Noah is striding toward me, looking distressed.

I furrow my brow. "Hey. What's up?"

"Can I talk with you?"

"Sure," I say slowly, and go back into my office. He follows me in and shuts the door behind him. "Am I in trouble?" I ask.

"What?" he says distractedly. "No, of course not."

The tension in my chest eases. "Okay, good."

"How did it go Friday night with Alden Meyer?"

How did it go? *Well, boss*—even though Noah's technically my partner, not my boss—*I stripped him down, put him in my bed, fed him breakfast the next morning, and got a chubby when he asked me to be his sex teacher. Other than that, it was a normal evening.*

"Fine. I took him back to my place to sleep it off."

Noah gives me a look.

I hold up my hands. "I didn't do anything with him, I swear."

But I might want to.

My thoughts freeze for a moment, since Alden is off-limits in so many ways. But I've learned not to be ashamed of every horndog idea that enters my brain, especially when it relates to such a gorgeous guy. Moving along ...

"Is he going to be okay? You don't think he has a substance abuse issue or anything, do you? Do we need to look into some employee assistance?"

Oh my God, Noah's the sweetest boss on the planet. He genuinely cares about his employees and wants them to be well. "He's fine. He's a lightweight and tried to keep up with us when he shouldn't have, that's all."

"But he knows he doesn't have to, right? I don't want him to think that's some sort of condition of employment."

"Relax. He was just trying to fit in."

"He doesn't have to do anything to fit in, though. He can simply be himself."

I smile at him. "I'll make sure he knows that. I think you'll see a different Alden at this Friday's happy hour."

"Okay, good." Noah leaves, looking relieved, and I wander down to Alden's office. He's sitting at his desk, absorbed in typing something. One of his curls is in his face—reminding me of when I put him to bed Friday night—and he looks super cute.

"Hey," I say. "You doing okay?"

His face lights up when he sees me, and something swells inside my chest that I haven't felt in a long time. "I am. What are you doing today?"

I tell him about the case I'm working on, and he tells me about his plans for streamlining our expense reimbursement process, and I only realize I've spent too long on nonbillable time when Sam comes over to ask about a motion we need to file. I wave apologetically at Alden. "See you later."

Alden waves back, and again I get this funny wiggle in my stomach. I follow Sam to his office, where we discuss the project and divide up the work. When I finally get back to my desk, I sit down, but before I start drafting, there's something else I need to do.

I made a list of things I hashed out with my mom—and some things that were very much not appropriate to discuss with her. But Alden can work up to actual sex. For now, he just needs to get into the right frame of mind. I think I can help him do that. I pull out my phone.

# CHAPTER 9

*Alden*

As I work through bank statements and check off transaction amounts, I keep wondering what on earth I was thinking on Saturday.

At the time, propositioning Danny seemed like a good idea. But now it seems like an exceptionally bad one. Because I'm going to see him every day in the office. And he knows what an inexperienced ninny I am.

Except he was kind about it. Except he seemed willing to help. Except I'm so desperate to *not* be so desperate.

So maybe it was a good idea after all.

He stopped by this morning, just to talk, and it was easy. Ever since I got over my initial reaction to his blazing hotness, things have been easy with Danny. But maybe they're getting easier overall as I settle into this work environment.

A voice startles me out of my thoughts, and I see Shelby's kind face peeking through the doorway. "How are you feeling today?"

"Uh, I'm okay," I stutter. *You can talk to guys, Alden. Even cute twinks like Shelby. You can do this. You've talked with him before—he's safe.*

"You were feeling no pain on Friday."

I clap my hands over my face. "I'm so embarrassed," I groan.

"Don't be. You're not the first person who's had one too many at the office. Especially if you're not used to it, it can be easy to overindulge."

"I'm never drinking alcohol again."

"Maybe just go easy on the amount."

I nod. "Deal."

"How'd it go with Danny?"

"Fine." It was more than fine, but I don't want to let anyone else know that.

"I heard he took you to his house. What's it like? We all want to know. He's the most infamous player, but he never takes anyone to his place."

"It's nice. I don't think he's there too much, though, because he doesn't have art on the walls. He has good furniture, though."

Shelby makes a "Go on" gesture. "Dish. I want to know all about the love lair."

I shrug. "There's nothing to tell. He slept on the couch. I'd drunk too much—which you know already—and woke up with cotton in my mouth. He cooked me breakfast and then drove me home. He has a friendly cat."

He eyes me suspiciously. "Hmm. That sounds innocent enough."

"It was innocent!" I don't sound innocent at all, even though it's true. Nothing happened, because why would it? I'm not who Danny wants.

Except I asked him for sex lessons. Should I tell Shelby about that?

I look at him, this pretty guy with his platinum hair and big eyes. Maybe when I've known him a little longer.

* * *

My cell phone flashes on my desk, and I get a special thrill when I see that I have a message from Danny.

**Danny**: Your first homework assignment is to tell me what you're looking for in a man.

I frown. What does he mean, what I'm looking for? I want a man who isn't straight or in a relationship. Beyond that, I'm not in a position to be choosy. But I suspect if I text him that, I'll fail, because it's the wrong answer. And if I think about it logically, it's not true. I'm not settling for someone whose beliefs are diametrically opposed to mine or who was shitty to my mom or who I could tell would be abusive—to whatever extent you can see that beforehand.

I've never really thought about what I want. I've just focused on the fact that I don't have *something*. I'm not exactly sure what that something—or someone—is.

**Alden**: I don't know.

**Danny**: Think about it. You have 24 hours to tell me.

**Alden**: Sheesh. Bossy.

**Danny**: That I am.

**Alden**: Okay. Does the 24 hours start now?

**Danny**: It does.

**Alden**: I'll do it when I get home from work.

**Danny**: That's why we're calling it homework.

\* \* \*

That evening, after a quick meal with my mom, I sit down at my desk, fire up my laptop, and open a new document. What am I looking for in a man?

I start typing. I want him to not make fun of me. I can see Danny rolling his eyes when he reads that. It should be a given, right?

I want someone who appreciates me for me. Who doesn't want me to change. I want someone who's patient with me and balances me out.

And I want him to look like ... Actually, I don't care what he looks like. I just care how he makes me feel. Although with both the looks and the feels, the only picture that's coming up in my mind is Danny. Someone who listens and is caring.

I'm interrupted by a text from Mason, who's in Paris, apprenticing to be a pastry chef. It must be before dawn there, but bakers get up early.

**Mason**: How's the new job?

Such an innocent question. That now calls for such a complicated response. What do I tell him? The safe-for-work bits, like I love the job I'm doing and the people I'm working for? Or the part where I got drunk and now have a sex tutor?

**Alden**: Good.

**Mason**: That seems evasive.

**Alden**: Because it is?

**Mason**: Is that a question or a statement.

**Alden**: Both?

**Mason**: Lol.

My phone rings, and it's my bestie. "I decided our texts are going nowhere," he says. "So, what's really going on?"

I gulp. "Hi, Mason."

"Yes, yes, hi, Alden. What's going on?"

"Nothing. You?" I can feel his stare through the phone, so I give in. "I love my new job. I'm working with amazing people, and they have a very cool business model and philosophy, and I like the work I'm doing."

"I'm sensing a 'but.'"

"But I have a crush on one of the attorneys," I mumble.

"That's so cute! Are you going to ask him out?"

I choke. "Me? Ask out an attorney? No. I'm a bookkeeper, not a god."

"Pretty sure attorneys aren't gods, either."

"He is," I mutter. Then I take a deep breath and get it over with. "I also maybe accidentally kinda got drunk at the firm happy hour and he took me home with him to sleep it off and now I'm even more infatuated. And I'm getting lessons in how to be a playboy."

I swear Mason is blinking. Then, finally, "No way."

"Yeah, I know. I totally misjudged my tolerance for alcohol."

"No, I mean, you got someone to give you lessons, eh? Is he going to teach you how to go after the hot attorney?"

"Um, well, actually, he is the hot attorney."

Mason screeches, and I hold the phone away from my ear. "I love that!"

"I'm not sure I do. I think I might be in over my head."

"What has he asked you to do so far?"

"Describe my ideal man for him."

"Oh really? Who is your ideal man?"

"Him."

"So say that."

"Nope," I say quickly. "That's cheating. And besides, he doesn't need to know."

"Well, what else you got?"

"That my ideal man is male and doesn't make fun of me."

Mason pauses. "Good start."

"I'm Hopeless," I whine. "I don't know what to say."

"Did you capitalize that? You did, didn't you?"

"Kinda."

"Are you looking for someone who is more of a friend? Or do you want passion?" He says that with a ridiculous French accent, and I laugh.

"I just want someone I enjoy being with. Is that bad? I don't really care what they look like, although I want to find them attractive. But I'm attracted to a lot of people, you know?"

"Yeah," says Mason. "I know. You'll find him. Or maybe your teacher daddy will do the trick."

"That's not going to happen."

\* \* \*

The next day at work, Danny comes into my office right at twenty-four hours after he sent the text.

"Have you done your homework?" The way he says "homework" is so deep and dirty it makes me think he means something else.

"I wrote down what I want," I say. "So, yes."

"Read it to me."

It takes me a moment to open the document on my phone. I clear my throat and glance up. He looks amused. "Ready?"

He nods.

"I want someone who is male and who won't make fun of me," I dutifully read.

Danny snorts. "Those things are given. This list needs to be more aspirational."

"Well, give me a minute."

"Sorry. I got impatient. Hit me."

"I want him to like me when we wake up in the morning and when we go to bed and all the time in between. I want him to want to tell me things and trust that I will support him. I want him to listen and not tell me that what I'm feeling is wrong. I want him to accept me for who I am. And I want to love him back with all my soul."

I glance up. Danny's eyes are warm and welcoming. I could swim in them.

"I want him to be patient with my inexperience."

Danny nods. "Okay, good start. We can work with this. And how inexperienced are you? Have you ever held hands?"

"Just with my best friend."

"Have you danced with a guy?"

I shake my head. "No. No one ever asked me, and I didn't ask them."

"Were you too shy?"

"Yes. And I was focused on my studies. The socially awkward don't do well at parties and things like that. I've been to a few weddings and b'nei mitzvahs, but I stayed away from dancing."

"Do you think you'd like to dance?"

"I don't know. Maybe. I like music."

"Dancing's fun and sexy. You can feel the rhythm in your body, and you get to be close to people." He gives me an evaluating look. "I think we're going to take you dancing."

I open my mouth to say no, then remember I'm not doing that right now. "Okay."

"You don't need to be a pushover, Alden. If you really don't want to do something, that's fine. Speak up for yourself. But I'm going to ask you to try new things, because it's good for you."

I gulp. "Okay."

He taps my desk with his finger a few times. "I have to go to court now, but today's homework is to talk to a stranger. Not just any stranger. Not, like, a waiter or cashier. It needs to be someone you don't *have* to talk to for a transaction. Someone you could potentially take home with you—or go home with. Maybe they're sitting on a park bench. Or by themselves in a restaurant."

I want to ask how I figure out who to pick, but that might be the point of the exercise. Maybe I'm overthinking this. "Okay," I whisper.

He grins at me. "I'll check in on you." And he leaves in a cloud of handsome man.

I go back to entering numbers on a spreadsheet, waiting for a decent time to go to lunch. Might as well get my homework done early.

Danny's words echo in my head as I walk into the coffee shop in the basement of our building. Although most people grab what they want and go, there is some seating. Being new here—and being me—I haven't hung out here much, and anyway, I don't know how to go up to someone and talk to them.

This is going to be a disaster.

But I need to do it and report back. I suppose I could just say that I did it, but I'm not one for cheating. And I like how Danny is trusting me to give it a shot.

After I get my drink and sandwich, I take a deep breath and scan the room. A kind of cute guy is sitting by himself playing on his phone. He's got a vibe about him that I can't quite read, but I can't read anyone well. So I might as well try.

"Is this seat taken?" I ask, pointing to a place next to the guy at the long counter. The coffee shop is empty enough, it being not quite noon yet, that I have plenty of places to choose from, so it's obvious I'm trying to pick this guy up.

Not that I know how to do that.

The guy looks up from his phone and smiles at me. "Um, no. Unless you want it. And then it would be taken by you."

I nod repeatedly. "Okay, yeah."

This is going well. He didn't say no.

I don't know if he's gay, but that's okay. I can just talk to a stranger. That's the assignment.

Settling in next to him, I take a sip of my soda. I open my mouth to try to start a conversation, but the guy beats me to it. "Have you heard about our lord and savior Loki?"

I try not to groan. "Um?"

"I'm a follower of Loki. Here, I have some literature." He pulls a pamphlet out of his bag and slides it over to me.

*Great job picking someone, Alden.*

But I dutifully take the pamphlet, because I'm not going to be rude, especially when I'm the one who came up to him, not him to me.

Danny laughs hard when he finds out what happened. It's the end of the day, and he's in my office again, his big body taking over the space.

"Good for you," he chokes out, when he can finally talk. "That's part of the process. You have to figure out which people you actually want to spend time with and which ones you don't.

You found one you don't." His face softens. "But I'm proud of you for approaching a stranger. Full marks."

"I didn't ask him on a date."

"That wasn't the assignment. That wasn't even extra credit. Because you have to figure out who you like before you can do that, and I don't think you know."

Actually, I think I do know. And he's standing right in front of me trying to teach me how to go ask someone else out.

"I still feel a bit like a failure," I say.

"You shouldn't," he says. "Hey. Come here." He holds his arms open, and I snuggle into him.

I'm not a huggy person. I'm normally kind of prickly, but this feels good. His body is solid against mine, and I can feel his pulse in my ears. I can feel mine, too. There's just something about *him*. "Thanks," I mutter.

"Can I ask how many times you've hugged a guy?"

"Not that many."

"Maybe you should book a massage."

I step back. "Have a stranger touch my naked body?"

"A massage therapist is a professional, so it's much more like having a doctor touch you than a random stranger, and it's important for you to get used to being touched before you find someone to fuck. And as a bonus, it will leave you feeling better, more invigorated, and more relaxed. The massage therapists sometimes have a harder touch than you might imagine, but it's really good—I promise."

"I dunno. I think I'd still be nervous."

"Want me to go with you?"

"Really? You'd do that?"

"It's no hardship to get a massage. And it's no hardship to hang out with you. I like you, spreadsheet man. So is that a yes?"

"Okay."

"Super. I'll book a couples massage. That way you won't ever have to be alone with someone you don't know."

Red flags wave in my brain. "What's a couples massage?"

"It just means we're in the same room getting massages at the same time. No biggie."

"'No biggie,' he says. That means three people seeing me naked instead of just one."

Though it would also mean I'd get to see Danny naked.

"It's not like that. They're very good at keeping you covered. They only expose the part they're working on, and they don't do too much on your front—no chest or stomach area." He smirks. "Or lower. We won't be going to a 'happy endings' place. It's a reputable massage spa."

"Okay," I say quietly. "That's fine. Is it expensive?"

"Don't worry about it."

"That means it is, which means I'll worry."

"My idea, my treat. And it really isn't that expensive. It's just a little indulgence. Less than dinner and a night in a bar." He takes a look at his watch. "Crap, I have to finish up a brief. What are you doing tonight?"

"Um, tonight? Nothing."

"Then let's get together after work."

I look around to make sure he's talking to me. Even though we're the only people in the room.

"Yes, you." He chuckles. "Okay, that's another thing we're gonna work on."

"What is?"

"Your assumptions. I'm not a psychologist, but I think you don't believe that people truly want to hang out with you."

"I never said that."

"But that's how you behaved. Like there was no way I'd be interested in spending time with you." He frowns. "Do I have that wrong?"

"No," I say. "You have it right."

"Then come to my house tonight. We'll work on it."

I swallow and nod. Spending time alone with Danny feels like a date. Even though I know it's just because of our deal and so he can have content for his social media.

Still. Part of me swoons.

# CHAPTER 10

## *Danny*

Alden is perched on the edge of my couch like he's ready to bolt for the door.

Standing in front of him, I cluck my tongue and shake my head. "Is it okay if I do something?"

"Wh-what?"

I put my hands on my hips. "I don't want you to be afraid of me."

"I'm not afraid. I just get nervous."

"What if we do this?" I sit my ass down in the middle of the couch and drag him over so he's sitting closer to me. Not on my lap or anything. He's just three inches away instead of three feet.

"Okay," he whispers.

"Okay." I settle back into the cushions. "Look. I'm not going to force you to talk. But it'll be easier for me to help you if I know a little more about you. And some of the stuff I want to talk about might be uncomfortable. Is that okay?"

"You can stop asking me if it's okay." Alden takes a deep breath. "You know what? You have my consent. Ask away. If I don't want to answer, I'll tell you."

I nod. "Thanks for trusting me. I want to ask you about sex.

Because maybe we're barking up the wrong tree here. Is sex something you're even interested in? It's okay if you're not. Don't feel like you need to be anything other than who you are."

His chest rises and falls. "For a while I wondered if I was maybe on the ace spectrum, but I don't think I am. I'm interested in sex. I imagine it, sometimes. I watch porn, and I like it."

"Me, too." I smirk at the mental image of Alden watching porn. It's an appealing thought. But I'm here to help him, not fantasize about him.

"I read *The Joy of Gay Sex*, and I could picture myself doing those things." He coughs. "Some of them, anyway."

I raise an eyebrow. "I haven't read that. I wonder if I could learn something."

"I bet you could have written it."

I grin. "Likely so. Okay. I just wanted to make sure we weren't setting you on a path for failure. There's nothing that says you have to have sex or have a relationship—or have to have sex *to* have a relationship. We could work on your self-assurance without getting into the sexual side of things."

Alden's eyes get big. "But I want to have sex. And I want a relationship."

"Fair enough. You understand, though. If you were ace/aro, I didn't want to be pushing you into something that wasn't ever going to be right for you."

"I have romantic feelings toward people. I get crushes. I just get too mortified to talk to the people I'm crushing on."

"Then we can focus on that." I scrub my face. "Look, I'll tell you anything you want to know about me or about sex. So please don't feel like I'm prying. I'm simply trying to figure out who my student is. Do you masturbate?"

Alden nods. "Yeah. Most days."

If that isn't a sexy picture. "Me too. Okay." I knock my shoulder into him playfully. "I think you're hot. You should have no trouble with this when I'm done with you. The guys will be falling at your feet."

"I'd settle for one guy." He sighs. "This has always felt so complicated, and I just want it to be simple. I'm gay, and I've never had a physical relationship with anyone. I want to see what the fuss is about."

"What would you do on your ideal date?"

Alden tilts his head to the side, and it's adorable. "I don't know. I've been on dates—just not a *second* date. I get nervous in places that I'm not familiar with."

"We can work on that." I pause as something occurs to me. "We should be recording some of this. Or I should be taking notes for a video."

Alden gulps. "You can record my voice. Just keep the camera on you."

"Are you sure?"

"Yeah. Can I see the video before you upload?"

"Of course." I stand. "Hang on." I stride into my office and come back with a little tripod. "I bought this off Amazon. Let me set it up so I don't have to hold the camera."

He settles back on the couch. "Go for it."

I pull out my phone and set it into the tripod. "Ready?"

He nods.

I smile at him, then turn the camera on and smile at it. "I'm Love Tutor Dan, and I'm here today with my pupil, who's going to talk about his first homework assignments and receive his next one. I'm going to call my student, um. What should we call you?"

"John."

"Right. John Doe. John, the first project I asked you to do was to describe your ideal man. How did that go?"

"It was hard. I haven't really thought about it before, other than he's a man and he would hopefully like me."

The camera is focused on my face, with Alden off to the side and out of frame, and I'm sure my genuine affection for him comes across. "Now that you've had time to consider the question, who is your ideal man?"

"Well," he starts, "actually, my ideal man is someone like you."

My heart rate increases. "But I'm a player."

"No. Well, maybe you are, but you're also caring, hot, kind."

"I promise I didn't pay him to say this," I say to the camera, my cheeks heating.

"You didn't, but you asked me to tell the truth. I'm shy and awkward, and I'm not the kind of guy people give the time of day to. The fact that you're helping me tells me something."

"You're selling yourself short. There's no way that anyone who gets to know you for real would ever let you go."

"Wow," he whispers. "That's exactly the kind of thing my ideal partner would say."

For a moment, I'm a little envious of this fictional ideal partner, because he gets to see all of Alden's sweetness. "Okay, moving on. What do you find hot in a man?"

Alden swallows hard. "I'm not sure. You're very sexy, but you're off-limits because you're my teacher."

"And because I only do one night, and you're too good for that."

"I don't know. I might not want to be too good," he says cheekily.

I hold up my hand for him to slap. "Give it here. That's exactly the kind of attitude that will help. But besides me, who else?"

He shrugs. "I want someone who'll spend time with me. Who won't mind that I still live at home," he adds. "I want to be with someone who likes to be quiet sometimes. I don't know. I just want to experience all the things I've put off."

"While you and I have talked about this, let's tell the viewers. What do you think about dancing?"

"I'll try it."

"I'm assuming you've never downloaded a hookup app?"

"I'm scared the moment I do, I'm going to get dick pics. It'd be like racing at the Nürburgring, only instead of having a Bugatti Veyron so I'm competitive ... I have a horse. I wouldn't be able to keep up."

I squeeze his knee. "I think you'd be able to keep up just fine." And he likes cars? I make a mental note.

He's fidgeting, looking uncomfortable. But we might as well keep talking about this, because it's not going to get any easier if we avoid it.

"Do you think you're up for all kinds of sex ... eventually? Oral, frotting, anal?"

He turns this delicious shade of pink. "Yeah. I think so. I wonder what it'll be like to have someone else touch me, though. How will they know what to do? And how will I know what to do to them?"

"Ah, see, you don't normally do it *to* them. You do it *with* them. That's the secret. You're both in it together. That's the fun part."

"Oh. I hadn't thought about it that way."

We talk about his awkward experience with the Loki worshipper, and that seems like a good place to end. I grin at the camera. "Until next time."

After I turn off the camera, I give Alden a high five. "How was that?"

"Um, it was okay. You did most of the work."

"But I think viewers are going to love to hear from you. If they can't see you, that will just up the intrigue factor. They're going to want to know everything about you."

"Okay, if you say so."

"I'm sure of it. Let me process the video, and I'll show it to you. Then, if you're happy with it, we can upload it."

"Sounds good."

As I tinker with the video, we talk about how much we both love Formula 1 and cars in general. Eventually, with his approval, I manage to post the video, but it doesn't get many responses.

How come I'm not going viral immediately? What am I going to have to do?

\* \* \*

The next morning, after court, I stride into Alden's office and sit down in his wooden guest chair. I whistle. "Wow, this place looks so much better than it did a week ago."

Alden grins. "It was a mess. But that's no problem for me." His face drops. "Unlike talking with men."

I gesture to myself. "What am I, a cat?"

He gives me a little wave. "You don't count, because you're my teacher. Not a prospect."

Why does that sound bad? It's exactly right, yet my chest aches with this prickly pang. But I laugh it off. "Thanks a lot."

"You know what I mean. You're doing this to teach me how to hook someone else."

"Yes, and soon you'll have plenty of experience talking with guys." Alden waits expectantly. He's so sweet. How can someone not have picked him up yet? "So your next homework assignment is to get a makeover."

He swallows, and for a moment I'm mesmerized by his Adam's apple going up and down. Then I recover. "Don't feel bad. You're beautiful just as you are. But to help with upping your mojo, I think you should have a few new outfits." I pause. "And maybe a haircut."

"Going to turn the squashed cabbage leaf into coleslaw?"

I stare at him. "Are you saying you're a squashed cabbage leaf?"

"My hair is."

"Your hair's gorgeous. Guys will be drooling to get their hands on it." I get a vision of Alden on his knees, with me tugging that mane. I suppress a groan. "All I'm saying is that if you want different results, you might want to try something new. And everyone feels better with a good haircut."

He looks at me with those wide eyes. "Okay."

"Okay?" I don't know why it makes me so happy that he's trusting me with his image.

"Do what you like. I'm not the one who has to look at me—everyone else does. Might as well make it pleasant for them."

"Can we take a few 'before' pics?" I ask. "For posterity?"

Alden smiles. "Sure." I take several photos of him, and he looks adorably uncertain.

I kind of want to keep him all to myself.

* * *

On Saturday afternoon, I take Alden to the shop in Los Feliz where I get my hair cut. As I park, he leans over and whispers in my ear, "I thought you'd go somewhere fancier. Or a hipster place. This seems … normal."

I grin. "I've known Jessamyn since we were in school together. She knows what she's doing, and she's always been stylish."

Alden seems nervous, biting his lip and fussing with his hair, but then he sucks in a deep breath and lets it out. "Do your worst."

We walk inside, and Jessamyn greets me right away. "Danny!" She tilts her head to the side. "What are we doing? You don't really need a cut yet."

"It's not for me," I say. "It's for my coworker, Alden."

That term doesn't feel quite right, but I don't know what else to call him. My sex prodigy?

She gives him the biggest smile. "Oh, wow. Are you handsome! Come and sit. Let's talk about what you want done."

With a final look at me, Alden climbs into her barber chair, and she wraps a cape around him.

"What were you thinking?" she asks.

He shrugs. "I don't know. I don't think all that much about my looks."

"Dios mío. You have better cheekbones than Cillian Murphy."

Jessamyn fans herself. She pulls some of Alden's hair back and runs her fingers along his cheekbones, which are prominent and, yes, gorgeous. "If I just do some shaping here," she gestures, "and a bit of texturizing, we can keep the curls but make it more manageable." She gives him a penetrating look. "How open are you to using some product in your hair? Not a lot," she adds hastily, seeing his bewildered look. "Just some cream."

Alden shrugs again. "Tell me what to do. I'm the student."

She claps her hands. "Yay! Then let me get to work."

Jessamyn leads Alden over to the bowls, where she shampoos his hair. I play with my phone in the waiting area. I didn't really have to come with him, and I don't have to stay, but I want to. I like spending time with Alden. I want to show him support. And, frankly, I can't wait to see what he ends up looking like. I think he's going to be amazing.

After a while, I glance up, and she's almost done. My jaw drops. I can't believe the transformation. While Alden was already beautiful, having his hair tamed makes him ... sexy. I saw that in him from the start, but now the rest of the world is going to see, too.

For a moment, I regret it. I liked being the only one who saw him this way. It's the best thing for him, though. I quickly Zelle Jessamyn the price of a cut, plus a generous tip. She glances down and gives me a quick smile when her smartphone watch pings with the payment.

"You look amazing!" I say. "What do you think?"

Alden is studying himself in the mirror, a smile on his face. "I like it." He tugs at a curl, which is shorter and in control, but still very Alden. "I think I can keep this up."

Jessamyn finishes, and when she whips off his cape, she holds out her arms. "You okay with a hug?"

"Yeah," he says, smiling. "Absolutely."

"Um, how much do I owe you?" he asks.

"It's taken care of," she says, and winks at me.

Alden spins and looks at me. "What? I could pay for it."

"It's a present," I say. "Consider it a bonus."

"I have money," he grumbles.

"I know you do. Just let me do something nice for you, okay?" I whisper in his ear. "That's part of this, too. Part of being confident is letting yourself accept things. Presents, invitations, dates, dances. *Blowjobs*."

He sputters, and Jessamyn laughs. "What are you two talking about?"

"Nothing," I say. "Just a game he and I have going on."

"Come back anytime. I'd love to see you both again. You make a cute couple."

"We're not together," Alden says.

Jessamyn just nods. "Okay."

When we get back to my car, he keeps glancing in the mirror on the back of the visor. "I can't get over how I look like myself, only better."

"Makes sense to me." I pull out my phone. "Do you mind if we do a video? We can keep you off-screen."

"That's fine," he says. "Go ahead and record."

I pull out my camera and start talking about how part of being confident is feeling like you look put together. And we're in phase one, which was a new haircut. "My protégé seems to have liked the experience. What did you think, 'John'?"

"It was scary—guess I didn't know what would happen or if she would make me look even geekier—but I'm glad I did it."

We chat about how his haircutting experience was, and then I shut down the video.

"Now it's time for the next part," I say. "Clothes. Do you mind showing me what you already have?"

"You want to come over to my house?"

"Yeah," I say. "I mean, that's where your clothes are, presumably." He hesitates, and I wonder what I did wrong. "Sorry," I say. "I don't mean to intrude."

"No, it's not that. Just, my mom's in treatment for cancer, so she might be kind of worn out."

"I'm so sorry," I say immediately. "We don't have to—"

"No. She's almost done with chemo, and the prognosis is really positive. I want her to meet you. If you're okay with that."

"I'd love to."

We drive to Alden's house, which is in what would once have been a nice, middle-class neighborhood of Los Angeles, but nowadays prices are through the roof everywhere.

"Mom," Alden calls as we walk through the front door.

"In here, sweetie."

I follow him into the living room, where his mother is sitting in an armchair reading a book. She gives him a big smile, and he goes over and drops a kiss on her head. "This is my coworker, Danny."

"Nice to meet you," I say, shaking her hand.

"Likewise. Wow, your hair, Alden! You look wonderful!"

"Danny took me to his hairstylist," he says. "I asked him to help me with, you know. Self-confidence."

I grin. "He was already a handsome guy. He just needed a little direction."

"Thank you," she says. "It's nice to be able to see his eyes. I haven't been able to do as much with him—"

"I'm an adult, Mom. Don't you fuss about me." He sighs. "Anyway, Danny's going to help me with clothes, too, and he wanted to see what I had first."

"You're the one he stayed with the other night?" She gives me an appraising look. One I know well from my own mother.

But nothing happened, so I keep my expression neutral. I nod. "That's right."

She seems to accept that. "Are you going to stay for dinner?" she asks me.

I don't know what the right answer is. I want to stay, but does Alden want me to?

He shrugs. "You can if you like. Not sure what we'll have."

"Then yes, I'd love to stay," I say. "I can help cook."

"Oh, he's a keeper, Alden."

I grin to myself.

"Mom, he's just a coworker." He scrubs his face. "Let me show you my closet."

# CHAPTER 11

## *Alden*

Danny stands in my bedroom, one hand on a hip, watching me as I pull clothes out from my closet.

"I like that," he says, pointing to a blazer. "And I bet those skinny jeans would look super hot on you."

"Really?"

He nods. "You may not need to do much shopping. You just may need to be brave enough to tap into the guy you thought you were when you bought these. But we'll get some new things, too, to round out your wardrobe." He pulls out a T-shirt and reads it. "'I swear by my pretty floral bonnet, I will end you.' What's this?"

"It's a *Firefly* shirt. Old TV show."

Danny smiles. "Okay. Will you show it to me sometime?"

"I'd love to. It has the best quotes."

"What are some of your favorites?"

"There are a few funny math ones, but I think my all-time favorite is when the captain says to one of the crew, 'My days of not taking you seriously are certainly comin' to a middle.'"

Danny laughs, and it warms me. He pulls out one of my suits and holds it up to me, inspecting it. "Where did you get this?"

"Warehouse store."

"I can tell. It needs to be tailored. The suits I've seen you wear have the crotch too low and the sleeves too long. I know a guy. We'll bring your suits to him so he can tailor them to fit your body. I promise you'll feel better in them when that's done."

We pile up my clothes to take to the tailor, and I check my phone for the time. "Want to help make dinner?"

"Of course," he says, and gives me this big grin.

There's something soothing in the fact that I know he's out of reach. Because I know I can never try for him, I'm not awkward around him anymore. That, and the whole already having seen me at my worst thing.

So Danny is starting to become a friend. A sexy, gorgeous friend I have the hots for.

We go to the kitchen, and I hand Danny a package of marinated steak tips, then start pulling out ingredients for a salad. "Do you mind being in charge of the grill? We have a stovetop one."

"I'm good with meat," he says, and there's that naughty spirit I want to tap into.

While he heats up the grill pan, I wash and chop vegetables. He pitches in wherever he can.

When we all sit down to eat, my mom beams at us. "Danny, thank you so much for helping."

"Thanks for having me over."

"How is work?" she asks. "What's it like being a lawyer?"

"I love it—the formalities of the courtroom, putting together all the pieces of a case and figuring out how to present it to a judge or jury. Hell, I even love those old, downtrodden midcentury modern courthouses with their terrazzo flooring, smoke-stained ceilings from decades ago when it was legal to smoke inside, and rickety elevators that crap out on you when you have a hearing at eight thirty, eleven flights up. Something about those places—all the stories every day in all those courtrooms—really gets to me, and I love being a part of it." He turns to me. "What do you think of the office, now that you've been with us a little bit?"

"It's the best place, I swear. Someone's always doing something interesting," I say. "And I've never worked at a place where the higher-ups take the time to chat with the staff about what they're working on."

Danny nods, biting into his steak. After he swallows, he says, "Yeah, we're all part of the same team. Or maybe we're all little boats in the same flotilla, headed the same direction."

"Do you have good clients?" Mom asks him.

"Very much so. I tend to like our clients and believe in what we're fighting for. I think it would feel soulless if I were trying to defend something I didn't believe in. Although the lawyer in me thinks that could be an interesting challenge."

"Can you tell me about any of your cases? Or is that all confidential."

"The identities of my clients are generally not confidential." He twists his lips. "For example, I represent a gay porn star who is suing for sexual harassment."

She sets down her fork and focuses on him. "Oh, that's interesting."

"We have to overcome all sorts of prejudices with that one, but I'm hopeful we can win. Just because he gave his consent for one thing doesn't mean he gave it for everything, especially when he was clear about what he would and wouldn't do, and with whom."

"Go get 'em," she says.

Danny nods. "The wrinkle, though, is that the studio is suing Velvet back for breach of a 'personal services' agreement." He chuckles. "Yeah, *that* kind of personal services. Ordinarily, you can't sue someone for specific performance of a personal services contract because of the Thirteenth Amendment against involuntary servitude. But because he's an actor, he's a unique 'commodity,' which is treated differently. They're trying to show he turned down projects he was under contract to act in, so they've lost profits and he owes the money. They're saying no one else can, uh, *perform* like he does."

Ain't that the truth. Although, while Velvet's as hot as hell, he's got nothing on my fantasies about Danny.

"Of course, the reason he refused those projects was because he didn't want to perform with the dude who was harassing him. So it's messy."

"How can the other attorney even represent this studio and the sexual harasser?" Mom asks.

"There's two sides to every story," Danny acknowledges. "While I like to go in there all fired up that I'm on the side of truth and justice and the other person broke the law, I'm sure there's another interpretation. And even if the other guy is a horrible human being—one, he's still entitled to legal representation, and two, sometimes the attorney can effect change from the inside. I like the opposing counsel, and I know her heart is in the right place. I have faith that justice will prevail, no matter how naive that sounds."

"So, when's the trial?"

He chuckles. "Not for quite a while. Months, or even years."

Mom sits forward. "What will you do in the meanwhile?"

"Oh, that's not the only matter I'm working on. I have plenty to do. I have another case that's going to trial soon." He turns to me. "You won't see me for days when that happens. I live and breathe the case when I'm in trial."

"Does that mean Velvet just has to wait?" I ask, continuing to ignore the fact that we're talking about a porn star with my mom.

"Yeah," Danny says with a "What can I do?" gesture. "LA courts are backed up. He won't get to a jury for a long time."

"Well, I'm glad you're helping him," Mom says. "And that you're helping Alden. When are you going clothes shopping?"

"Tomorrow," I say.

At that, she gives him an assessing look. "Don't change my son too much," she warns.

"I won't," he assures her. "I just want to help him be more himself."

That wins him a slow nod. "Then I approve. Tell me more about yourself," she says.

"I grew up in South LA. My dad died when I was four. Car accident. I don't have too many clear memories of him. My mom raised me on her own after that. She's a teacher at the elementary school I went to, so she was done for the day by the time I got out of class and I didn't need a babysitter too much of the time. She's my inspiration. Never lets anything get her down."

I nod. "My dad wasn't around, either."

"He and I divorced when Alden was a baby," my mom supplies.

"Right," I say. "So I don't really have any memories of him. He never did weekend visits or anything. I guess when he was done, he was done."

I feel like the lack of a father figure in both of our lives means something. Danny seems to have handled it by going out and conquering the world. I handled it by folding in on myself.

I like having Danny at my mom's table. With his good humor, dancing eyes, and easy smile, he's charming her like I knew he would.

After dinner, my mom excuses herself, and Danny and I go out to sit on the patio. We're drinking plain water, because I don't plan to drink anything stronger for a long time, and he seems not to mind.

"I know we've talked about how you have no experience with men, but did something happen?" he asks. "Something bad, that made you feel undesirable or like you couldn't be relaxed on dates?"

I scrub my hand over my face. "Not bad like *bad*. But, well. Yes." I tell him, in halting, aching words, how I almost got kissed by my high school crush but instead fell into the pool. And how his friends made fun of me, that day and for the rest of my high school career.

"What a complete and total asshole," Danny growls.

"Teenagers are so fucking mean sometimes. And crap from school can stay with you for a long time."

"Ninth grade sucks." I look up at him. "But I figure you were always popular."

"I was popular, yeah, but my high school boyfriend dumped me on prom night."

My jaw drops. "Are you serious?"

He nods. "It sucked. Actually, that's an understatement. I thought we were in love. After that, I vowed that I'd never open my heart to anyone again."

"I'm so sorry," I say. "That must have hurt so much."

Danny gives me a half smile. "It made me grow up."

I want more details, but I can tell by the way he's sitting that this isn't something he wants to talk about. "Thanks for telling me."

He shrugs. "It's in the past. I'm mostly over it."

"How did you get over it?" I ask.

Danny gives me a long look. "Maybe I didn't," he admits, "because it still informs my behavior. I think we both have some of the same things going on."

"Have you kept in touch with your ex?"

He shakes his head. "I started off the night by giving him a promise ring, and he broke up with me before we even got to dinner. I didn't really want to stay friends after that."

"That's awful."

He shrugs, then squares his shoulders. "But let's talk about you. You want some more homework?"

I nod. "The haircut was nice. What's next?"

* * *

The next morning, Danny picks me up in his shiny red Porsche. "I can't believe you want to spend your whole weekend with me," I tell him.

He shrugs. "I enjoy shopping, especially if I have a goal. And we have a goal. We're also going to have help, so it'll all go smoothly."

I'm beginning to realize that's part of the issue. So many times I haven't asked for help because I thought I could—or should—do it on my own. And when I did ask, I asked the wrong person.

Now I have this whole support team, and I like it. First, we go to Danny's tailor, who agrees that the crotch of my suit pants was too low and the jacket's sleeves were too long. I guess I'm not going to dress like the host boy from my date with Sumner. That seems so long ago, even though it's only been a few weeks.

Next, we drive to a boutique on Melrose, and like Danny's hair salon, once I step inside, it's not as scary as I feared. Danny has a good eye for my comfort levels, because this place is hip, but not so fashionable that I feel entirely out of place. I can see myself wearing some of these clothes.

The guy working there bounces out from behind the counter, all flirty with Danny, and I bristle.

But then he turns to me, equally welcoming. I almost look around to see who he's smiling at before I realize it's me.

So I lift my chin. "Hey." I try for nonchalance.

"My friend Alden here needs some new clothes," Danny says. "Quirky chic, so I figured this place was perfect. Can you help us?"

"Oh, absolutely. Let's get you some fabulous outfits."

Soon, the two of them push me into a changing room with a pile of clothes in my arms and start bringing me more items, one after another.

I try each one on. Even the things I think I'd hate.

And I discover that I love wearing bright red jeans. I feel amazing in a velvet blazer. I step out to show an outfit to Danny, who's sitting on a bench outside the changing room. "These pants fit well," I murmur, turning around.

"They do," he agrees. "They make your ass look biteable."

I put a hand on my hip. "Really?"

He stands and takes a step toward me, grinning. "Makes me wonder yet again why you've never been kissed. You're way too sexy."

"I think you're the only one who sees it."

"Not true. The salesman sees it, too."

There's a look in Danny's eyes. I must be mistaken, but it's almost like he's going to kiss me.

But that's absurd. I just don't know the signs.

I step back into the changing room. Danny follows me in to help grab clothes I've tried on and rejected and make space for more.

Without thinking about it, I drop my pants to try on the next pair.

But then I remember Danny is standing right here. Heat flashes in his eyes as he looks at me in my tight T-shirt and briefs.

"I knew you had that secret," he murmurs.

"What secret?"

"You wear very nice underwear. I noticed it when I undressed you at my house." He holds up his hands. "I didn't touch, other than the minimum to get you comfortable. But"—he grins—"you look really hot."

I feel warm all over at his praise. "I, um. Thanks. Just because I don't know how to get a guy doesn't mean I don't *want* to know. You know?"

"I get ya."

I can't do anything but nod, because my dick is starting to chub up, and I don't want him to see. I bend over and pick up another pair of pants to try on, and Danny makes a stifled sound.

"I'll wait for you out there. Let me know what you decide on." He slides through the curtain.

After I finish trying on what seems like everything in the store, I pick out the items I like the most—several pairs of colored jeans, a few patterned shirts, and two slim-fit blazers, and take them up to the counter.

"You two are so cute," the clerk says to Danny. "Bring your boyfriend back anytime."

I open my mouth to correct him, but Danny gives me a look. I guess he's right; it doesn't matter what this clerk thinks.

When we step out onto the sidewalk, I'm almost giddy. "Makeover, huh?"

"You didn't need too much of one. Just a few tweaks. Upgrading small things can sometimes make all the difference." He opens up his phone and types while we walk back to the car.

"What are you doing?"

"Buying you some Armani underwear. They're the best."

My mouth drops open. "You don't have to do that."

"You're welcome." He stops and gazes at me, and again, I get the feeling that he wants to kiss me.

"Actually," I say slyly, "I love those. Thank you." I can feel my cheeks heat, but I soldier on. "I really like sexy underwear. So, I, um, have a collection. Tom Ford, CK. Even a few wild ones from Andrew Christian. Jocks, too."

He shakes his head. "And you're a virgin."

"Not for lack of wanting. Just for lack of knowing, you know, what to do. For a while, I was worried something was wrong with me. Or I wasn't really gay. Because how did I know if I was gay if I hadn't been with a guy? But, I mean, it's obvious what turns me on."

Danny smiles at me. "Whoever ends up with you is going to be in for a huge treat."

His kind words warm my heart ... and other places. "I just hope I can find someone, period."

"No," he says. "You shouldn't settle for anything or anyone less than what you really and truly want. You deserve the best." He whistles and looks at me. "And no one knows that under those clothes is something ... Fuck, that's hot." He stares at me. "Are you sure you've never been kissed?"

"Not a real kiss. I mean, cheek kisses from relatives."

"That's not what I'm talking about."

"Then, yes. I'm sure. I've never, ever been kissed."

"Do you want to be?"

Is that an offer? My heart starts beating so fast I almost pass out.

# CHAPTER 12
## Danny

I want to kiss Alden. I want to claim his mouth. I want to find out what he tastes like. I want *him*, with his big eyes and his inherent sweetness.

I scold myself.

Alden's first kiss needs to be with a person he chooses. And he needs to be comfortable when it happens. I've pushed him far enough out of his routine for a bit. He can have a breather.

"Of course I want to be kissed," he says.

"If you could plan your first kiss, where would it be, and who would it be with?" I ask, channeling my thoughts into something more productive than fantasizing about the "who" being me and the "where" being right here, right now.

Alden stops, dropping his shopping bags and putting one hand on his hip, raising the other to scratch the back of his neck. "I have no idea."

"Use your imagination. Would you be on a mountaintop? In the middle of a crowded room? At a train depot saying goodbye?" I think Alden might be a romantic. And maybe I'm teasing him a little.

He thinks about it for a moment. "None of those. Or— I don't think it really matters where, does it? I have no idea."

"What about who?"

"I'm not answering that."

I tilt up his chin with my finger, looking into his whiskey-colored eyes. "Alden, be honest with me."

He reddens. "No."

"Please," I wheedle.

"Fine. I want it to be you." He meets my gaze, defiant, and a zing of electricity rockets through me.

"I'm not sure that's a good idea," I say slowly.

"Why?"

"Because don't you want your first to be someone who you could ... " Actually end up with. Have a relationship with. I don't say the words, but I think he gets the idea.

"Danny, I'm at the point where I just want to be kissed, and you're hot, so there you go."

I want to drag him into my arms right now, exhaust fumes and random pedestrians be damned. He's eminently kissable. He has this way of biting his lip and giving me a shy smile that makes me want to do very dirty things to him. Plus, his unsullied innocence is captivating. It's not that he's sexually inexperienced—or it's not *only* that—but how he's so willing to let me guide him.

If he really wants a kiss, who am I to second-guess him? I can credit him with the agency to know his own mind.

Even though I'm concerned he may later regret this choice, I'm not sure I'm a strong enough or a good enough human being to say no to him. Because I want to kiss him for me, too.

"When do you want your first kiss?"

Alden lets out a frustrated noise. "It's all built up in my mind now. It's annoying. At this point, I want to get it over with."

"That's not the right attitude."

"I know. I'm being super romantic." He rolls his eyes.

"Well, there's no time like the present," I point out. "Do you

117

LESLIE MCADAM

want to do it right here on the sidewalk?" My pulse has ratcheted up so I feel it in my ears and eyeballs.

"What?" Alden's jaw drops, literally drops, and he's so adorable, I can't even stand it.

"Do you want me to kiss you?"

"Are you kidding me? I told you I don't want to be made fun of."

"I'm serious. Yes or no?" I can't help the gruffness in my voice. And I can't help but focus on his plump lips. I step closer to his slim form. I want to touch him. I want to run my fingers through his hair and trace his jaw. I want to press against him, hip to hip.

"Yes," he whispers.

Before I can stop myself, I lean over, slide my hand behind his head, and kiss him. I've got a little bit of scruff right now, and it scrapes against his smooth skin.

He stands there like a fish, and I chuckle against his soft lips. No chance of him parting them for me to slip him the tongue. God, he smells good, though. "It's okay to kiss me back," I say against his mouth, then lean back, studying him. His eyes are closed, and he looks so sweet. Like he's waiting for a prince. Not me.

Alden reddens and opens his eyes, then sighs and bites his lip. Now I want to bite it. "But how?"

"Just give it a try. Trust me. You know how to kiss instinctively, I'm sure of it."

He hesitates, then seems to pull resolve from somewhere deep. I smile. "Is it a problem? You don't have to if you don't want to."

Shaking his head, he whines softly and then tentatively puckers up and stands on tiptoe to kiss me. We're touching only at the lips, our bodies forming an archway.

I step into him, getting us much closer. Chest to chest. Hips to hips. And, of course, mouth to mouth.

And I take control. With one hand on the back of his neck and the other at his waist, holding him to me, I whisper, "Let me in."

He parts his lips slightly, and I plunder his mouth.

Now, it's on. He lets me explore his mouth while he explores mine—tentative at first, then getting bolder and bolder, tongues dancing and swirling. Little sparkles zip across my skin, so intense that I imagine they must be visible.

We change the angle, and I move forward, bags forgotten, walking him with me to the side of the building, where I kiss the daylights out of him.

It's the kind of kiss I remember from when I was a teenager—but better. The kind of kiss that seems to say, *I want you. You're mine. I don't have the words to express how I feel, so I'm going to do it by connecting our lips as intimately as I can—and somehow, that will make our hearts connect, too.*

And now he lets out this growly little groan. We break apart, panting.

"Wow," he whispers. "Okay. Kissing. Yes. Achievement unlocked."

I smile. "Are you okay?"

He grins. "Yes." And before I can do anything else, he launches himself at me again.

This time, he's braver and bolder, his mouth hot and greedy, his hands—simultaneously tentative and firm—exploring my body, traveling down my back until they hover above my butt.

"You can touch me anywhere," I whisper, kissing his neck and trailing kisses over the exposed skin behind his ear.

His hands cup my ass, and I feel him get harder against me. I was already turned on, but this is driving me wild, and I grind my equally hard erection against his.

But then I come to my senses. He's new to this. We're out in public, and it's the middle of the afternoon. I can't dry hump him. There's no one gawking at us, but that doesn't mean someone can't see.

I don't want to shove him away, either, and honestly, my brain isn't working too well right now. Because my body is telling me *more, more*. But I know I need to keep it in check.

It's hard, though—ha—because he's so kissable. I hold him to me tightly, making out with him like we're high school kids in the back of a car. And it feels so, so good.

"Fuck, Alden. You're incredible," I say when we break apart at last.

Alden is adorably rumpled, his hair messy and his lips red. His pupils are huge, and he looks dazed. So I kiss him again, lightly. Gently. No tongue. Soft, chaste kisses to let him know I don't want to stop, but I also don't want to overwhelm him.

"You're a natural," I say. "What do you think?"

"I like this kissing business."

We pull apart, and I grab one of his bags and hold it in front of me to hide the tent in my pants.

Because Alden turns me the fuck on. Something about his innocence and openness just does it for me.

But it's not me he needs. He needs someone real, someone long-term. And I can help him with that.

"Feel better? Now that you don't have the pressure of never having done it before?"

He gulps. "My first kiss. Yeah. Okay. That's done."

"You checked the box?" I tease.

He nods.

I'm playing it off, but the truth is, I want to keep kissing him. Something about my lips being the first to touch his is making me very possessive. And I don't know what to do about that.

# CHAPTER 13

*Alden*

Back at Danny's car, I get in the passenger seat, my head reeling. I lick my lips and gape at him. "Do all kisses feel like that?" I ask in wonder.

He gives me a gentle smile. "No. That was a good one." He huffs out a laugh. "A *really* good one. Sorry to ruin you for life."

"Thanks a lot," I say sarcastically.

"It goes both ways. You may have ruined me, too. Time will tell. Maybe I'm just doing a good job at teaching you to be a man slut."

"You know, that phrasing is offensive. Because it implies that sluts are women by default, and you have to call out the alternative. Like a female comedian."

He nods. "I know. I even gave Charlie crap about it before. I'm not always consistent."

"And also it implies that being a slut is a bad thing."

"I don't think being a slut is a bad thing," Danny says. "I personally think it's pretty fun."

*Fun.* Judging by the way Danny's looking at me, I think he wants to take my clothes off. I know I want to take *his* clothes off, but I don't know whether Danny would be willing to do more with me.

"Should we, um." I gesture vaguely between us. But he gets it.

"Alden, if you were a guy I met in a club, I would've had you naked within hours." I blink in surprise. "But you're not. And I don't do more than one night. You're not the kind of guy for that sort of thing. You're a guy some lucky man is going to want to come home to and have again and again and again."

"So it's for my own sake you won't sleep with me."

"Well, when you put it that way ..." He scratches the back of his neck. "Actually, it might be for mine. I don't know if I'd be able to stay away from you if we had sex. To be honest, I want to kiss you again already."

"You can," I say quickly. Then, "I'm sorry, I'm sounding too eager. I'm probably supposed to play hard to get."

"You don't need to play games. You can be honest with people, and it can work just fine."

"Are you? Honest with people, I mean."

"I try to be up front, yeah. Generally I tell them what I'm looking for: one good fuck. And that's that. To be fair, I have had a few repeats, but they weren't ever consecutive nights. Just, some guys are hot, what can I say? But then I get with them again and remember why I don't do relationships."

I nod and swallow hard, wondering if that's really what he wants.

"Look, Alden. I know you're ready. Let's go find you the right guy."

I can't help thinking that the right guy is sitting here next to me. But he doesn't feel the same way, and I don't want to force him into something he doesn't want to do. Even for demonstration purposes. "I know you said you don't want to get your heart broken again. But do you ever think of looking for the right guy for you? Someday?" I ask.

He sighs. "I have to admit I'm getting a little tired of the constant chase. I don't think I'm ready to settle down, but I do want something different. It just wasn't working for me the last time I hooked up with a guy."

I don't want to know the answer, but I ask anyway. "When was that?"

He frowns and taps his finger against his lower lip. A plush lower lip I've now tasted. I'm trying to figure out my favorite part of our kiss, and the only conclusion I can come to is … all of it. I'd expected a quick kiss, not a make-out session that was as hot as the sun.

But me being bowled over doesn't mean that he is. I'm surely not the first person he's kissed like that. Maybe I'm not even the first person he's kissed like that *today*.

He finally says, "Um. Hmm. Weird. It's been a while, actually. Not since before you stayed over at my house."

I stare at him. "I thought you hooked up every night—or at least a few times a week."

He grins. "There are weeks like that, yeah. But I'm not a machine."

"Are you spending too much time with me? Am I taking you away from getting some?"

"I don't miss it," he says. "If I needed to find someone, I would." He gives me a friendly shove. "You're fun to be around, and I enjoy spending time with you. I guess I let it get away from me." He grins. "I'll take you home."

When he pulls up in front of my house, I pause before getting out. "Thanks for helping me."

"It's a pleasure." He leans forward, then stops, as if he was going to kiss me but thought better of it. I wish he *would* kiss me. Instead, he puts his hand on mine. "Do you want to try going to a club next? Or is that going to be too big of a step for you?"

"I'll try it."

"Next weekend?"

I nod. And again, I really want to kiss him.

He just smiles. "Enjoy your new look. If you want, this week you can try talking with someone else you don't know. Hopefully you'll have better luck and can avoid weirdos who invent their own religion. But your next homework will be to go with me to the club, so you can have a bit of a breather, if you like."

"Okay," I say, hoping my voice doesn't sound too wistful. "See you at work."

"See you."

* * *

"Alden?" Mom calls as I walk in.

"Here," I call back.

Do I look different, now that I've been kissed? Will she be able to tell?

Probably not. Even though I'm still burning from Danny's touch—in a good way. Like he's made me come alive. Kissing him was so, so hot.

"How was shopping?" she asks.

"It was more fun than I expected. I got a bunch of stuff." I hold up the bags.

"Then let's do a fashion show. I must say, I'm happy with how this Danny is treating you. It's how you deserve to be treated."

"He's just a friend, Mom. Or a coworker."

"Mm-hmm," she says, not sounding convinced. I let it slide and model all my new clothes for her.

When I'm done and back in my room, my phone buzzes with a text from Mason.

**Mason**: Checking in on you. How's the love coaching going?

**Alden**: I finally got kissed.

**Mason**: SCREECHES

**Alden**: Even though that's in writing, keep it down!

**Mason**: I'm so happy for you! Who? Some guy in a bar?

**Alden**: No, it was Danny.

Three animated dots appear and disappear. Then they appear and disappear. And this repeats for a long time.

Finally, a text comes through.

**Mason**: Wow.

**Alden**: That's all you have to say?

**Mason**: It's not every day you get kissed by your crush.

**Alden**: I can't have a crush on him anymore. He's just helping me out. It doesn't mean anything.

**Mason**: Did you like it? The kiss, I mean.

**Alden**: It was the best kiss I've ever had.

**Mason**: It was the *only* kiss you've ever had.

**Alden**: But seriously, it was really good.

**Mason**: This is better than if Sean Moses had kissed you in high school. Remember him?

**Alden**: Of course.

**Mason**: Did you know he ended up going to jail for cooking meth?

**Alden**: No! How did you find that out?

**Mason**: My mom's friends with his mom. Good thing he wasn't your first kiss. Good thing you waited for someone better.

**Alden**: That kind of changes my world view. All this time I figured I was Nobody because Sean never kissed me.

**Mason**: When in reality, all this time you were Someone.

**Mason**: How is this going to go in the office? I mean, now that you kissed?

**Alden**: I have absolutely no idea.

**Mason**: Then good luck, my friend. Let me know if you need anything.

He's right. How am I supposed to behave tomorrow at work? I mean, we made out. Is that going to change things?

I sit at the desk in my bedroom with a video game loaded, but I'm not playing it. All I'm doing is reenacting the kiss. Over and over again.

I've read so many kisses in books and seen so many in movies.

125

But none of that substitutes for the real thing. Danny's lips on mine. He didn't seem like he was in any hurry to get away from me. If anything, the more we kissed, the more it felt, well, passionate. Like we both couldn't get enough.

I haven't tried many things that made me crave *more* like that. Apparently I'm no good at drinking.

But kissing? I could get used to kissing. Very, very easily.

And I can't. Not with Danny, at least. He's not going to kiss me again. That's the first and only thing I need to know.

CHAPTER 14

## *Danny*

I pull into my garage and tell myself that kissing Alden wasn't a mistake.

I don't believe in mistakes.

All my clients have made what other people would call mistakes in some form. Whether they got involved with someone awful or made a professional decision that didn't go the way they wanted, there's a point where something went wrong. It's my job to put their lives back together—in legal terms. I can't go back in time, but I can do my best to mitigate the effects of their decisions. So they don't sting as much.

I can't see kissing Alden as something I need to go back and fix. Even though I want to do it again and again.

He brings out a protective side I didn't know I had. He's been embarrassed, and he's shy, and between the two, he doesn't want to put himself out there. But he has so much going for him. He's sensitive about the fact that he takes care of his mom, but I admire his loyalty. I take care of my mom, too. Or we take care of each other.

He's smart and kind. I also like how he trusts me. If I could bottle that trust, I'd keep it in reserve and bring it out whenever things are going badly.

But I've agreed to share it with the world. I pull up my Ad/VICE profile. I have twenty-seven followers, and while a few comments are negative, most are positive or coming on to me, like, "U hottie suk my dik."

Classy.

Still, I'm in this to win it, and I have to start somewhere. I turn on my phone and set it on the tripod to shoot a video, then settle in on my couch, my best side angled forward. Not that I have a bad side. "Hey, everyone, I have some news. I kissed my pupil. We weren't supposed to do that, but here's how it happened." I let out a deep breath. "Actually, I'm not one to kiss and tell, so this is kind of hard. All I can say is, I'd been wanting to kiss him. So when he said yes"—I shrug—"I had to. And wow, was it the right choice." Maybe raw, unfiltered honesty can help with the views and give Alden a confidence boost. "One of the top ten kisses of my life. Actually, it was number one. Better than my first kiss. Better than anyone else. It had this innocence about it, but it was hot, too.

"So what comes next? I think he's ready for some real-world experience. After all, he's doing this to learn the skills he needs to get himself a hot guy. I have to say, he has kissing down."

Much to my delight ... and disappointment. Because someone else is going to get the benefit of those skills. Oh well.

I click off the camera, review the video and edit it lightly, and then send it to Alden.

**Danny**: Is it okay if I post this?

I wonder if he's going to play it cool, but he surprises me by reading the message right away, and after enough time for him to watch the video passes, the dots start dancing.

**Alden**: Yes.

I laugh hard. Alden is just so ... Alden. There's no bullshit with him. No games.

**Alden**: And wow. Best kiss ever? You're really playing this up for your audience. That's fine. You can make me sound better than I really am.

Shit. Do I assure him I meant every word? Or do I laugh it off and let it go?

**Danny**: You're good, Alden. I'll follow up with you on Friday to make sure we're still on for the weekend. My usual hangout is One. Will that be okay with you, or do you want to go somewhere else?

Why is my heart racing? This is no big deal. Everyone knows me at One.

But I never show up with anyone except Charlie. And the thought of Alden going home with some random guy makes my stomach churn. Still, I need to follow through with our arrangement.

**Alden**: Should I drive on Saturday? I don't want to walk into the club by myself.

**Danny**: I can pick you up.

**Alden**: What if I end up going home with someone?

**Danny**: Are you ready for that?

**Alden**: Not really.

**Danny**: If it happens, you can take a Lyft. Otherwise, I've got you.

I rub my face, questioning yet again what I'm getting myself into.

\* \* \*

When I pick him up Saturday night, Alden opens the door wearing one of his new outfits. He takes my breath away.

"What is it?" he asks, picking at the brightly patterned dress shirt. "Is something wrong?"

I shake my head slowly. "No, not at all. Quite the opposite. You look gorgeous."

A grin spreads across his face, and his cheeks go pink. "Oh.

Thank you."

"Ready?"

He nods. "I think so. I'm a little nervous."

"Don't be. I've got your back."

This past week, I've been exceptionally busy in court, although I made it a point to stop by Alden's office every day to check in on him. Everyone's noticed his makeover, and Charlie took me aside to ask if Alden was the subject of my Ad/VICE videos. He also made fun of my 103 followers.

"It'll snowball, my friend," I told him. "Like compounding interest. It just takes time."

"Uh-huh. Early adoption is a thing, too, and you're late to the party."

"Pfft," I said. "I got this."

Truth be told, it is annoying to have only a few followers trickle in, like I'm a baby social media person. Which, I suppose, I am. At any rate, I'm not going to let Charlie know it's getting to me. If I lose, I'll survive the stakes, even though it would be embarrassing. Still, I like to win.

And I want to see Alden succeed.

He's twitchy as I drive, his knee jumping and his fingers tapping. I want to tell him to relax, but I'm pretty sure dismissing his feelings is the last thing I should do.

"You don't have to go to the club if you don't want to," I say instead.

He shoots me a glare. "No, we're doing this."

"All right, but it's okay if this makes you feel ... however. Stressed or excited or anywhere in between. I know you asked me to help you be more like me, but really, you just need to be yourself and try a few different things. That's all. If you hate clubbing, you never have to go back."

"But wouldn't I be failing if I did?" I can hear the smile in his voice, even though I'm concentrating on traffic. "I want to pass your course."

"Your grade depends mostly on class participation. All you have to do is show up with a good attitude." I reach over and squeeze his hand. "You're already acing everything."

His voice is small. "Okay." And then, a moment later, "Thanks."

When we walk into One, the music is thumping. Julian Hill's latest release, a catchy dance song, is playing. While I've been here so often I know every inch of this place better than I know my own house, I can tell Alden's uncomfortable. I don't want that for him. But I don't know any way to help except to give him a moment to adjust.

"So, Julian Hill is really Sam's boyfriend?" Alden asks, his mouth so close to my ear that I can feel his breath.

I want to turn my head and kiss him, but instead, I reply, my lips grazing his skin. I don't miss his shiver. "He is. Sam came to work with us a little bit ago, and he fits right in. I think his old firm wasn't the best for him. Julian comes into the office sometimes. You're sure to meet him."

He grins. "That would be very cool."

We make our way through the crowd to the bar. A lot of guys try to catch my eye, but I'm focused on Alden. I'm sure the regulars are wondering why I brought a date, but I don't really care.

"Want a Coke?" I ask, shouting over the music. At the last happy hour, he stuck to sparkling water. I don't blame him.

"Thanks."

I come up behind him and put my hands on his waist to steer him closer to the bar. In doing so, I'm reminded how much smaller than me he is. He might weigh a buck fifty soaking wet.

I like how he feels, though. And I really like how he smells. I like the bounce of the curls on top of his head.

He shudders under my touch, and I like that I did that to him. That he's not unaffected by me. Because I'm affected by him.

Except, wait. He's supposed to be looking for someone else. Not me. All this is just to teach him what to do with other people.

I wave down the bartender and get our drinks. Then we turn our backs to the bar and check out the dance floor on this level.

He goes up on his toes and says in my ear, "Can you show me how you do it?"

Frowning, I make a motion with my hand for him to continue.

"I want to see you pick up a guy," he explains.

I blink. "I thought that was your assignment tonight."

"I want to observe first."

A few of the guys sitting at the bar are the types I would normally go up to. But I feel like that would be disrespectful to Alden. Which is ridiculous, because he just asked me to do it.

But I don't want to leave him alone. Truth be told, I'm not in the mood to pick someone up. Lately, I've been wanting something else, but I don't want to analyze why.

"I'll do it later. For now, dance with me," I say. And before he can say no, I lead him out onto the dance floor.

Once we're there, he stands still, looking bewildered. "I'm not sure ..."

"It's easy. Follow my lead." I tug him into me, holding him low on his waist so our pelvises match up, and start moving with the beat.

I may not have thought this through. Because once I have Alden in my arms, I want him to stay there. He starts to move with me, and, little by little, he loosens up. It's adorable. He has some rhythm.

"I can't really dance, but I do get how music works," he says into my ear as one song segues into the next. "It always made sense to me. Like math and accounting."

Only Alden could talk about accounting on the dance floor and make it sound really good.

"Are you going to point someone out?" he asks, a couple of songs later.

"What?"

"Are you going to point out someone you're going to ... you know. Talk to? How are we going to do this?"

"Oh, right." I tug him to me one last time, then push him back. "Let's get another drink."

He nods. "Okay."

We go over to a quieter section of the bar where we have a view of the whole place and prop ourselves up on barstools. The place is hopping with all sorts of beautiful people. But none of them is right for Alden.

Then I realize I can't decide that for him. That's his choice to make.

I lean over and say into his ear, "Sorry, I'm not finding anyone" —else—"I'm interested in. Do you see anyone you want to talk to?"

He takes his time looking around, then shakes his head. "Just you. But I'll try harder. I'm sure I can do it."

He's leaning on me a bit, and I like it. I like the way he smells when he's a little sweaty and a little messy from dancing.

And I get this sudden urge to kiss him.

But we can't do that. I'm his teacher, and we've been over kissing already. Now he can find someone else to practice with.

That thought makes me want to growl.

I'm about to say something—I'm not sure what—when a guy I recognize comes up and stands right in front of me, his back to Alden. "Danny! Hey! How are you?"

Giving him a chin lift, I shrug. "All good. And you?"

"I'd be a lot better if you came home with me again."

It's pissing me off that he's ignoring Alden. I reach around behind him and grab Alden's hand. "Sorry, that's not going to happen."

Alden plays along, standing up and coming closer to me. I move aside to make room for him so that he's kind of perched on my thigh. Not quite sitting, but I'm definitely claiming him.

The guy—I don't even remember his name—frowns, somewhere between disappointed and affronted. "I see how it is." He shrugs and gestures at Alden. "Good luck with your new boy toy."

After the interloper walks away, Alden turns in my arms, and my hands automatically wrap around his waist and pull him in for a hug. "Thanks," I say as quietly as I can into his ear. "You saved my ass—again."

He giggles. "Is it bad for me to say that it's a nice ass?"

I laugh. "Don't flirt with your teacher. But full marks for the line."

Alden's eyes are dark in the dim light, the multicolored dance floor lasers flashing across his face. His full lips are parted. He adjusts his position in my lap, and I can tell that he's hard. I'm getting there, too. Something about his warm body against mine. The scent of his skin—Irish Spring soap, if I'm not mistaken, and the sweetness of the Coke he was drinking. He goes to take a step back from me, as if acknowledging that we're getting into dangerous territory, but I don't let him.

I like him in my arms. What can I say?

When Alden licks his lips and smiles, I lose control. I haul him forward so he's practically straddling me, and he parts his lips. My tongue dives into his mouth, and he matches the action, and *fuck*, I want him. He tastes like ambrosia. My hands make their way down to his ripe ass and squeeze.

We break apart, panting. "This okay?" I ask.

"Yes," he gasps, rubbing up against me.

"Just wanted to be sure." I chuckle. "Even though I know we shouldn't be doing this, it feels so fucking good. Better than with anyone else."

"I have nothing to compare it to," he murmurs against my ear, darting out his tongue to lick the shell.

"Trust me."

And for a moment, I wonder what it would be like to have access to this guy every day. I like him, and I like how I feel with him, and I want to know more about him.

Which, of course, violates all my rules. But I'm a lawyer. I'm sure I can find a loophole.

CHAPTER 15

*Alden*

D anny and I started kissing, and I don't want to stop. Also, I'm so pent up I might burst.

I don't know what I'm doing. At all. I'm way out of my depth, physically and emotionally. The second one might be more important, because I know this doesn't mean anything to him. Whereas, since I have a crush on him, it kinda sorta means something to me. So I need to stop.

But I can't.

His big arms hold me to him, and all the club noises and movement and bodies just fade away. I don't know anything other than him and what it's like to be embraced by him.

He's solid and soothing—and at the same time wildly exciting. We move away from the bar and toward the dance floor, kissing as we go, so it's clumsy but hot as hell.

Is this my real life? I need to pinch myself. Instead, I let him grip my ass tight as I rub against his zipper, our hard cocks pressed together.

"We have to quit it," I gasp, "or I'm going to come in my pants."

Danny grins wickedly. "I want to see that."

"What? I'll make a mess!"

But something about the idea is turning me on. I've only ever come in my bed or the shower—not where anyone else can see.

And I'm very close. I can only take so much—Danny's dancing is arousing, and the kissing has been working me up, and the friction on my cock is driving me wild. The music's loud, and there are bodies moving all around us.

I glance to each side, and it's not like anyone's paying attention to me. Sure, I'll be a mess, but it's so dark in here, I'm not sure anyone would be able to tell—especially not in these jeans.

Danny makes the decision for me with his intoxicating words. "I'm just saying, it would be fucking hot to see you come. Not going to pressure you. But if you happen to rub against my hard dick ..." He's hauling me up now, grinding with me, all sexy and dirty. It's more than dancing. His lips nip at my ear. "And if it feels good." One hand slips inside my pants and touches my bare ass. "Then enjoy it." Between the music and the motion, the rubbing and his hands all over me, his words and his kisses—I let myself go.

My dick pulses through an orgasm that's like the pinnacle of my life so far. Pleasure suffuses my body in waves, and Danny doesn't miss a beat. He watches my face and shivers, then dives in and kisses me deeply as my body shakes and my brain zaps out.

When he finally pulls back, he growls, "Fuck, that was amazing. Need to get cleaned up? Or do you want to go home?"

I don't want to do either. I want to stay here with him, dancing and imagining that this intimacy between us could be real, could last. But the warm spunk in my jeans will get gross and sticky soon enough.

"Let me clean up, and then take me home?" I ask.

He gives me a light, gentle kiss. "Sure."

Holding my hand, he tugs me to the bathroom, where I clean up as best I can. When I'm done, I wash my hands and stare at my face in the mirror. My cheeks are flushed, and my lips are swollen from kissing. My eyes are at half-mast, drunk with pleasure still. But my hair looks good. And my shirt hides the wet spot on my jeans, so I can make my way out of the club without too much embarrassment.

But then I remember. "What about you?"

"What about me?" Danny asks in his low rumble.

"You didn't come." I reach for him, uncertain whether I should, what, jack him off? Blow him? I don't know what to do.

He grasps my wrist. "I'm okay. Don't worry about me. Let's get you home."

I nod. Before we leave, though, I stand up on my tippy-toes and wrap my arms around his neck, giving him a huge hug.

"What's this for?" he asks with a chuckle.

"Just, thank you. I feel better. I handled being in a club without passing out. And even though this"—I gesture at my damp crotch—"is awkward, it was fun while it was happening." I shoot him a grin. Then my face falls. "But, crap, I was supposed to pick someone up. Or you were."

He studies me. "Would you want to come clubbing again?"

I nod.

"Then that can be next time."

"Who'd've thought that I'd like being in a dance club?" I muse. Now that I'm more comfortable in my own skin, being here is easier than I expected. Like I'm not fading unnoticed into the darkness and shadows because everyone is looking at the bright lights.

I'm starting to have some confidence. I'm starting to feel like, while this isn't my thing, and it doesn't have to be my thing, I can make my own place here. Not by turning myself into someone I'm not, but by finding the parts of me that enjoy this experience.

Because I do like music—and more, I like looking at the people dancing. I like observing. I'm not so good at being part of the scene ... but maybe I don't need to be part of it. Maybe I can just be me.

"You never know until you try. But you fit right in." He gives me one more kiss and then holds my hand as we walk outside to get his car back from the valet.

The whole time, all I can think is that Danny's acting the way I want a boyfriend to act—sexy, supportive, kind—and I need to stop those thoughts.

We're quiet on the drive home, but that's another thing that works with Danny. I don't feel like I have to chatter with him. He's ... easy to be with. When we get to my house, just like when he took me shopping for clothes, I pause before I get out. "What are we doing next?"

"I have some ideas. I think you should ask a guy on a date. What would you want to do if you went on a date? Go to the movies? Dinner?"

"I'd probably take him to a Dodger game," I admit.

"You like baseball?"

"Like a fiend."

"Did you know I used to play? In high school. Pitcher."

"So you mostly pitch? You don't catch?"

Danny grins. "Did you just make a dirty joke?"

I shrug and grin back at him. "Maybe. Do you want to go with me? To a Dodger game? I can get tickets."

"And now you're asking me on a date?"

I nod, feeling smug. "I guess so."

"Then let's do it. Pick a weekend afternoon game, and let's go."

At work the next Friday, I'm taking a break and searching for Dodgers tickets when Shelby walks in. "You're looking so good these days!" he says.

I touch my curls. "Um, thanks."

"Any reason, or you just feel like changing things up?"

"Actually," I say, drawing the word out. "Remember how you said I should ask Danny to teach me?"

Shelby's mouth drops open, and a lock of platinum hair falls into his face. "No way! Did he deflower you?"

"What? No! He's just giving me some tips. He helped me get this haircut and go shopping, and he took me to a club." I flush at what happened in the club. I've been dreaming about that nonstop.

"Well, that's very sweet of him. Is he doing it out of the goodness of his heart?"

I shake my head. "No. He has a bet going with Charlie about going viral on social media, so he's documenting my changes on that."

Shelby looks like one of those dolls that you squeeze and their eyes pop out. "OMG. Why? Are you okay with that?"

I nod. "It's anonymous. He's not showing my face or anything."

Shelby's silent for a moment. Then he says, "Alden, can I ask you something?"

"Sure."

"Why do you want to change?"

"What do you mean?"

"I mean, why do you want Danny to teach you to be more like him? Don't you just want to be the best Alden you can be?"

"I do want to be the best Alden I can be. That's the point. I think I've been holding myself back out of fear, and I want to not be scared anymore."

"But do you need to be more like Danny to do that?"

"I think what I'm asking him is to help me be more like myself."

Shelby gives me a long look. "Hmm. Okay, I think I understand. You're not trying to copy him. You're just trying to develop a part of you that's maybe underdeveloped?"

"Or completely undeveloped. But yes. That's exactly it."

He nods. "I get it. Okay. Carry on." He reddens. "Not that you need my approval. But you have it, just in case."

"Good," I say with a smile.

Danny raps on the door. "Hey," he says breathlessly. He nods at Shelby. "Hey."

Shelby's expression goes secretive. "Hey there yourself, big guy." He waves at us. "I'll be tootling off. Have fun, you two."

Danny watches him as he goes. "I told him," I say. He raises an eyebrow. "That you were helping me with my hair and wardrobe and stuff," I clarify.

"Oh, cool." He holds out his phone. "I got us reservations for a couples massage. Will five o'clock work? We'd miss happy hour."

I don't really care about happy hour, and the more excuses I have to hang out with Danny, the better. "That's okay."

"Then we'll head out at four thirty. Do you need to let your mom know where you'll be?"

"I'll text her," I say. "Are you good with going to the Dodger game tomorrow?"

"Absolutely."

I click to purchase the tickets.

He puts his hand on my shoulder. "The massage is going to be relaxing. I need it after the hearing I had today. And"—his voice drops—"you can gain experience with someone else touching your naked body."

While I want that person to be Danny, I'll take what I can get.

CHAPTER 16

*Alden*

T he spa is the exact opposite of the dance club Danny took me to last weekend. It's calm and quiet, sleek and sophisticated, all sage green and cream. Danny and I are welcomed and given water with cucumber and berries in it.

"This actually tastes okay," I say after taking a sip.

"That's good. Don't you eat fruits and vegetables?"

"Sure. But not normally in my water."

"Oh, the worlds I'm going to open up to you." He squeezes my shoulder.

We relax in the waiting area until our room is ready. Other people lounge around us wearing robes embroidered with the name of the spa, I guess because they're hanging out post-treatment or staying at the spa all day for facials or whatever.

This is a lot classier than the places in my porny fantasies. Apparently Danny only does nice things.

Or, at least, he does nice things with me. That's something to think about.

"Villaseñor couple?" the receptionist calls quietly.

Couple.

Alden Villaseñor.

I could handle changing my name, actually. I've heard enough Oscar Meyer jokes to last a lifetime. An end to the wiener jokes would be nice.

Focus, Alden. Go get, um, naked with Danny. In a very small room. Where a stranger is going to rub you and make you feel good.

Who thought this was a smart idea?

But I dutifully get up, leaving my spa water behind, and follow the perky receptionist down a tastefully low-lit hall that smells like ... something spa-ish.

They open a door, and I peek inside. Like the rest of the spa, the room is modern and soothing, with plants, quiet music, and a few lit candles.

Jesus. I think I actually have seen this porn scene.

But the receptionist is no-nonsense. They show us where to put our clothes and tell us to climb up on the massage tables, face down, with the blankets over us.

I take a deep breath. So, all I have to do is take off my clothes in front of Danny.

Easy.

I don't know if I should turn around and give him privacy, or if that would seem prudish.

He's seen me in my skivvies before. And I've seen him in boxers.

But he's watching me as he undoes his tie and hangs it on the chair, then starts unbuttoning his dress shirt. And my mouth goes dry. Where did that spa water go? I *needs* it. Because under that shirt is the sexy torso I've been dreaming about.

I know Danny works out. He's mentioned it before, and I've seen a gym bag in his office. The time I saw him when I was all hungover, I wasn't unaffected. But I missed the full impact because of how bad I felt.

Now, I'm feeling great, and if I keep staring at him, I'm liable to get a boner, and that will make getting a massage oh so much more uncomfortable.

So, instead, I start undressing quickly, not the slow striptease that Danny seems to be doing. While he isn't watching me, he's not *not* watching me, either. Like, I can tell he knows my eyes are on him. And I can tell he thinks it's fun.

Fun isn't what I'm experiencing.

Danny opens his mouth as if to say something, then seems to think better of it and doesn't.

Instead, he strips off his shoes, pants, and—oh God—boxer briefs, giving me a view of his taut naked ass, then climbs under the thin blanket, moaning a little as he stretches out.

That moan is going to make it hard for me to take off my own pants.

And also, "We have to take off our underwear?" I ask.

"Up to you. It gives the massage therapist better access. They can do these moves from your hips down to your feet and whatnot. But if you're not comfortable, don't do it. A massage is about pleasure and stress relief, so anything that will make you tense is a bad idea."

I decide to bite the bullet.

Grateful for the muted light, I shove down my briefs and climb up on the table. He can see my bare ass, too, and I wonder if he looked. After I situate myself, I glance over, and he's grinning unrepentantly.

"What?" I ask.

"Nice cakes."

I redden.

Then we just lie there, naked mere feet from each other, in a dark, scented room with quiet music playing.

I might fall asleep. Either that or go from semi to full chub. Or both.

After a moment, I let out a big yawn and try to turn it into a sigh. "Sorry." I giggle.

"That's nothing to be sorry about. That's the point. To relax."

Unfortunately, relaxing apparently means blurting out the first thing that comes to my mind, which happens to be, "Do you think people have farted while getting a massage?" Then I wince, because way to be a dork, Alden.

He chuckles. "I bet it happens all the time. Daily. Here." I look up and see him sliding his hand from under the blanket and reaching toward me. It takes me a moment to extricate myself, but I mirror his movements and take his hand. "Don't worry so much," he says. "I'm not going to judge you by any noises you make or things your body does. You're not yucky. You're just Alden."

He squeezes my hand and then settles his own back under his blanket, giving me the smallest glimpse of an expanse of tanned skin.

There's a knock on the door, and two muscled, hot men come in.

And my mind goes *there*. There to where this becomes some kind of orgy. Even though I know that's ridiculous. One orgasm with another person, and now sex is all I think about. I mean, I used to think about it before, but now it's constantly on my mind.

One of the guys puts his hands on the back of my neck. "Do you have any places you don't want to be touched or that I should otherwise be aware of? Allergies? Anything that hurts?"

I mutter a no, distracted from my dirty thoughts by the sensation of another person's hands on me.

Strong hands.

Strong hands covered in oil. Making their way down my back. Following the muscles and ligaments or whatever.

I groan, and it's loud. I hear Danny chuckle. "You okay there?"

"Yes," I say into the cloth-covered doughnut pillow. "I'm fine."

"I think we can do better than that," Sven says.

His name isn't Sven, but I wasn't paying attention when he said it, and he sort of looks like a Sven. I sink into the massage. I let myself enjoy the rhythmic sensations of hands on my body—of Sven rubbing the muscles of my arms, legs, back, feet, and even my scalp.

"Danny," I murmur after a while.

"What, babe?"

*Babe.* "This is amazing."

"See? I knew you'd enjoy it."

I turn over per the massage therapist's urging, and as I do, I can see the other guy still working on Danny's muscled back. While part of me is self-conscious because my back is nothing like that, at least I can enjoy the view for a little bit.

Also, at least I don't have an erection. I was worried I'd turn over and be tenting up the blanket.

But then Danny moans.

And yep. There's my cock. Great.

I can't even shift to hide it, because the masseur has the blanket pulled down so far. But he tells me to move my legs. I think he knows what's happening and is trying to help me.

So, there's that.

I let Sven work my arms and my legs. He runs firm fingers over my face and plays with my hair, drawing strong fingers over my scalp.

And then, with a light touch to the top of my head, he says, "Done. We'll let you rest. Take your time getting up."

Both therapists quietly leave the room.

Danny and I lie in silence for a few moments. "What do you think?" he says after a while.

"I think you were right. I needed to be touched."

He turns his head to me, and I get the full force of his grin.

"I also think," I continue, "that I need to get laid."

"That's the whole point of this exercise, no?"

"Yes." I shiver. "But having someone touching me. It felt so fucking good."

"I'm glad."

"Do we really need to get up?"

"We do."

"Then okay. Just ..." I squeak an embarrassing noise. "It was kind of um, erotic."

"It was." Danny gestures at his blanket, and, oh God, he has an erection, too.

"Do you want me to leave you by yourself for a moment?" I ask.

"It's fine."

"Or you could take care of it. Oh my God, I said that out loud. And it's probably not something you should do in a place like this. I wouldn't want the workers to have to deal with the mess. But, I mean, I could leave and you can— Or I don't have to leave."

Shit.

He grins, wide and wicked. "First off, who told you that you should only have sex in places where you're 'supposed to'? And second, have you ever seen another man come? Besides on a screen?"

I shake my head.

He scrubs his hands over his face. "I can't believe I'm doing this, but yeah, you can watch. Just don't tell anyone at work. I don't want them to think I'm sexually harassing you."

"You most definitely are not."

He blows out a breath. "I'd better be fast. And clean up after."

But instead of the quick motion I'm expecting, he slowly trails a hand down and plays with his balls through the blanket.

And fuck.

That's the most erotic thing I've ever seen. After a few moments, he slips his hand under the blanket, and I can see his movements, starting off slow, then picking up the pace.

My dick throbs, close to bursting, and I think I might come without having touched myself, which would be embarrassing.

I watch as Danny's hand moves faster and faster. Then he

throws his head back and grunts, and it's so fucking sexy I want to scream.

I almost do. Instead, I hastily reach under my own blanket and jack myself until I come all over my fingers.

We both sigh and then laugh.

And then I say, "I feel so much better. Thanks for this."

"You're welcome, Alden." He looks at me. An emotion I can't name flickers in his eyes. But instead of saying anything more, he grabs a box of tissues and hands me a few. We both tidy up and toss the evidence into a small trash can in the corner.

He tilts his head. "Do you want me to give you privacy to change? Because truth? I want to see you."

"That's okay," I whisper. We both hop off the tables, and before I can talk myself out of it, I reach for him. His naked warmth pressed up against mine ignites every nerve in my body. We're all oiled up and relaxed, and I kiss him deep. I never want to leave this room, this moment.

But there's a gentle knock on the door, so we break apart and get dressed, giving each other sheepish grins. With one last kiss, we're on our way.

"**G**O DODGERS," Alden cups his hand to his mouth and yells. "GO!"

I stare in amazement at my little nerd bookkeeper, who is indulging his wild baseball side. When he told me he liked baseball because of the statistics, I figured he'd be mild-mannered at the game.

Uh, no.

He quivered in excitement as we got closer and closer to Chavez Ravine. After going through security, he immediately got sidetracked by the team store, even though he came in a Tommy Lasorda jersey and a baseball cap, carrying a mitt.

He looks cute in a jersey.

When we got to our seats, we discovered mine was broken, so we talked to a service rep, and they ended up putting us right behind home plate.

Oh, man.

Now Alden won't shut up. I sip my twenty-dollar can of beer while he lets out a stream of invective so foul, I'm about to remind him there are twelve-year-old children here.

But he's *so* into it.

"Fuck!" he screams, as the Giants' slugger dongs one out of the park.

Then he looks at me, as if remembering I'm here. "Hi," I say. "I'm Danny. Your date."

"Oh my God, I'm sorry."

"I love it," I say. "I love to see your passion."

He nods vigorously, cracking open a peanut and letting the shell drop onto the concrete below our seats. "I just ..."

"You don't have to explain. I understand."

I like baseball fine—though these days I'm more of a basketball kind of guy—but watching anyone enjoy something they love is a thrill. Alden's right there with the players, absorbed in the game. Every once in a while, he squeezes my hand, but in a stadium with fifty-two thousand other people, we're discreet about PDA. Even in LA, better safe than sorry.

Still, his enthusiasm is charging up my libido. Because this isn't the calm, quiet Alden from the office. He's letting it all out. And if he can let it all out at a baseball game, then he can let it all out in bed.

I like my logic. Because I'm so attracted to this guy, I can't stand it. From seeing him change clothes to kissing him, to practically dry humping him on the dance floor, to getting off while he lay next to me, naked beneath a sheet—I'm about to explode.

Fortunately for our seatmates, there are plenty of distractions to keep me from tackling him. Dodger Stadium is a riot of noise and images and the scents of nachos and beer. It's like an old-school browser with all kinds of pop-ups and too much information all over the place. It's hard to pay attention to what's happening on the field when there are gold low riders bouncing on the DodgerVision screen to let the crowd play some trivia game.

The Dodgers score a few runs. The game moves along, but I'm more interested in watching Alden than anything else. He fills out the scorecard in the program and pays attention to every pitch, narrating to me the whole time.

"Are you this intense when you watch games on television?" I ask at some point.

He gulps and nods. "Yeah. Sorry."

"Don't apologize. Passion is my favorite thing in the world."

"I was scared you'd think I get too into it."

"I think that's part of what makes you you." I shrug. "I know you've asked me to help you change, but I don't really want to change you at all. I just want to boost your self-esteem. The way you are is more than good enough."

He smiles at me. "I wish I could kiss you."

"Later."

Then he turns and starts clapping with determination as the latest Dodgers star saunters up to the plate. The pitcher for the Giants has this weird throw, sidelong, almost like an underhand softball pitch.

Only it goes 92 mph and is absolutely precise. It looks hard to hit. I mean, any MLB pitch looks hard to hit, but this seems impossible.

Alden grips his armrest and then scoots forward. And farther. And farther, until he is literally on the edge of his seat, lips parted, watching as the pitcher throws, the batter swings, and—

"OMG GOOOOOOOOOOOOOO, YES!" he yells.

The line drive rockets just over the left field wall.

"We're killing them!" He's whooping and hollering and standing up in his seat, watching and clapping as the runner trots home, where he's greeted by his teammates, who all slap him on the butt. That might be my favorite part of baseball. That and the scruff on some of these guys. My God, they're delicious. Alden hugs me in celebration, saying, "Being able to do that makes this the best game ever!"

At the end of the night, when the stadium plays "I Love LA," we stand and clap and let the music, crowd noise, and strobe lights overwhelm us.

Then we take the long walk back to the car. Once we're there,

Alden scrambles over the center console into my lap, getting right in my face. I chuckle, loving his boldness.

He puts both hands on my shoulders. "You're the most amazing person. I know I wasn't the best date. I'm sorry for ignoring you."

"I wasn't ignored," I say. "I was amused. We were both into it. You were slightly *more* into it—although I do like baseball. I just like you better."

His eager tongue delves into my mouth, and before I know it, I'm scooting my seat back so we don't hit the horn. We get a few wolf whistles as pedestrians stream by on the way to their own cars, but I don't care.

When we break apart, I murmur, "I love seeing you come out of your shell."

He's hard, and so am I. He feels good in my hands. Against my body. He tastes like peanuts and sweat, and you'd think that would be a bad combination, but you'd be wrong. He tastes real and like Alden, and it's a heady combination. Every time we kiss, Alden gets more confident ... and more desirable.

But I'm supposed to be helping him to kiss other people. Not me.

"I like kissing you," he admits. "I'm sorry if I'm being too forward."

"You're not," I growl. I lean up to kiss him again, my hands gripping his ass.

"If we keep this up, I'm going to explode," he admits. "And while that was fun once, I don't want to get all messy again."

"Sex is messy. You're going to have to get used to that."

"But maybe not outside a Dodger game," he says, giving me a lighter kiss, which deepens into something that elicits a growl from me.

I haven't explored just kissing with anyone in so long. I normally kiss enough to get things going and then skip to the fucking.

But with Alden, I enjoy it. I like exploring his mouth. I like how hot he makes me feel.

Still, Alden's right: we probably shouldn't let this get any more involved here on the street. "I want you," I whisper. "Do you want to come home with me?"

He opens his mouth and then shuts it. But he doesn't say anything. Instead, he scoots over to his seat, puts on his seat belt, and nods, pointing forward.

I laugh, start the car, and cut off as many drivers as I can to get to my house as fast as possible.

# CHAPTER 18

# *Danny*

I usher Alden into my house, close the door, then stop and hold him, leaning down and kissing him softly.

I want us to already be shedding clothes on the way to the bedroom, bumping into furniture and not caring about anything except getting naked. I want to push him down on the kitchen table and make him feel things he's never felt before.

But I need to be more careful with him. I need to focus on his pleasure, his level of comfort. Even though we've talked about all sorts of sexual acts, I want him to lead tonight.

The sensual kiss is making my cock even harder than when I was watching Alden strip at the spa. I pull back to take off my jacket and set down my keys, wallet, and phone, then wrap my arms around his waist, tugging him close. "Alden?"

"Hmm?" he says into my chest.

I pull back and tilt his chin up so he's looking at me. "What would you say if I told you I want to be the first man to suck your dick?"

"I, I, I would be okay with that. I mean, if you wanted to. You know." He blinks rapidly, then laughs. "Oh my God, I can't even be cool about it."

"I don't want you to be cool about it. Or, rather, I already think you're cool."

"Then ... I might come in my pants from the mere idea of you doing it."

"Okay."

He blinks again. "What you do you mean, 'Okay'?"

"If you come in your pants, I'll just have to wait a few minutes." I grin. "I like it when you come in your pants."

"Holy shit."

But he's given me the green light, and I'm not going to insult him by questioning him any more. If he wants to put the brakes on, I'll stop, and he knows that.

So I fall to my knees in front of him and nuzzle his crotch. He's hard behind his zipper. I whisper, "Fuck yes," and leave an open-mouthed kiss on the fabric. I look up, searching his eyes. "I can't wait to taste you."

He nods so many times I'm worried his head may fall off. I smile against his hip.

"Please. Put me out of my misery," he mutters.

I unbutton and unzip his jeans, then slide them and his underwear down far enough to have access to his dick.

It's a very handsome dick—ruddy at the tip, thicker than mine but not as long. I get off on how hard he is. How I can *see* how much he wants this.

I part my lips and wrap my mouth around him, going down as far as I can. Remembering my first experiences on the receiving end, I fully expect him to come immediately.

"Oh, God," he whimpers. "That feels ..."

I figure, if this is going to be fast, I might as well make it feel as good as it can, so I loosen my throat muscles, breathe out through my nose, and give him a good, hard suck.

"*Fuck.*"

I love hearing him come undone. I can tell by how rigid he is, his cock straining, his thighs quivering, that he's going to unload.

It hits me hard that I'm the first one to do this to him. While I've given and received plenty of BJs, this one feels monumental, brings out the caveman in me.

I suck his dick and think, *Mine.*

But I don't just mean his dick. This *man* is mine—or I want him to be. I want to be the one to take care of him. I want to help him come out of his shell, and I want to support him when he does. I want to see him shine. I want to let him be himself, because from all I've seen so far, I think he may be the most genuine, cute soul I've ever met.

I haven't had feelings like this since high school.

Somehow, with Alden, I feel safe. Because everything is out in the open between us, I'm not under pressure to be something I'm not or live up to some rep I've developed. I can focus on him.

And I really like focusing on him.

I pop off long enough to whisper, "It's okay to come. You don't have anything to prove." Then I take him deep again, this time making sure I don't lose eye contact.

With a glorious, delicious moan-groan, he pulses in my mouth, and I greedily swallow the warm, salty release. Then I suck him gently, feeling the twitches and aftershocks of his O.

I grin up at him.

He slumps against the nearest wall. "So *that's* what I've been missing out on all this time."

I stand up and kiss him deeply, ignoring my own hard cock. At the same time, I help him pull his pants up, not wanting him to feel embarrassed.

When we break for breath, he shakes his head. "I don't have words."

I hug him. "That's okay. You don't need to say anything." I realize he's trembling, and I kiss the top of his head. "Hey, baby. What's wrong?"

"I don't want to cry, but that was earth-shattering," he mutters into my chest.

"If you need to cry, it's okay." He's still shaking, so I hold him tighter.

"I feel like I've crossed some boundary. Some watershed that was holding me back from being an adult."

I don't reply or urge him on. I just keep him safe in my arms. He sniffles, and I snuggle him closer, my biceps locking him in place.

"Thank you," he finally whispers.

I let him go enough to tilt up his chin with my finger and kiss him softly. "It was my pleasure."

Then he blinks again. "What about you?"

"I'm fine," I say.

"No, really. Can I at least explore you? I've never touched another guy's dick before."

"Sure," I say. "What do you want to do? My body is yours for the taking."

"Can I just touch you?" he asks.

"Of course. Want to go to my bedroom?"

He nods.

We walk down the hall holding hands, and I'm nervous. I've never felt nervous before sex. At least not for a very long time.

But this is Alden, and he's starting to mean a lot to me. If he doesn't feel the same as I do, that would suck. I need to click back into my usual MO—that this is only sex.

That thought makes my stomach hurt. No, I can't do that. I like being close to Alden and want to make him feel good.

When we get to my room, I gesture at the bed. "How do you want me?"

He hesitates only a second before saying, "I want to explore your body. Can you, um, take your clothes off?"

Said in his casual but careful way, it makes my dick throb. "Sure," I reply, leaning over to kiss him.

Since he seemed to like the peeks he got at the spa, I take my time, unbuttoning my shirt slowly and setting it down on the back of a chair. Then I slip off my shoes and socks and unbutton my pants.

My dick is tenting my underwear, and he sucks in a breath.

"You're so hot," he whispers.

I shed my underwear and crawl onto the bed. "Do you want only me naked, or do you want to be naked, too?"

He shrugs. "You decide."

"Take off your clothes, everything but your briefs, and lie on the bed," I order. Then I backtrack. "If you're comfortable with that, I mean."

He nods. "I am." He takes off his shirt, and I get to see his lean body again. He's wearing the teeny-tiny briefs I bought him. I ignored them earlier in my haste to suck him, but now that I take the time to appreciate the view, they make his dick look huge and his ass look perky.

I whistle. "You're so fucking sexy."

He gives me a shy grin. "Thanks."

"Did you wear these for me?" I tug gently at the elastic.

Alden shrugs. "You know, for years, I've worn nice underwear for me. But ... yeah, this was the first time I had a hope that someone—you—would be seeing them."

That thought makes my chest swell with pride.

He whimpers. "This is like a porno, only it's real."

I grin and kiss him, then flop onto my back, my head on a pillow. Gesturing to my body, I say, "Do your worst."

Carefully, so carefully it makes my heart ache, he reaches out a finger and traces my jaw. He looks into my eyes and smiles shyly. Then he leans down and kisses me.

Damn, I love it when he takes the initiative. I want to dominate the kiss, to flip us over, to take him. But I'm not going to. I just hold his hips loosely, and he kisses the side of my mouth and my jaw. And then he starts kissing my neck.

"Oh, God." I moan. I seriously moan, because his lips are so soft—and this is one of my erogenous zones. "That feels amazing."

He grins against my skin. "Good. I'm not sure what I'm doing."

"You're doing fine. More than fine, actually. You're incredible." Now I'm babbling, which I never do.

But his lips and fingers start tracing down my arms, my torso. He touches my nipples tentatively, then reaches down and licks one.

I shoot upward in pleasure. "Fuck."

"Did I do something wrong?"

"Not at all," I gasp.

"Then what is it?"

"Lots of men have licked my nipples, but it's never felt like that."

"I'm just trying to follow the things that seem to make you jump. And the things that I imagine feel good."

"Your imagination is incredible, then," I pant out.

He explores farther, at first skimming over my skin, then coming back stronger and more emphatic.

His skin brushes against mine as he takes his time, touching me, exploring my chest, my abs, my hips—first with his hands and then following up with light kisses.

"Fuck, baby, you are so fucking sexy."

Alden stops. "I never imagined someone would say that to me."

"Stop worrying about your imagination, because reality is so much better."

He smiles. "I agree." He moves to straddle my legs and then looks his fill. I'm propped up on a pillow, my arms behind my head, which makes my abs pop. My hard dick is lying against my stomach, and he's raking his nails gently through the hair on my upper thighs.

I wonder if he's anxious, but before I open my mouth to let him off the hook, he bends down and licks me.

I barely keep from bowing off the bed. His tentative, warm,

wet tongue feels amazing on my sensitive flesh. I hiss, and he startles.

"Was that bad?"

"No. It was so, so good. Keep going. Don't use teeth, but anything else is okay."

Like a cat, he licks up the underside of my dick with a wicked look on his face, then settles in to give me the sloppiest, most enthusiastic blowjob of my life. He's moved lower, and his junk is pressing between my shins through the fabric of his briefs. It feels like his dick is perking up again already.

I'm in turns enthralled by him and distracted by how good it feels. He settles into a rhythm with his mouth and hand, and I say, "Baby, you don't have to finish me with your mouth."

He looks a little relieved. "I want to, but I don't know what I'm doing."

"Then let's try this." I move so I'm on my side, facing him, and line him up next to me. "Take your briefs off."

Alden slides his underwear down his thighs, and as I suspected, he's pretty much hard again. Benefit of being four years younger.

I grip both our cocks, and he groans. "Damn."

"Wait, let me get lube." I reach back and fumble in the drawer until I find the bottle. Then, wrapping my fingers around our dicks again, I stroke us simultaneously, and the way his body feels against me, the slick and friction and pressure, it's too much. I'm going to blow.

It's clear he's enjoying this, too.

Can I hold on long enough to get him there? I wouldn't normally doubt my stamina, but there's something about Alden that makes me lose control. I abandon my dick for a bit and work on his, stroking him firmly, focusing on the head and watching him come apart again. When he starts fucking into my hand, I can see he's getting desperate.

"Ready?" I whisper. "You can come with me, right?"

He nods rapidly and gives me a messy, tongue-filled kiss that makes me growl.

I want this man.

I jack us off together until I hit my own trigger, nearly whiting out. I keep stroking him, using my come as even more lube, and in a few moments, he comes, too, and then we both lie back on my bed, chests rising and falling as we catch our breath.

I go to hug him but realize we're pretty messy, so I wipe my hand off on a corner of the sheet and clean up our bodies as best I can.

Then I kiss him. We move so I'm on my back and he's half on me, and it feels ... right.

And then he leans into me and kisses me again. "You're the best teacher I could've asked for."

My stomach drops. Because while that's exactly what we are, teacher and student, I'm starting to think I want us to be more. Now that I've gotten to spend time with him, have seen glimpses of who he really is, I want to know him better. I want to take care of him. I want to enjoy him, and make him smile, and ... maybe ... take a chance on something real again.

I tug him close. "Let's rest and then try for another round."

"Sounds good to me."

# CHAPTER 19

*Alden*

For the second time in my life, I wake up in Danny Villaseñor's bed. It's still disorienting, but this time I feel ... calm and sated. I feel comfortable.

I feel *hot*, because he's wrapped his whole body around me—his arms tugging me to him, one leg over mine, and his nose in the back of my neck. His hard dick pokes me in the ass. His cat is curled at our feet and hops to the floor when I stir.

I could get used to this. I like being overheated and in a man's arms. Not just any man—it's Danny. Danny, who centered all his attention last night on bringing me pleasure twice—with his tongue and with his hand.

But he's been teaching me to act on instinct, so that's what I do. I turn so we're nose to nose, and he stretches his back, adjusts his arms so he's still holding me, and then blinks his eyes open.

"Hey," he whispers, his voice groggy from sleep.

"Hi," I say back, feeling shy for some reason.

The shyness doesn't last long, because Danny tips me onto my back and settles between my legs, kissing me.

"Don't you care about morning breath?" I ask, once we break apart for a moment.

"Nope."

I find that I don't care about it, either—neither one of us has particularly bad breath. And the warm weight of Danny over me and between my legs is making me feel ... *things.*

Like, is this my life? My crush is kissing me. Actually, my crush is rubbing his hard cock against mine slowly and deliberately, in this erotic dance. And it's all I can do to hang on and enjoy the sensation.

Danny reaches between us for my cock, giving it a tug. Then he grabs the lube. I watch in happy disbelief as he proceeds to slick both of us up.

He settles against me again, kissing me everywhere he can reach —my neck, my collarbone, my jaw, my lips.

"You feel so fucking good," he whispers into my cheek, his hand moving between us.

"Nghh," is all I manage.

But it isn't just the fact that Danny's touching me in ways that no one else has. It's the intimacy of this moment—a sleepy Sunday morning, with no one around, no responsibilities. I'm in his wide bed with its soft sheets and the sun peeking in through the shades. There's no sound but our heavy breathing and the slick slide of his hand on our cocks.

And he's *watching* me in a way no one else has. He's looking at me like I'm his entire world ... which is such a dangerous thing to think. Because I know, for him, this is solely physical. He's told me that many times. This is how he is with everyone. It's a way to get off. Well, and he's teaching me, preparing me to have sexual relationships with other people.

I can't help thinking, though, that this means more. When he kisses me so gently and deeply. When he seems more focused on my pleasure than his own.

But maybe that's why he's so popular.

I shove all those negative thoughts to the side. I've somehow managed to get into bed with my ideal man. He's been my first kiss, my first orgasm with someone else in the room, my first blowjob ... and he's the first man I've ever woken up to in the morning. I'm turning my brain off and enjoying this.

Because I'm scared it won't last—because it *won't* last. Orgasms never do.

I kiss him back, gently at first, and then deeper. My hands explore his skin. I get bolder and bolder, not just running them along his shoulders or down his back and sides but down to his ass, with an exploratory dip between his cheeks.

He pauses for a moment and grins at me. "Go for it."

The truth is, I want more than his body, but that's me being greedy. I'll take what I can get.

With tentative fingers, I explore the cleft of his ass, his balls, his taint. Danny hands me the lube, and I use some to take over jacking him. He groans in pleasure. "Yes. God. That feels good, Alden. Here, let me."

Danny rolls us so he's spooning me, his dick between my legs and his hand reaching around and grasping my length.

I keep getting lost with him. Lost in desire and pleasure. Lost in fulfilled promises and dreams coming true. I have to remind myself that this is only for right now. Only to teach me how to be with another guy.

But it's easy to forget.

Soon enough, between the friction of his hand and the warmth of his body, I'm coming, the O taking me over in a burst of tension and then release. Danny pulls away from me and starts to jack himself furiously, but with a grin, I take over. When I get him to come, I watch his head fall back and his eyes flutter shut, and I think yet again that he's the most beautiful human I've ever met.

Once he comes down from the high, he ignores the mess we've made and again crawls up over me, kissing me hard and deep, then soft and sweet. "Take a shower with me," he whispers.

I'm having those dangerous thoughts again. I want this to be real, even though I know that it can't be.

* * *

After we've cleaned up and I'm sitting at Danny's bar while he cooks pancakes, his cat winding between our legs, I sip my coffee and ask, "Am I still a virgin?"

He tilts his head. "What? Why do you ask that?"

"Just wondering. Does what we've done count as sex?"

"Pretty sure that, one, virginity is an outdated concept generally used to oppress women, and two, you can make your own rules. I mean, if you're gay and you're never going to put your penis in a vagina ..." He shrugs.

"But, um, anal sex. Do I have to have that to not be a virgin?"

"No. Plenty of gay men aren't interested in anal. If it's something you want to do and you feel you haven't completed your punch card because you haven't done it, that's a different issue." He gives me a gentle smile. "I can tell this is bothering you. I'm afraid I don't have all the answers, but I'm willing to listen."

And this is why he's dangerous. Because he doesn't dismiss my concerns out of hand or tell me shit that isn't true. He discusses things with me like what I care about matters.

I sigh. "The concept of virginity is so confusing. I've just always kind of assumed losing it was important. And it bothered me that no one seemed to want to touch me."

That elicits another smile. "Oh, I assure you I want to touch you very much."

"That makes me happy."

"Good. I want you to be happy." Danny comes around the counter, tugging me to him. "If having anal sex is important to you, we can talk about it. Have you been thinking a lot about it?"

I give him a look. "Of course." Besides the fantasies I've had since I was a teenager, if it feels that good to be inside Danny's mouth, what would it feel like for him to be inside me? I bet it'd be overwhelming in the best way.

"And who you want to do it with?"

Now I redden. "Yes." It makes my heart thud.

His voice takes on his sexiest register. "Can you share with the class?"

"You, of course." It's barely a whisper.

"Okay," he whispers back. "We can work up to that. Some-time. When you're ready." He holds up his hands. "I'm done saying no to you." He looks calm but eager. Like I gave him a present. "Have you thought about what you'd like to do? And yes, I'm talking positions. Where? How? Do you want to top? Bottom? Both?"

"I always figured I'd bottom, but I want to know both."

"I normally top, but I'd bottom for you. Would that feel safer to you?"

I pause. "Yes," I say eventually. "I think it would. But I'd feel safe with you no matter what." His eyes catch mine. "I don't really want to do it with anyone else. I mean, I suppose eventually I'll have to. When you're done with my lessons. Or whatever." I grimace.

"Hey," he says. "This doesn't have to be about the lessons you asked for. This can just be ..." He shrugs. "Who we are when we're together. I'm okay with you being the only one I'm with. While we're doing this." He points between us.

I look up at him in surprise. "You are?"

"I don't want you to worry." He holds up his hand. "I'll still give you tips or whatever so you can practice with other people, but I don't want you concerned I won't be available when you need me. Plus, I don't want you worrying about diseases. I get tested often and use condoms, but I'll get tested again."

"This kind of feels like something is happening between us," I blurt.

He gives me the gentlest smile. "That's because I think it might be."

Holy shit. Does he mean that? Should I ask what he's really saying, or will that only shatter whatever magical dream we're in right now?

"Shelby is going to ask questions. How are we going to play this at work?"

"How would you like to play it?" Danny asks. "I'll do whatever you want. If you want people to know we're ..." He makes a gesture. "Messing around. Doing things. I'm okay with them knowing you're mine."

*You're mine.*

I know he means temporarily, but God, it feels good to hear it. I've had no experience with relationships. Is this too fast? I'm supposed to stick to our plan of him teaching me.

Even though I don't want anyone but him.

* * *

Monday morning, I step off the elevator on Weston & Ramirez's floor and stop short, because Sam Stone is standing there, kissing the biggest rock star in the world.

I clear my throat, and the two of them break apart.

"Sorry," Julian Hill says in his British accent.

Sam looks sheepish. "Sorry. Jules, this is Alden Meyer, our new bookkeeper. Alden, um, this is my boyfriend, Jules Hill." A man who needs no introduction. "He has a thing about elevators, so I'm going to accompany him down. There's no paparazzi in the lobby, are there?"

I shake my head. "Not that I saw."

"Fantastic," Jules says. He reaches out a hand to shake mine. "Lovely to meet you, Alden." He's tall and slim, wearing a green-and-blue-striped sailor shirt with buttons on the shoulders and black jeans. Sam's in a suit with a polka-dot bow tie. They enter the elevator together.

And while I should be bowled over by the fact that I just met a major celebrity, I'm more excited that I get to see Danny today. Even though I saw him yesterday. And basically all weekend.

I really do have it bad. I stop at the reception desk to say hi to Shelby, who has his head down and seems busy with some kind of art project. I knock on the desk. "Hey."

He looks up, startled, and then gives me a big grin. "Morning!" He narrows his eyes. "You look very happy today."

I shrug. "Yeah, I mean, I guess so."

"Hmm. Did something happen?"

I press my lips together.

"Oh my God, something did happen!" he squeals.

"Shh, keep it down. I'm not one to kiss and tell."

"But Danny is, right? If it's him, I mean. I can just find out on his Ad/VICE account, can't I? So, what happened?"

Did Danny do a video? If he did, he didn't send it to me. I'll have to ask him.

I take a quick glance over each of my shoulders to see if we're being overheard, but the coast is clear. "We've kissed and messed around a few times. Sort of."

Shelby raises his dark eyebrows so high they get lost in his white hair. "A few times? As in repeats with the king of one-time club hookups? That's unprecedented."

Nodding, I shrug again. "Yeah. I mean ... I don't know what I'm doing, but it's good."

His focus on me sharpens. "And he hasn't ghosted you?"

Digging in my pocket, I pull out my phone and show him that Danny texted me a good-morning GIF earlier today.

Shelby's mouth drops open. "Well. Hmm. You may be taming the beast. Still ... I don't want you to get hurt. He's a playboy. A good playboy, but a playboy."

"I know you mean well, but—"

"Do you have enough experience to know what Danny really has in mind?"

Ugh. I hate this. Because he's right: I don't know. I've never had any sort of romantic or sexual relationship before, so how can I tell what it's supposed to be or not?

I want to trust what Danny said. But I'm starting to second-guess myself. I wish these things were easier. I want a spreadsheet where I could plug in the numbers and know the result.

Human interactions are so much more difficult.

Shelby sees my expression, and his face softens. "Hey," he says. "I didn't mean to burst your bubble of sexy-man happiness. I'm just being realistic."

"I don't know that there's anything realistic about feelings."

"That could be." I can see him thinking about it. "I don't want to see you hurt."

"Me neither. But it seems to me like I'm going to be hurt or I'm not, and either way, I can't do anything about it."

"That's a fatalistic attitude."

"Or a realistic one. Which is what you just told me to be." My voice drops. "I like him. I like what we're doing together. And I can't help any of that. So I think I just need to ride this as far as it's going to go." I hear myself say "ride," and my cheeks heat.

Shelby notices and grins. "Okay. I'm sorry. I didn't mean to bum you out. I care and wanted to make sure you were warned, is all. But maybe I'm being an ass."

"Maybe you aren't. Maybe that's simply the way the world is."

"But how is it with him?" he asks. "For real. Because he's kind of a legend, so maybe I'm a wee bit jealous."

"He's magnificent."

He truly is.

"Wow," Shelby breathes. "That's something. I knew it was true."

Just then, Danny walks in. "Hey," he says, and he squeezes my shoulder, like he's avoiding PDA in the office but he can't stop touching me. I don't want him to stop, either.

"Hey," I say. I'm pleased my voice doesn't squeak. "What's up?"

"I wanted to turn in a few receipts. Had to advance fees at the courthouse, so I put it on my card."

"Okay," I say, taking the papers and staring at him. Then I blink.

Shelby is watching the two of us, looking amused. "Oh, you two are so cute. I can't stand it."

Danny whips his head around. "What?"

"Don't deny it, Mr. Villaseñor."

"I'm not denying anything. But I don't want it all over the office, either, because I don't want Alden to be tarnished by my reputation."

"You couldn't tarnish me," I say.

"You're still new," he insists.

"Don't assume that just because I'm new to this I don't know what I think or feel."

"Fair," he admits. Then he looks both ways and brushes a very quick kiss on my lips. Apparently, since Shelby knows, Danny isn't going to hide.

"Whoa," Shelby says. "It's true."

Danny gives him a quick grin and strides off.

"I revise my opinion," Shelby says. "That's a whole new side of Danny. I think he's so into you that no one else even competes. And I'm proud of you for being the one to capture his heart."

"Now I think you're going too far in the other direction."

Maybe I don't need to let anyone else's opinions into this relationship. Maybe I can just let Danny and me be who we are.

It's time for me to get to work, but before I do, I point to Shelby's desk, where scissors, folded-up paper, and tape are strewn about. "What's all that?"

He smiles broadly. "Okay, so you know our client Johnny Haskell?"

I nod. "I love him. Uh, his work, I mean." I feel my cheeks going pink.

"Me, too. At any rate, if any client ever needed a hug, it's Johnny, and he normally makes sure to come here when I'm working so I can give him one."

"Do you have a thing for him?"

"No, it's platonic. I told you, I only attract them if they're unavailable. Johnny's single and gay. At any rate, I'd told him I'd be here today, but I'd forgotten about a dentist appointment. So I'm making him a hug book." He holds it out.

He's taken blue construction paper, folded it in half and stapled it, and then taped on all sorts of cheesy hug pictures from the internet. T. rexes hugging with arm extenders. Cats and cartoon dogs hugging. It's the most wholesome thing I've ever seen.

"You're going to make him cry," I say.

"He deserves to feel loved."

I smile at him and go down to my office with a warm feeling in my chest. Not only am I getting more comfortable in my own skin and with my love tutor, I'm surrounded by pretty nice people, too.

If only it could all last.

# CHAPTER 20

# *Danny*

After work, I go over to Alden's house and help him cook and clean for his mom. Then we sit outside, drinking water—because Alden—and talking. There's a nervous flutter in my stomach, because I know we need to discuss a few things, but I don't really want to. Still, part of being a lawyer is not avoiding the uncomfortable stuff. I'm not helping people if I can't give them bad news.

So I do the stiff-upper-lip thing and say it. "We haven't been having you interact enough with people other than me."

Alden nods. "Yeah, I know."

"Should we do a video about this conversation?" I ask. We've been falling behind. I haven't wanted to talk about what Alden and I have been doing together. This, though. This is the point of the exercise.

And my follower count is stuck at 357. Nowhere near the number I need. Still, I'm not giving up.

"Sure," Alden says. Though he gives me a bright smile, I can tell he's not into it.

I'm not sure I am, either. In fact, I haven't recorded anything in a while. I guess because it felt too invasive. I haven't wanted to hurt Alden, and it feels like I might if I keep going with the videos.

So I put my phone away. "Nah, let's do it later. But I do think we should work on you going out with someone else. Do you want me to set you up with someone?"

The idea seems so wrong.

He shakes his head. "I've been set up too many times. I don't want to do that again. It never works out."

"The point of this was for you to be comfortable around other people. You're a lot more confident now. You might have a completely different experience on a date than you have in the past."

"The point of this was for me to become a player."

"I don't feel like I'm doing very well at helping you with that, since, you know, you've only messed around with me."

Alden bites his lip. I can tell he wants to say something, but he's holding his tongue. "Okay," he finally says.

It's like the way he texts.

"Is being a playboy what you want?" I ask. "Not what you think you should want, but what you truly want?" He looks at me, and I can see the anguish in his face. I want to kiss it out of him. "Talk to me."

He sighs. "Deep down, I think what I want is to be comfortable in my own skin. And you're helping me get there. I'm not stuttering or tripping as much as I used to. I look in the mirror, and I like what I see. Things are starting to feel better. I don't know if I'll ever be good at asking a guy out, but I think I could do it."

"Practice should help with that." Just because I'm thinking of him as mine doesn't mean he really is. I'm like a mama bird, teaching my hatchling to fly. Sooner or later, I'm going to have to shove him out of the nest and trust that he's not going to hit the ground. "We can start small. What if we go to a coffee shop, and I'll sit at a table in case you need me. I'll do some work or something.

But you can just go talk with whoever. Hopefully it won't be a Loki worshipper."

He nods. "Okay. We can do that tomorrow at lunch."

\* \* \*

The next day, with a heavy heart, I go with Alden to Southwinds Coffee at lunch. While I'm tempted to put my arm around him and claim him as mine, I can let my baby bird go. I think.

We order separately, even though I want to buy him everything he desires. We shouldn't look like we're together. This way, he can grow. It's better for him.

He gives me a small smile, and then I go to a café table for a date with my laptop and a brief, and he heads off to find someone to sit next to.

I can't help watching him more than my screen, though. He stands for a moment, holding his iced mocha and sandwich, then spies a young guy with glasses who's sitting by himself at the long bar, drinking a latte.

I hate the guy immediately.

But Alden smiles and points at the stool next to him. The guy smiles back, gesturing for Alden to sit down, and I want to punch something.

I can't tell what they're talking about, but I notice their body language. The guy perked up when Alden approached him. Alden isn't anywhere near as fidgety as he was when I first met him. Although I don't think he'll ever be a smooth operator, I'm proud that he seems to be getting through a conversation with this guy without tripping over his tongue. Or anything else.

After a while, the guy pulls out his phone, and Alden does something on it. Probably giving him his number.

That pisses me off, even though it's exactly what Alden should be doing.

I try to focus on the brief I have to write, but the words on the screen are meaningless. When Alden finishes his meal, I can't stand it anymore. I slide my computer back into my bag and stride over to him.

"Alden!" I say cheerily and wrap an arm around his shoulder.

He gives me a confused but wide smile. "Hey, Danny. This is Joel."

I shake his hand in a death grip. "Nice to meet you."

"You, too," Joel says. "Alden has a lead on where I can get an original *Firefly* hat."

"That TV show you like?"

Alden hops off his stool and nods. "Yeah."

The guy eyes where my arm ends up—around Alden again—and he seems to get the idea.

I should feel evil about sabotaging Alden, but I don't. He did what we came here to do: he talked to someone. I just don't want him to get farther than that. Is that really so bad?

The guy gathers his things. "Nice to meet you, Alden. Danny."

Alden gives Joel a little wave. "See you around?"

"Sure."

After the guy leaves, Alden gives me a weird look. "Ready to go back to the office?"

I nod.

Alden follows me out of the shop. When we get into the elevator, thankfully alone, he asks, "What was that about? I thought I was doing okay. I didn't need a rescue."

I rub my hand over my face. "I'm sorry."

"It's no big deal. There was no spark. I didn't think he was someone I'd want to get together with. But he could be a friend."

"That's not what he was thinking."

Alden puts a hand on his hip. "If I didn't know any better, Danny, I'd think you were jealous."

I gulp. The elevator doors open, but we don't immediately get out. "Yeah. I think maybe I was, a little."

The doors close again, but the elevator doesn't move. Alden pulls me to him and gives me a hard kiss.

Then he hits the open button, and we step out.

I'm not totally sure what just happened, but I think I'm happy about it.

* * *

When I walk into a partnership meeting later that afternoon, Charlie corners me.

"What the hell is up with you? How come you haven't been out with me in ... a long time?" He says "a long time" meaningfully.

I shrug. "Busy."

"Uh-huh. Busy with our bookkeeper," he whispers loudly.

I shrug again.

"You haven't been going to the club. You haven't been stumbling in here smelling like sex and alcohol. Are you finally getting your life together?"

"I never come to work smelling like sex and alcohol."

Noah looks over at us. "Uh, yeah. You do. Or did, at any rate."

"I have perfect hygiene."

"And a tendency for quickies," August says.

I snort. He's not wrong. I built my reputation by making my way through the town.

And yet.

*And yet.*

Now I don't want to. I just want Alden. And that's a scary thought. I've never not wanted to look for something new before the sun comes up.

Charlie studies me. "If I didn't know better, I'd think you were starting to catch feelings."

I'm not going to insult Alden by denying it. "I like the guy. What can I say?"

He raises both eyebrows. "Fascinating admission coming from you, counsel."

I glance around. The meeting hasn't begun, and the other partners all seem interested in Charlie's and my conversation.

I need to change the subject. I notice August is texting, but Noah is steadfastly ignoring his phone even though it's buzzing repeatedly in his pocket.

"How come you never check your phone when anyone's around?" I ask.

Noah shifts in his seat. "Um, no reason."

"Uh-huh."

August coughs. "All right. Well, it's inappropriate shit. And that's all I'm gonna tell you."

I grin. "Wait, what? You and Noah send each other inappropriate texts all day?"

"Not all day! Just ... judiciously timed ones. We have rules."

I nod at him. "Okay, whatever."

"Trust me, you don't want to know."

I hold up my hands. "Fine. Be that way. Can we start this meeting, please, and avoid discussing my personal life?"

I get a few knowing grins, but they start the meeting.

For the next few weeks, Alden and I see each other every day at work and, most of the time, both days on the weekends. When we're apart, I miss him, although work does keep me busy. It's hectic, especially since I'm getting ready for a trial. Not Johnny's, but another employment case. Still, I manage to steal kisses now and then.

Alden ends up spending the night three or four times a week. Now that his mom has had her last chemo treatment and he knows she's doing better, he's more comfortable taking time for himself.

I map every inch of his body, learning every erogenous zone and sweet spot, and tease both of us by figuring out just how fast —or how slowly—I can blow him. Every time I touch him, it feels like a gift. I finally get to make my vision of Alden on his knees before me real, my hands raking through his curls as my cock slides in and out of his beautiful mouth, his trusting eyes locked on mine. He does everything he can to make it good for me, and his sincerity makes me weak in the knees. He's not quite a master at blowjobs—he has a gag reflex that doesn't let me fuck his mouth for long—but his solid attempts make my heart move in a way it never has before.

We still haven't been doing anal, even though he's asked. As much as it pains me to deny him anything—and as much as I want to fuck him—I keep telling him we need to wait. I tell myself—and him—that I want him to be absolutely sure. But the truth is, fucking him would be a final exam of sorts, and I don't want this class to end.

\* \* \*

It's Saturday night, and Alden and I are on my couch. I haven't seen *Firefly*, so we ordered pizza and are watching the show together, with a running commentary from Alden about the characters, how he wishes there were more episodes, and how pissed he is that certain people involved with the show have turned out to be less than savory.

While I'm sort of paying attention to the on-screen action, I'm mostly focused on Alden. When we're done eating, I tug him into my lap because I can't stand having him even a few inches away. And once he's there, I can't stop my roaming hands. They go under his shirt, tracing his smooth skin. They dip inside the waistband of his jeans. Finally, he turns in my arms so he's lying on top of me, and we're making out like teenagers, grinding against each other.

"If you were any other man," I growl, "I'd be balls-deep inside you right now."

He pulls back. "Why am I different? Is there something wrong with me?"

I knife up and kiss him. "There's nothing wrong with you. You just deserve better than me."

"Stop it," he says. "You told me we could do that. Are you changing your mind? Because we can do it and still have our arrangement."

I look at him, emotions warring within me. Because I want him. I want him bad. And it's not just lust. He's slaked my lust plenty of times.

I want *Alden*.

"Please," he says again. "Please."

# CHAPTER 21

*Alden*

"Please, Danny," I beg. "I want to know what it feels like. I want to do this with you. You *promised* me you'd do it if I couldn't find anyone else. But it isn't that. I don't *want* to do it with anyone else. I want to know what it feels like with you." I want the intimacy with him, even if it scares me.

"Okay," he says, and it's less like he's relenting and more like he wants it as much as I do. Then he kisses me softly, just a sweep of his lips against mine. But the tenderness in the move makes me ache.

Everything about him makes me ache. And perhaps that's the point. He rolls us off the couch and to our feet and takes my hand, tugging me with him down the hall. I shiver in happiness.

In the bedroom, he starts undressing me, slowly, methodically. First, he tugs at my shirt, and I move so he can pull it over my head. Then he shucks his own shirt off, eyes fixed on me. He leans in for a kiss, then mouths my shoulder and my neck, running his hands over me and making my skin come alive.

"Alden," he says. My name on his lips is like nothing I've ever experienced before. It's like he *sees* me. He sees *me*.

I help him when he fumbles with the button on my jeans, and when he unzips me, I sigh in relief.

He takes his time shimmying my underwear and jeans down. Then, when he's between my legs, he looks up at me and grins.

"What?" I ask.

"It's right here. I can't not take a lick."

I'm not sure how I got through life without blowjobs. I was missing out on something so sensual, so incredibly *nunghhhh*, that I couldn't even imagine it.

But I wonder if it would be the same with anyone else.

Danny licks and sucks me like it's a real treat. He laps me up, gripping his own erection through his jeans. The knowledge that I arouse him arouses me.

"Get naked," I say. "Please."

With a curt nod, he backs off of me and stands. Foolish, Alden.

But after a few efficient movements, he's naked, too. And then I'm holding his fantastic body against mine.

Models are nice and all. But there's something about the realness of Danny's body that just does it for me. His tanned skin and brown nipples. The little bits of hair below his belly. The way his thighs are muscular and hairy and his calves are triangles of goodness.

You can tell he works out, but his body doesn't have the overdone perfection of those diehards who eat only protein and won't even inhale near fries. Danny enjoys himself and looks good while doing it, and if that isn't a way to live, I don't know what is.

"See something you like?"

I blink. He's caught me staring, and I'm not abashed, because he's worth staring at. He knows it, but he also has some vulnerabilities I wasn't aware of before we started getting together.

He's been hurt before. And I don't want him to hurt again.

I grin at him. "I do."

That makes him flush, and his nipples get harder. I get onto the bed on my knees, and I tug him to me and kiss him. Because

I'm not going to sit tight while he does things to me. I want to be an active participant.

Even if I'm not totally sure what I'm doing.

(I'm not at all sure what I'm doing.)

His tongue in my mouth makes my dick harder. I'm not sure how that mechanism works, but it does. Boy, does it. And now I'm leaking, and he's leaking, and he reaches between us to grab our dicks and jack us both at the same time.

I'm not taking for granted having someone else touching my body, and it gets me so excited. When I'm in his hands, I know I'm well cared for.

"God, that feels good," I groan.

"All right?" He studies me.

"More than. Trust me to tell you if that changes."

"I can do that." He grins. Then he kisses me. It starts soft, but it soon turns harder, wetter, more passionate. I reach around him and grab his ass. I like the firm feel of his butt cheeks. The muscle there, but also the small amount of padding that gives me something to hold on to.

He is so fucking sexy.

I can't believe I get to do this with him. Alden of last year, last job, last clothes would never have dreamed he'd be able to touch a man like Danny. But he's mine, at least for tonight.

I need to stop thinking about what this means. And honestly, that's easy when he's doing these things to my body.

He pushes me over so I'm sprawled on the bed and goes back down to lick my cock.

"You're good with fucking me?" he asks.

I blink. "I mean. I guess. I don't know what I'm doing. How do I know what angle and how fast and how to make it good for you?"

"You listen." He studies me yet again. "Plenty of people don't have any interest in being fucked, and they figure out how to top just fine. It's all about communication. But if you feel like that would make you too nervous, I could do it to you instead. Would you like that? Me inside you?"

I nod. "I'm scared that it will hurt, but yeah."

"It's a foreign feeling, especially at first. But your body will get used to it. And then you'll understand what the shouting is all about." He kisses me. "We'll go slow."

"Okay."

"Can I prep you?"

"Sure." I'm proud that I don't stutter.

He pats the outside of my thigh. "Turn over."

I flip onto my stomach, and now that this is happening, I'm feeling rather exposed. But then Danny's strong hands are on my shoulders, and his lips are between my shoulder blades as his cock nestles between my ass cheeks.

God.

He kisses his way down my back, his hands moving surely—not tickling, and not a massage, exactly. More that he's letting me know where he is and what he's doing.

I appreciate it more than he'll ever know.

Then his lips reach the base of my spine, and he hums against my skin. "You taste so fucking good."

I guess I'll take his word for it, because I'm not going to argue with a guy when he's this close to my ass.

He grabs my cheeks and spreads them, and I squeak. I had thought he was going to use lube, but apparently ...

His tongue touches my hole, and I clench up.

"Shh," he whispers. "I'll take care of you. Just concentrate on letting me know what you like and what you don't like. Okay?"

I nod.

He chuckles and gives me a lick.

"Oh my God."

I say thanks to past Alden for having the foresight to take a really thorough shower earlier. While I've experimented a little bit with my hole, I'm not all that knowledgeable or experienced with it.

This is next-level, though. Danny leans into it. His tongue caresses me, getting me used to having someone touching me there.

"How can this feel so good?"

At least that's what I mean to say, but I think maybe I just moan into the pillow and wantonly shove my ass in his face.

Danny growls, seriously growls, and it's even hotter than I'd imagined. Because have I imagined this? Sure.

Does it feel anything like I thought it would?

No. No, it does not.

He licks and then gently circles my hole and presses his tongue into me. That feels like the intrusion he was talking about. He kisses my butt cheek. "Still good?"

"Yeah." My voice is raspy. "I am."

"Okay. I'm going to get some lube. This will feel a little cold."

"Okay."

I hear the snick of the bottle and the squidge of liquid in his hands. And then his fingers are on me. Some of the lube runs down my taint and onto my balls. I'm trying to stay calm and relax. But with the lube comes a finger inserting itself more insistently.

I feel like I'm in a doctor's office. No joke. I thought it would feel sexier. My erection flags, and I start to think this may have been a mistake.

But then Danny starts talking.

"Shh, Alden. This will take a moment. Your ass hasn't had anything like me in it, and you need to stretch to accommodate me. But you will. You are quite possibly the sexiest thing I've ever seen. Do you realize how you're gasping and moaning?"

I didn't.

"It's the ultimate turn-on. For you to be responding to things I'm doing to you."

"Yeah?"

"Yeah." He lets out a puff of air against my skin. "There we go." And I realize his finger isn't making me uncomfortable anymore. He adds another one. He's moving gently, going slowly and letting me get used to him.

I can see why this is a big deal.

After a while, his fingers inside me go from being just okay to being something I want more of.

"It's not enough," I whine.

"That's a good sign. You're getting there." He adds some more lube and another finger. "I don't want this to hurt. I'd rather overdo the prep, especially for your first time. When you're a pro, you can do this with spit or whatever. But right now, that would hurt you bad." He kisses my ass again. "You're almost there."

His fingers brush against something that sends sparks flickering through my brain and makes my dick perk up.

It's unfathomably good. I was determined—I was doing this no matter what. Even if it hurt.

But the care that Danny is taking with me is almost too much to bear. I don't know what it's going to be like with him inside me.

I need to find out.

"Just fuck me."

He nods against my back. "Okay."

I blink. "So easy?"

"So easy. You're ready. Or, at least, I think you are. I'm still trusting you to speak up if it's not okay."

"Okay."

I look over my shoulder and see him kneeling, ripping open a condom and sheathing himself. He's looking down as he does it, but then he looks at me and the radiance on his face is palpable. "Thank you for trusting me with your body." He pours more lube onto his cock. Are we going to be bathing in lube? I guess so.

I nod.

"I've asked a million times, but I want to be sure. You can still change your mind—now or a minute from now or at any point. Do you want me to do this?"

"Oh, God. Yes. Please."

"Okay. Relax and breathe and bear down on me." He lines himself up with my entrance. I smell the latex. And I feel him enter me slowly, the invasion drawing all my attention.

And, okay. Yeah. It hurts.

I suck in a breath.

"It burns, right?"

"Yeah," I gasp, tears stinging my eyes.

"Want me to stop?"

"No." I'm holding my breath, so it's hard to talk. The feeling is indescribable. Another man—*Danny*—up my ass. For some reason, my nose is starting to run. I think I might be crying—in a happy, relieved way.

"Okay." Now his voice is sounding strained. "You are so fucking tight. And you are so fucking beautiful. This ass. Your smile. Your body. Your humor."

I've never heard Danny babble. I think he's trying to distract me.

It's working. Something eases inside.

I let out a breath.

"There," he whispers. "I could feel that. Does it burn, still?"

"Not as much."

"Okay. I'm going to move." He does an experimental thrust, and it's weird. But then he pulls out and rearranges me so my ass is tilted up more. He enters me and tugs me up to him.

"Holy fuck."

"Now we're getting somewhere?" he asks.

"Yes," I whisper.

"Then hold on."

He eases out and eases in, and little by little, he increases the speed and the angle until he's flush against me over and over again and he's hitting my prostate, and I'm lost.

My dick is leaking. We're a mess of lube and my precome and I don't know what else. Probably my tears and my snot and his sweat.

"Fucking hell," he whispers. "This is so hot. But wait."

He pulls out, and I whine. "What?"

"I want to see you. Turn over." Again, he taps the outside of my thigh.

I roll onto my back, and he slides his knees under my thighs. He gives me a quick kiss and lines up again.

He pushes in, then leans down to kiss me. Then he pulls back and holds one of my hands.

"Ready?"

I nod.

This time I can not only feel what he's doing but see it better, and holy moly.

I like this a lot.

I like the sweat beading on his forehead. I like how his hair's all sexy and unruly. I like the passionate look in his eyes that tells me he's into this.

I like *him*.

"Here we go." He starts fucking me more rapidly, a hand on my cock, but when his strokes get ragged, I take over and he smiles.

I shuttle my hand over my dick, aided by all the lube that's dripped onto my body. He's slamming into me, and it's taking me to a place I never knew existed. One of pain and pleasure.

I am sure I'm babbling things. That he's amazing. That I love this.

"I'm going to come," I cry out.

"Good. Do it. Dunno how much longer I can hold out. It feels too good."

I fall into the pleasure, my body quivering. And I let myself go. "Oh, fuck! Fuck, fuck!" I scream, jetting all over my chest.

"Alden," Danny whispers, and he slams into me. I can feel the pulse of his release as he shudders over me and into me. And then his body trembles with little aftershocks that match mine.

He doesn't pull out but collapses onto me, and I wrap my legs around him.

"You're incredible," he whispers. "You're an honor. You're a pleasure."

And I think I hear him whisper, very low, "You're mine."

# CHAPTER 22
## *Danny*

I t's the middle of the night, and I'm shook. More than shook. I'm dismantled. Like my foundation has been knocked loose.

I've had a lot of sex. I'm good at it. I like getting a guy shuddering and swearing and thinking I'm his world.

I have never, ever had a guy look at me the way Alden did tonight. Like he trusted me with everything. Like I was worth being his first.

Alden offering himself to me felt like *more*. It felt like he was giving me a part of his fucking soul. And a part of me wants to pull away. Because this is getting a little too scary. A little too much like an emotion I swore off ten years ago.

But I could never do that to Alden. And besides, just because we're doing some kind of friends-with-benefits thing, that doesn't mean we're falling in love.

I don't want to trap him into being only with me when he hasn't had a chance to experience being with other guys. For all I know, Alden could feel like he has no other prospects. But anyone who's paying attention could see he's the best.

So here I am, cuddling a sleeping Alden, not wanting to move even though my arm is going numb. And I'm wondering what the hell is happening. The me of just a few months ago wouldn't have gotten anywhere near a situation like this.

I don't want Alden to leave, though. And I'm kinda talking *ever*.

Alden doesn't snore, but he has this soft, rhythmic breathing that I can't help listening to. It reminds me that this interesting person is alive. That he's flesh and blood. That a life force pumps through his veins.

I like how his body feels against mine. He's smaller than I am, but I don't feel like I'm going to break him. More like he's someone I can protect and take care of.

I like the idea of taking care of him.

My dick is thickening as I remember Alden's cries when we were moving together, the slickness of his skin and the way he trembled under me. How good it felt. How I felt connected in ways I don't normally feel.

I sigh, contentedly and deeply, and let Alden's steady breaths soothe me to sleep.

\* \* \*

I wake up a little too warm, nestled against a body that smells of sex and sweat, combined with Alden's soap and his own unique scent. And that I now know more intimately than I did before last night.

"Alden," I say, my voice creaky. "Hey."

He's facing me, our knees touching, and he's studying me, looking concerned. My stomach drops. Does he regret what we did?

"Morning," he says carefully. "How are you?"

I blink. "I'm great. You okay with a hug?"

He looks surprised. "Of course." He cuddles into me.

I speak into his neck. "I can't get enough of you." Then I slide a hand down his back and squeeze his ass. "Are you sore this morning?"

"It feels funny, yeah."

"Is there something I could do to make you feel better?"

My sweet Alden grins. "Kiss me?"

"That," I say, "I can do. With pleasure."

He's like a purring cat under me, because of course I push him onto his back and settle in between his legs. He's all warm and sleepy.

This is awesome. Why did I never spend the night with a man before Alden?

Oh, right. Because none of them was him.

He's hardening against me, and I woke up hard. I reach between us. "This good?"

"Yes," he hisses, and I don't know if it's from my touch or my question. "Please get me off. *Please*."

I chuckle and reach for the lube to jack us. "I've turned you into a monster."

"I am. I can't get enough."

"Maybe not. But I'll give it my best shot."

\* \* \*

After a shattering orgasm each, and a much-needed shower, I sit with wet hair at my kitchen bar, sipping coffee while Alden makes waffles.

My phone buzzes.

**Charlie**: You were AWOL again last night, dude. You still spending all your time with bookkeeper boy?

**Danny**: Yep.

**Charlie**: Sounds pretty boyfriend-y to me.

**Danny**: Could be.

Except I'm still afraid it can't. Sure, everything seems great, and Alden says he's not interested in anyone else—but I thought Brian wasn't interested in anyone else, too, right up until the moment he ended it.

**Charlie**: Wow.

I click out of the text application and check a few email messages. Then I scroll through my phone and find the photos of Alden before he got his hair cut.

"Check this out," I say, holding my phone up to him. He has flour on his nose, and I love it.

"I look like such a geek," he says.

"No. You were hot back then, too. But you didn't have the confidence you do now."

He grins and shrugs. "Yeah, that could be."

I tuck my phone away and watch him putter about my kitchen. It's the kind of domestic scene that would normally scare me.

I'm not scared at all. He's someone who takes care of people. And maybe it's not just me helping him gain confidence and experience. Maybe we're both taking care of each other.

That's awfully relationship-y, but I think that's okay. Because maybe I want a relationship with Alden.

But any lawyer knows you can't change the terms of an agreement unilaterally. You need mutual agreement on terms. So I'll have to discuss it with him. After waffles. And maybe more kissing.

Except I don't, because what if he says no?

# CHAPTER 23

*Alden*

**M**onday morning, I sit at my desk, staring at a spreadsheet.

This is normally where I'm in my element. Being one with the numbers. Able to organize. Categorize. Determine where things go, how the numbers add up and where they belong.

I'm feeling like I don't make sense anymore. Like I don't recognize myself.

Danny has woken up my body. I know that sounds like a cliché, but before he and I started this ... whatever we're doing, I didn't understand what touch could truly feel like. I mean, sure, I've stroked out plenty of orgasms. But it's different when someone else gives it to you. It requires so much trust. That it will happen. That they won't suddenly stop when you're about to blow. That they'll stay with you through the experience and help you come down.

And having him inside me ... My prior fumbling was nothing like having a real live dick in my ass. Evidence of how turned on he was. Rigid and yet forgiving. *Human.*

I can't work. All I can do is daydream about what we did this weekend, and I really hope I'm not getting the wrong idea.

I'm getting the wrong idea.

I don't care, though. If I'm going to go down, this is the way to go: with him wrecking my body. I can't wait to feel the delicious ache of him inside me again.

I'd figured it would hurt, but people seemed to like it, so I expected it would also be pleasurable. I didn't know it would be soul-connecting.

It's not that I was waiting around for a man to give me meaning. More that I felt like I was missing out on something that everyone else understood and I didn't.

Because I was—still am—awkward and anxious and shy, I push people away, sometimes intentionally and sometimes involuntarily. But Danny seems to be the exception to everything. He's easy to talk to. Relaxing—at least, when he's not making my heart race and my body tremble.

I look up, and he's standing in the doorway.

"Hey," I say quietly. "How are you?"

He gives me a big grin. Then his face falls. "What's wrong?"

I shrug. "I missed you last night."

He comes into my office and closes the door behind him. "I missed you, too. I wished you were with me."

"You could've called me." I hate how needy I sound.

But Danny doesn't seem to mind. "I wanted to see if I could still sleep without you." He shrugs. "It turns out I can, but it's not anywhere near as fun. So I suggest you keep coming over as often as you like."

He leans in to kiss me, but I stop him. "What if someone comes in?"

He eyes me. "Do you care? Because," he continues, "if you want to keep our getting together quiet for the time being, I'm fine with that. I'm fully expecting that if anyone else finds out what we're doing, I'll get about six Mafia-style 'If you hurt him' lectures from our coworkers and probably my mom. But that's okay, too, if it's what you want. So don't hold back on my account."

"I don't know what I want," I admit. "There is some benefit to not having everyone all up in my business. But I'm not ashamed of this"—I point between us—"educational experience, either."

"Then let's play it by ear. We don't need to make an announcement, but we won't deny it if it comes up."

"Sounds good." I lean in and kiss him.

I love kissing him. I don't ever want to stop.

After he leaves, the good feeling that came into my office with him stays for a while, but then it subsides.

We haven't promised each other anything. I need to remind myself that I'm exactly where I wanted to be: getting sexual instruction from a master. I know the rules. This is just him helping me out and teaching me how to not be stuck in my shell.

And boy, is he doing that.

* * *

That evening, I'm moping about my room when Mason texts, asking if I'm around. When I respond by calling him, he answers with, "What's wrong?"

I sigh.

He waits. Then, eventually, he asks, "Are you going to tell me, or am I going to have to drag it out of you?"

I squeeze my eyes shut. But I did call him, after all. I need to spit this out. I fill him in on the things Danny and I have been doing together lately—not just the sex, but the evenings on his couch watching baseball, the morning runs around his neighborhood before picking up fresh bagels and going to visit my mom, getting up early to watch Formula 1 races around the world. "When I asked Danny to be my sex tutor, I figured, I don't know, that we'd talk about things," I say. "That he'd tell me what to do with some other guy, maybe be my wingman so I'd feel less scared approaching someone. Not that he'd be the one I fell in love with. I mean, I was already there with a crush, but I figured I could ignore that. I've had crushes before. They happen. But the way he's cared for me, how much time he's spent with me, when he could be doing literally anything else ... I'm gone for the guy."

"Wow," Mason says, and I can't tell how to interpret that. While he's my best friend, he isn't a number or equation, so I don't always understand him.

"What does 'wow' mean?"

"It's an expression of surprise."

I sigh. "Don't be sarcastic."

"All right. I meant it sincerely. I ... was not expecting to hear the two of you were spending that much time together. Do you have any idea what he's thinking?"

"Not really. He treats me really nicely."

"I'd have to beat him up if he did anything else," Mason says.

"From Paris?" I scoff. "But I do appreciate the protectiveness."

"De rien."

"But what do I do?"

"What can you do? You can figure out how he feels about you. The best way to do that, bee tee dubs, is to ask him. Or you can stew in your own juices and suffer."

"I don't like that second option. But the first sounds scary."

"Relationships are scary, Alden. Because you're putting yourself out there, and you might get rejected or hurt."

"Not if you beat Danny up from Paris."

"That would be only if he hurt you, so by definition, it wouldn't work."

"Hmm." I scrub my hand over my face. "I don't think he's going to hurt me. Not intentionally, anyway. I know I wasn't supposed to fall in love with him. What we agreed is that he would teach me how to be a player, and I'd let him record me."

"How's that been going? Do you like being recorded?"

"Um, now that I think about it, Danny hasn't recorded anything in a while—at least not with me there." I scroll on my phone and don't see any new videos. "It's like he gave up.

Although he does have two thousand followers, it's nowhere near the millions I believe he needed for his bragging rights."

"Huh."

"What does that mean? You're as hard to read with your 'huh' as your 'wow.'"

"'Huh' means I wonder if he stopped out of courtesy to you. Like he didn't want to be invasive once he saw where it was going. It seems like he wanted to protect you."

"Huh," I say, and Mason laughs.

"What kind of 'huh' is that?" he asks.

"The confused kind."

"What if," Mason says slowly, "he's starting to care for you the way you care for him?"

"Impossible," I reply immediately.

"Why is that impossible? You're easy to care for. You're sweet and fun. So long as he doesn't get between you and a baseball game, you're fine."

I smile at that, even though it seems hard to believe. Not the part about baseball—that makes perfect sense. But the concept that Danny could have feelings for me.

"We went to a Dodger game together."

"Marry him."

I laugh, but there's a pang in my chest. "He told me he doesn't do feelings. That he was hurt before, so he never has more than one-night stands. That—"

"Did he have more than a one-night stand with you?"

"He said that while he's teaching me he'll be exclusive, but I don't have to be—not that I want anyone else."

"And you didn't think to tell me that?"

"I guess not, no."

"That's huge, my friend. Players don't restrict themselves like that. They're just in it for themselves and then they move on to the next guy. That's showing a tremendous amount of care for you."

"Mason," I say warningly. "This is dangerous talk. You're

getting my hopes up, and I can't afford to get my hopes up. I have to be doing the opposite of that."

"You need to be a pessimist?"

"Well, that way I'm less likely to be disappointed."

"It's such a depressing way to go through life, though. I say be bold, Alden. Be bold, and let yourself love."

"Just so long as you're there to pick up the pieces at the end," I mutter.

CHAPTER 24

*Danny*

Alden and I are at his mom's house, sitting outside on the patio after having dinner with her. It's been a few weeks since he lost his virginity—as he would characterize it—and everything is chugging along. He hasn't said anything about wanting to see other people, and I haven't told him about these uncharacteristic feelings I've been having. Which means I surprise even myself when I blurt, "Do you want to meet my mom?"

Alden looks startled. "Um, sure. I'd love to."

I gulp. "Okay. She still lives in the house I grew up in. It's in South LA. Not as nice as over here on the Westside."

He shrugs. "How nice your mom's house is doesn't matter to me."

"Well, it's not the best neighborhood. There are bars on the windows."

"So, like, it's Los Angeles. I get it."

I keep babbling. "She normally makes al pastor for guests, but that's pork. Maybe I'll have her do carne asada. Would you like that?"

Reaching over, Alden takes my hand. "I feel like you're

worrying about this." He grins. "You're acting like I do, actually. I get all anxious."

"I'm anxious because I haven't taken a guy home to meet my mom since high school."

Alden's lips part, and his eyes go glassy. "Sure," he says quietly. "Okay. I'm honored."

When we pull up to my mom's the following Saturday, I see the house through different eyes. It's a small, old bungalow. While it's in decent repair, it's nothing fancy. I make sure it's painted and the yard is taken care of. She's got a great security system. But she won't move, because she's known the neighbors her whole life. I don't even know how she would handle being somewhere else.

But it's so humble compared to how I portray myself in the office. This is not custom suits and a house in a good part of town.

This is who I really am.

Alden squeezes my hand as we walk up. "This is cute."

I relax a little, and when my mom opens the door, she's her usual lipsticked self. "Mijo! Come in, come in."

I bend down to kiss her cheek, then step back to introduce Alden. "Mom, hi. Um. This is Alden. We work together." Is he my boyfriend? Can I call him that? "And we're kind of seeing each other."

"Is he the one you were going to give lessons in confidence?" she asks.

"That's me," he says with a smile. I'm so proud of how comfortable he seems around her. I'm the one who's nervous, and that's totally weird.

We step inside the house, which smells delicious. Mom offers Alden something to drink, and we all stand in the kitchen while she fusses with the tortilla press.

"You make these?" Alden asks in wonder.

She smiles. "They're better when they are fresh."

"Wow," he whispers.

"Tell me about yourself," she says. "How did you meet my Danny? Are you a lawyer, too?"

Alden tells her how he works at the firm but is a bookkeeper, not a lawyer.

"We always knew Danny was going to be a lawyer. He was arguing before he could talk."

"Mom, that's impossible."

"I could show you proof." She sets down a bowl and goes into the bedroom, then returns moments later with a photo album.

I groan. "No. Mom!" She swats my hand away and opens the book. There's a photo of me naked, sitting in the mud. "Great."

Alden chuckles. "You're cute. I'm astonished my mom hasn't pulled out the baby pictures yet."

"Oh, I'm going to ask her," I threaten.

"I was awkward then and am awkward now."

"You're way more confident these days." I kiss the top of his head and then realize my mother is watching. Her eyes are wide and happy. Oh well. Bringing him here feels like it means something.

Mom flips through the book until she finds a photo of me at about ten months old, standing up, insisting on holding a toy. "See? You were arguing, even without words."

I purse my lips. "What can I say?"

We offer to help Mom make dinner, but she shoos us to the living room, where we look through the old photos. When we come across some of my dad, Alden asks softly if that's who he is.

"Yeah. I don't really remember him."

"He was a good husband," my mom calls. "Although he let you eat mud, and I told him off for it."

"Mom!"

Her wistful expression makes me forgive her for any mortification she's causing.

And as I look at her, I realize her experience has affected my attitude toward love my entire life. Maybe more than Brian, even though he's the one I always blamed. Because she loved my dad with her whole heart and lost him.

I glance at Alden. Is he worth the risk of pain? While the answer frightens me, I'm pretty sure I know what it is.

Mom interrupts my thoughts by calling, "Let's eat!"

We all gather at the table, and Alden takes healthy portions of everything. That makes me happy, because I know my mom likes to feed people and she likes to see guests enjoying their food. But we don't make it far into the meal before she's back to making me feel like I'm fifteen.

"Alden, do you know how Danny came out to me?"

I scrub my face. "So we're doing all the old stories. Okay."

Alden gives me a gentle look. "I'm loving this, actually. Most of the time, I'm the only one who gets embarrassed."

"Not by a long shot." I sigh. "Continue," I tell my mom, then take a bite of my taco, knowing where this is going.

"Some fool child took a video of him kissing a boy at school under the bleachers, and Danny found out about it and came to tell me before I heard another way."

"Were you surprised?" Alden asks.

"No. He never seemed interested in girls."

"And it didn't bother you?"

"Never. What has bothered me is that I didn't know if my Daniel was happy. That's all I want."

"I'm pretty happy these days," I say, not realizing how true it is until I say it. Alden is everything I didn't know I wanted. I'm sure I'm staring at him with a dopey expression, so I focus on my meal.

Mom interrupts my thoughts. "Oh! Mijo. This came for you." She gets up and goes to the table by the front door, returning with an envelope.

She hands it to me, and I read the return address, my stomach fluttering. It's from the alumni association of my high school. I look up at her. "This is about my ten-year reunion, isn't it?"

"It could be." She gets a faraway look in her eye. "Remember how handsome you looked for your prom? You could dress up like that again."

I laugh. "No way. And thanks for bringing that up. It was the night Brian broke up with me."

Alden puts a hand on top of mine.

"He wasn't a good one for you," Mom says. "I know you loved him, but that was a high school love. It wasn't a long-term thing. You both had to find out more about yourselves before you could commit to someone else." She studies me. "Have you ever wondered what happened to him?"

I can't lie. "Yeah, I have." I open the envelope and read the invitation. The event is a few months out.

"Have you ever looked him up on social media?" Alden asks.

"No. I've been tempted, but I held back because I thought, no matter what, I'd regret finding out. If he's married or not, if he's done well or not. It doesn't matter. I don't want to think about him."

"He hurt you, though," he says. "Maybe you need some closure."

My initial reaction is to say no, shut this down. But then I think, what the hell? "Maybe I do. Want to go?" I ask.

Alden raises his eyebrows. "To your high school reunion? As your date?"

"Yeah." I'm ignoring my mom's pleased expression.

"If you want me to go with you, I will."

I smile at him. "Thanks."

We finish eating and help my mom with the cleanup. Once we're done with the dishes, I tug on Alden's sleeve. "C'mon. I want to show you something."

He looks at me questioningly but follows. I pull him down the hallway to my childhood bedroom. It's been turned into a guest room, with not much of me left, but I close the door and press him into it.

Then I lower my mouth to his.

He kisses me back hungrily. He's a pro now.

I'm sure if my mom walked by, she could hear us moaning, but I don't care. I need him. My hand snakes to the front of his pants.

"Danny," he whispers. "We shouldn't."

"We very much should. Can I suck you off?"

He shakes his head, eyes wide. "I don't want to do that to your mom."

I take a step back. "Yeah, I guess you're right."

"I know." He sighs. "But believe me, I could all too easily get carried away."

"Can we go back to my place and get carried away?" I sound like an overeager teenager, but that's what he does to me.

He grins and gives me a kiss. "Absolutely."

We thank my mom, who gives Alden a big hug and invites him back anytime. When we get to my house, I'm dealing with a different Alden than the one I met a few months ago. One who's sure of what he's doing. One who knows that he can have sex and enjoy it, rather than one for whom it was a great mystery.

What continually surprises me is how much I'm enjoying learning about him. When you go from bed to bed, you learn quite a bit about the human body, and I generally know how to make things feel good for another person. I didn't know how to make them good specifically for *Alden*, though. I didn't know how much he'd love to be kissed on his collarbone. When my lips touch him there, he arches into me like I've touched a live wire. I didn't know how he'd part his lips eagerly in anticipation of my kiss. Or how brushing my nose along his neck would make him shiver. He's never had much self-esteem, but that's changing, judging by the confident way he straddles me in bed and how he's stopped shying away from my compliments.

Over the past few weeks, I've been exploring the concept of monogamy, and I'm finding it to be fascinating. Rather than a broad, shallow field of knowledge, I'm getting to know Alden deeply, and I really like it.

It's not just his body, either. I know he likes sci-fi because he likes the science part, not the aliens. He likes to think that math can solve space travel questions. He's fascinated by car tech and can recite Dodgers statistics going back years.

But I'm also learning that I like who *I* am when I'm with him. And while I know we're only together because he asked me for advice, I can't help wanting ... more.

So we're in my bedroom, and before he can do anything else, I'm taking off his pants, sliding them down, and falling to my knees in front of him. Because I want to suck him off right here, right now.

He's so into it. And this is one of the reasons why we get along. Why I'll never get tired of him. Under that mild-mannered demeanor is a sex fiend ready to break free. And I love it when that happens, because he's so refreshingly sincere.

"Oh, fuck, oh, fuck," he whispers as I start sucking him in earnest. "Yes, Danny, oh my God, I can't believe how good it feels and I don't want it to end but if you stop I'll die."

I grin around his cock, then deep throat him and keep going, increasing the suction and speed until he goes off in my mouth.

I fucking love doing this to him, and it dawns on me how much I've changed.

Before, I'd been living my life for myself. Sure, I did things for my mom, and I took care of a cat. But both of them are pretty self-sufficient, TBH.

I haven't thought about making another person a significant part of my life since high school.

But Alden makes me want to change. I want to both cradle him in my arms and watch him go kick ass. I want to be his partner in every sense of the word.

Except, when I told him I'd be exclusive with him, he didn't offer the same thing back. And I can see why—it's not what he asked for. He wants a teacher, not a relationship.

Oh, the irony. And anyway, I'm not sure it would be right to tie him to me when he's just learning who he really is.

# CHAPTER 25

*Alden*

At the office a few days later, Danny leans over my desk and gives me a quick kiss. "You having a good day?"

His simple question warms my heart and makes me think dangerous thoughts. Because this is how boyfriends act, I'm pretty sure. But Danny's not my boyfriend. Just because he's not sleeping with other guys while he's teaching me doesn't mean we're together.

I think.

I can't help but remember what Mason said about this maybe meaning more to Danny, though. Should I ask him what our status is? Is that a dorky thing to do, or a sensible one?

Except he has enough on his mind with the trial, and I don't want to overwhelm him with me, me, me. I stick with the easy answer. "I am, thanks. You?"

While normal people can have this kind of conversation without a second thought, before I started working at Weston & Ramirez, I wouldn't have been able to make small talk like this.

I'm proud of myself.

He leans over, almost far enough to kiss me again, but there's a knock on the door, and we both startle.

It's Shelby, looking amused. "Hey there, do you two want to go to One tonight after happy hour?"

Danny's face falls. "Ugh. It sounds fun, but I need to finish going through opposing counsel's proposed jury instructions in my wrongful termination case. Are you going to go?" he asks me. "You should."

"Um. I guess," I say.

Shelby claps. "Yay! We get Alden! I'll ask the others." He scoots off.

"I may be able to meet up with you later," Danny says.

My smile widens. "Yeah? I'd love to see you." Although I blush, thinking of what happened the last time I was on a dance floor with Danny at One.

I can tell he's thinking about it, too, if the gleam in his eye is anything to go on.

But I don't want Danny to think I'm stuck to him like glue. I don't want to smother him. We've been spending so much time together, I haven't even been trying to talk to other people.

"Do you have any homework for me?" I ask.

"Homework?" He blinks, then recovers. "Oh. Yes." Is it my imagination, or does he not seem as enthusiastic as when we first started this? He rubs the back of his neck. "Um, why don't you see if you can dance with someone you don't know. You up for that?"

A weird mix of feelings runs through me. I'll admit I'm disappointed that Danny didn't do some kind of caveman "Mine!" roar and instead gave me a real assignment per our arrangement.

But part of me is wondering if I can do it—go up to a random man and dance with him. Because I'm going to need that skill when Danny and I are done, whenever that is. Have I gone far enough in my studies to be able to dance with someone I don't know?

I gulp and nod. "Okay. I can do that. If you want me to."

"It's not about what I want, Alden, it's about what you want. This is what you asked me for, right? To help you?"

"Yeah."

He nods. "All you have to do is get in a group of people danc-ing, then single someone out and dance with him for a little bit." He smirks and lowers his voice. "You don't have to do any more than that."

"What's that look for?" I ask, noticing his mirthful eyes.

"Did I ever tell you how I lost my virginity?"

"No!"

"It was with some guy I met at One."

"On the dance floor?"

"No." He chuckles. "In a limo, after. It was the night I got dumped. Prom. At any rate, don't feel like you have to be me and pick someone up. But," he adds quickly, "you could if you wanted to. You're fully capable."

"If that's what you want."

He opens his mouth as if to say something more, but before he can, Charlie hurries into my office and grabs him by the forearm. "We gotta focus, dude."

"I'll catch you later if I can," Danny says. "Trials are what they are." When he leaves, I feel like we didn't finish our conversation, but I'm not entirely sure what we were supposed to be talking about.

I do know, though, that despite being busier than God this week and me not sleeping over since he's been up all hours and needs any rest he can get, Danny's still stopped by and chatted with me every day. I love his attention. They say that someone who likes you makes the time to be with you, and he's been doing exactly that.

Then again, I need to not read too much into this. He's just nice. He's helping me out. That's all.

\* \* \*

I drive to One by myself, since I'm not planning on drinking. At firm happy hours these days, I stick to sparkling water, and I don't feel the slightest pressure to drink alcohol. I like being able to get to know my coworkers, though.

While it's still relatively early, there are people dancing, and I join a group of about a dozen people from the firm upstairs, in a quieter part of the club.

This feels like more of a friends' night out than an office party. I've never felt more accepted than I do at Weston & Ramirez. Since I'm the accounting department, basically everyone needs to talk to me at some point, so I've been getting to know all the attorneys and staff. I'd always thought that I was a shy introvert—and I still am—but I'm learning that I like to have fun, too.

A waitress comes by. "What'll it be?"

Everyone seems to recognize her, and many have usual orders. She takes her time chatting with all of them. When she gets to me, she clucks her tongue. "I'm Alice. And who are you?"

"I'm Alden," I say, without stuttering at all. "I'm the new bookkeeper at the firm."

"Nice to meet you, Alden. What can I get you?"

"Diet Coke?"

"You got it."

I instantly like Alice, with how she didn't bat an eye at me not ordering an alcoholic drink. It makes me want to come back.

We settle in, and Noah asks, "So, Alden, what do you think of the firm, now that you've been with us a little while?"

"I love it."

August elbows him, and Noah scoots just out of reach. "He's just fishing for a compliment," August says.

"What can I say?" Noah shrugs. "I like positive feedback."

"I can give you positive feedback," August says. "You're positively transparent."

Shelby catches my eye meaningfully. He's right. Those two need to get together.

I feel astonishingly comfortable with all these people. In high school, I went the full four years without being able to talk to anyone other than Mason. In college, I really only talked with my professors. But now I'm leaning back and listening and occasionally contributing to the conversation, and I might even be enjoying myself.

Danny's lessons have worked.

A few Diet Cokes later, I'm lurking at the side of the dance floor. Being with Danny has convinced me that I don't lack rhythm, despite my earlier fears. What I lacked was sufficient disregard for what other people thought of me.

Dancing makes me happy. Still, it's disconcerting to be out and about without Danny by my side. But this is what I'm supposed to be learning—to handle being alone in public and talking with available men.

A guy is nearby, also observing the crowd. He's reasonably handsome. He's not swaying like he's had too much to drink. He doesn't smell bad, either—not like pot or cigarettes or BO.

"Hey," he says. "My name is Robert." I look into his eyes.

"Alden," I respond, and shake his hand. His hand feels okay. It's not clammy or too hot. It's not too rough or too smooth. It's a good size.

*Huh.* This is what it's like to interact with another human being I don't know and see if there is potential—something between us.

"Are you from around here, Alden?" he calls over the music.

"Yes. You?"

"Cool. Me, too. Do you like this bar?"

"I do. My friends come here a lot." I see Shelby eyeing me from across the room, looking confused.

I don't know what I'm doing. But this is practice. It's what Danny told me to do.

I smile. "That's who I'm here with, actually, some friends from work."

"Want to dance?"

While all sorts of anxious thoughts run through my head—does it count if he asked me? Should I be dancing with someone else when I just want Danny?—I nod. The whole point of these lessons is for me to be brave enough to talk to nice guys.

I keep hoping Danny will show up, but I haven't seen him so far.

Robert and I start dancing, and while I'm not really into it, I'm also internally cheering. I'm acting like a normal person, dancing with a guy in a bar. He hasn't tried to seduce me into worshipping Loki, and I'm not making a total fool of myself.

He touches my waist, and I don't flinch.

It doesn't feel like it does when Danny touches me, but it's not *bad*. I look at Robert. Do I want to spend any more time with him?

I don't know.

I miss Danny. That's the bottom line, but I need to keep moving forward with my lessons. I can't waste my energy wishing for a true relationship with Danny when that's never going to happen.

So, when Robert pulls me close for a slow song, I let myself hold him.

How do I know different is wrong? What if different is just … *different*? Maybe I found a potential match.

It feels nice. Fine, even. Just not Danny.

Even so, we keep dancing, and at the end of the night, we exchange phone numbers. As Robert enters mine into his phone, I notice Danny standing at the bar, looking at me intently. I give him a smile, but Robert leans in to kiss me.

I startle and move, so his lips hit my cheek.

"So-sorry," I stutter, and I wince. Then I see that Danny is gone.

*Shit.*

"I just saw someone I need to talk to," I say, trying to leave quickly without being rude.

Robert nods. "Well, it was nice to meet you."

I take off running after Danny.

# CHAPTER 26

# *Danny*

The night air hits my face as I speed walk outside.

I don't like what I'm feeling right now. Time stopped when I watched Alden dance with some guy. And then almost get kissed.

Part of me is proud—that Alden's confident enough to go to a bar, pick up a guy, and dance with him. But my dominant emotion is jealousy, and it fucking sucks.

It needs to stop. I'm being selfish, and I shouldn't do that to Alden. I should be supportive of him and his growth. He has zero experience outside of me. I can't lock him down before he learns what the world is like.

I couldn't handle watching him, though, so I turned and booked it out of the club. I've never been a coward. I'm a fucking lawyer. I argue. I'm used to confrontation, conflict, strife.

But I don't want to get into it with Alden.

Except, as I turn the corner, he catches me, his fingers curling around my bicep. "Hey! Didn't you see me?"

I swallow hard. "Yeah, I saw you. It looked like you were doing great out there. Really balling."

He kicks the ground, but he can't hide his smile. "You've helped me a lot."

Despite everything, despite how rough I'm feeling, that makes me smile, too. Because all I want is for this man to feel good about himself.

He's standing with his shoulders back, his face flushed from dancing. His curls are messy and damp, but they're sexy. His clothes fit him well. "Why did you run away?" he asks.

I want to punch a wall. I'm not going to lie to him. But I'm also not going to tie him to me when he deserves to be free. "Because this was never supposed to be more than me teaching you how to date someone else. And you're ready. You've passed the class."

Except my words seem like they hurt him.

"I ... I see," he says.

I hold up my hands. "I really like you, Alden. As more than just my student. But you haven't been with anyone other than me. The whole plan was, I'd teach you how to pick up guys, and then you were going to take your newfound skills and knowledge and go practice them on someone else."

"But I don't want him," Alden says.

"Maybe he's not the right guy for you, but that doesn't mean the next guy you meet won't be. Or the one after that. You should go and meet other people so you can decide what's right for you."

His eyes flash. "Danny, you're being an ass. I'm not a child. I've been around plenty of people. Just because I was awkward as fuck —and still am, sometimes—it doesn't mean I haven't observed what I want and what I don't want. What I want is you," Alden says simply.

I want to believe him. Even though I started this thinking that when we were done with his lessons, I'd move on and go back to my old ways, I don't want to move on. I'm not done with Alden. I don't think I'd ever be done with him. But I swallow hard and say,

"Our contract is done. You passed the class. You can't go through your life having been intimate only with me."

*Even though I want you to.*

"Danny, I don't understand. Do you *want* me to go?"

"No, that's not what I want."

"But you're not even going to give us a chance?" he asks.

I throw up my hands. "I'm *giving* you what you need."

He wants me now, but it won't last. Because people don't stay. And I'm not even talking about Brian anymore. My dad abandoned my mom—not his fault, but she never got over it. If I fell, really fell for someone, and they left, I'm scared I'd end up like her: alone for the rest of my life.

Which I guess I am already—or was, before I met Alden. But that's too big a concept for me to worry about processing right now.

"Actually, you aren't giving me what I need." Alden puts his hands on his hips. "Because—like I said—what I want is you."

Fuck, he's so tempting. I have to say no. "I think we both need to take a step back and decide what we really want. Without the student-teacher dynamic."

*You. I want you. But I want you to be sure.*

"I already know what I want," he says. "But if you need space, fine. I can give it to you."

He spins on his heel and practically runs away.

I start to go after him, but it's better for him if I don't.

So I turn and keep going to my car.

\* \* \*

When I get home, Mamacita trots up to me, and I pick her up, petting her soft fur. My hand shakes, because I think I just broke up with Alden, even though we weren't actually together.

I pull out my phone and stare at my lock screen, which is a selfie of us. I should change that if I'm going out cruising, but the photo makes me happy. It sends the wrong message, though, I suppose.

I can't bring myself to change it. We look so content and comfortable together. Like we were a normal couple, having a good time. But I can't think like that. I can't trust that things won't change.

After I feed Mamacita, I take off my clothes and climb into bed. It feels lonely and empty without Alden. I got used to having a warm body sleeping next to me after years of never doing that.

I don't want just a warm body, though. I want to cuddle with Alden.

And I'm upset with myself for that. I should be grateful for the life I've built rather than try to have something that will never work out.

Mamacita curls up on what I've started thinking of as Alden's pillow.

*Fuck*, it's going to be awkward in the office next week. I always knew I shouldn't pick a flower where I work. I roll around on my sheets, utterly miserable.

I knew dating someone more than once was a bad idea. I never articulated it, but I knew emotions were going to happen.

Getting too close to someone can only lead to heartache and pain.

A little voice inside me says I'm already experiencing heartache and pain. I grew up without a dad, but I'm not sure my mom would have chosen differently if she'd known what was going to happen. I might not have let myself care so much about Brian if I'd known how things would end between us, but he wasn't the right one for me. It was me projecting what I was feeling onto him.

But am I projecting that onto Alden now?

Alden cured me and hurt me at the same time. He hurt me by making me believe in love again. That's a very dangerous thing.

I get out of bed and start pacing. Mamacita, confused, follows me around the house. I take in all that I've been able to achieve:

Nice clothes. A killer house. A fabulous car. Fame in the court-room and a great job.

And I'm fucking lonely as hell.

I throw myself on the couch and turn on the television, but I have no idea what's playing.

The next day, I wake up with a crick in my neck and hurt in my heart. Because what kind of fool throws away the best thing that ever happened to him?

This fool right here.

What I want, plain and simple, is Alden. I want a real, committed relationship with him. I want to wake up every morning next to him and go to sleep with him at night. I want to make breakfast with him and go to baseball games and do every-thing with him.

And I'm petrified to try. Because what if he leaves—by choice or otherwise?

I sigh and rub my eyes.

My house has gotten pretty messy while I've been focused on the trial, so I slump around picking up socks and sweats and underwear. I start laundry and gather my dishes and put them in the kitchen. I put my trash in the can and take it out. I do the dishes. As the suds rise up my arms and dampen my shirt, I think I'm doing some sort of benediction. A cleansing. This is what I want to be.

All clean. Too bad my love life's a mess.

My phone sounds, and my heart leaps, hoping that it's Alden. But it's Charlie.

"So, have you officially given up? I see you only have three thousand followers."

I groan and rub my hand over my face. "Fuck off. I guess I let my ego and my mouth run away with that one. Going viral is harder than I thought if you're not drinking cranberry juice on a skateboard and singing along to Fleetwood Mac."

"Get ready to be embarrassed," he says, crowing.

"Okay," I say listlessly.

"Hey." His tone changes to one of concern. "What's wrong?"

"Nothing."

"It doesn't sound like nothing." When I don't reply, he continues, "Does this have anything to do with a certain bookkeeper who has big eyes just for you?"

"Yeah."

I tell him what happened—how I let Alden go so he could experience the world.

"Dude, you're such a loser," Charlie says. "You know, you deserve to be happy and have nice things."

"I have nice things."

"Nice relationships. I've always thought that you were a little desperate."

"Fuck you. I'm not desperate."

"Um, yes, you were. You were going from man to man like they were going extinct. Nothing wrong with that when it's coming from a place of having fun. But I think, deep down, you want something more. And maybe you're afraid to try for it." *Yeah, no shit*, I think. Charlie sighs. "Just think about it. And then do what you need to do."

# CHAPTER 27

## *Alden*

I spend Saturday working around the house, doing chores for my mom on autopilot. She sees my eyes, red from crying last night, but she doesn't ask me any questions. Which is good, because I don't think I could answer them.

Why, if we did what we said we were going to do—Danny taught me how to be self-assured and prepared me to go out and date other people—does it feel so *wrong*?

It's because I went and fell for him. I'm completely in love with Danny Villaseñor. I love how he takes care of me. He's the kindest, most patient man I've ever met. He never mocks me. He doesn't belittle me or minimize my feelings. He does the opposite, making me feel like I'm his whole world.

My phone buzzes. Mason. When I answer with a gloomy "Hi, Mason," he immediately asks, "What's wrong?"

I sigh. "I fell in love with Danny."

"Right. You said that last time we talked, but you sounded a lot happier about it then."

"And I think he cares about me."

"Still not seeing the problem here. That's a good start, isn't it?"

"No, it's not."

"Tell me why."

"Because we never agreed to have a relationship, and what we were doing morphed into something more, and I think that scared him. He told me how badly he was hurt in the past."

"So you think he's too scared to love?"

"Yeah." My voice is husky.

"But people change. *You* changed."

"Yes, people can change, but will I be wasting my time if I wait for something that may not happen? He told me to go see other people. Hanging around until he changes his mind or has some sort of epiphany seems pathetic."

"Or, it's what people do when they like each other."

I groan. "I have to let him go. I can't be clingy."

"You shouldn't be clingy or stalkery, but you can try to make him understand you're not interested in dating other people. Don't make fear-based decisions, Alden."

"Even if he is?"

"Yes. Just because he's being a doofus doesn't mean you should follow his example. Talk to him."

"I did talk to him. And he said he wanted to take a step back."

"Well, I think you're making a mistake if you go along with that. I think you should pay for skywriting to tell him you love him. Or put it on the DodgerVision screen at Dodger Stadium."

I scoff. "That's a good way to get me super embarrassed."

"Love can be embarrassing. Ask me how I know."

"How do you know?"

"Do you remember Ben from high school?"

I think back. Mason had a crush on Ben at the beginning of our freshman year, but Ben switched schools. "Yeah, I remember."

"He's in Paris."

Despite myself, I let out a yelp. "No way!"

He tells me a story involving Ben, food poisoning, and a trip to the Rodin museum, and while I still feel crappy about my own situation, I'm happy that my friend might have a second chance at love.

\* \* \*

I dread going to work on Monday for the first time since I started at Weston & Ramirez. But Danny and I are both adults. We can behave rationally. I think.

Now I see why Noah was talking about a love contract so long ago. Wanting to make sure there was no blowback on the firm if a relationship fell apart.

I keep inadvertently looking for Danny, but his office lights are off.

Part of me knows that he's in trial, and that takes over an attorney's life. That he's going to be in court the entire day and preparing all night long. But I got used to him stopping by to check up on me, even when he was busy. So it feels like he's avoiding me.

That's probably the nicest thing he could do, because heaven knows interacting with him right now, with both of us knowing how I feel about him, would be beyond awkward.

I can't force him to do anything he doesn't want to do.

My stomach sinks when I overhear someone saying that they thought they saw Danny at One Sunday night. "He's not the kind to settle down," they say. "Some men just aren't. They need to be on to the next thing."

This whole experience has been a growing pain for me. I've learned that I can be confident, and I can look good and feel great about myself.

But I can't count on the other person feeling the same way I do.

When I get home, Mom is sitting on the couch, looking perky, but her face falls when she sees me.

"Alden, what's wrong?"

"Boy troubles," I mutter.

She opens her arms, and I settle in next to her. "Want to tell me?"

I do. I don't get too specific, but I tell her about my heart.

"He may be right, you know," she says. "And while you're welcome to live here as long as you want, I'm not going to need your help forever. I'm not kicking you out," she adds hastily. "Just, if you want to experience more on your own, I'll be fine here by myself. As long as you still come visit now and then."

"Thanks, Mom." I had been thinking of getting my own place, and it's a relief to know that she's okay with it. Maybe that's what I need to do. Then I can figure out who I am on my own, without Danny, Mom, or anyone else.

As much as I hate that idea.

CHAPTER 28

## Danny

I have yet another horrible night where I don't get any sleep at all, but I'm too tired to turn on the television or scroll through my phone. I'm exhausted from trial, and whatever brain waves I have left are spent thinking about Alden. I haven't been anywhere except court and home since I left him. So I just stare at the ceiling and pet my cat.

My three-day trial finishes, and Thursday, Noah and August corner me in my office.

I hold up my hands. "What is this? An intervention? I swear I don't drink that much."

"We know," Noah says. "But you're moping even though you won your trial. So what's up?"

Has it really been that bad?

"There is something going on, isn't there?" August asks.

I nod and shrug at the same time. "I've been kind of seeing someone."

"Alden," Noah says.

Not about to lie to my partners, I nod. "Yeah. How did you know?"

"Shelby," Noah and August say.

"Figures."

"Listen, Danny," Noah says. "You like Alden. And Alden likes you, right?"

"Yes," I admit.

"Then tell him."

"I have."

August and Noah look at each other. Noah says, "Okay, then maybe we should stay out of it. We just thought—"

"I appreciate your concern, but he and I have some issues we have to deal with."

"I mean," Noah goes on, "if I had the love of my life, there's no chance I'd let him get away."

Like Noah's one to talk. He's been pining for his best friend as long as I've known him. Still, "Why do you think Alden's the love of my life?" I ask sharply.

August stares at me long enough that it becomes uncomfortable. It's like he's trying to figure out what planet I came from and whether he can send me back. Then he glances skyward and shakes his head.

Alden can't be the love of my life. Can he?

I bite my lip. "But."

He whips his focus back to me. "But what?"

"But if he ..." I don't know what to say. All I know is that I'm scared to have him in my life and scared not to.

"What you should do is think about whether your life is better with him or without him," Noah says.

"With him."

"Then ask yourself whether you need to tell him that."

I nod and take a deep breath. "I suppose I do."

August says, "You do. You must know that he wants you. It's obvious, even for those of us who haven't talked with Shelby. We see how much time you spend with him—and how he lights up when you're in the room. The only way you'll get what you want is if you make yourself vulnerable. I don't know what happened to you to make you close yourself off like this, but you need to get over it."

I want to tell him that's rich coming from him, the guy with unrequited love for Noah that he's not even aware of. But he might not be ready to hear that. And apparently today is all about me.

Without Alden, my life is emptier. I miss his smile and the way he gets so animated at baseball games and how eager he is to share details about the TV shows he loves. The idea of being with him still makes me feel selfish, though. Like I'd be keeping him from living his life fully.

August apparently sees my thoughts on my face, because he nods. "I think you understand. What are you going to do about it?"

"Do?"

"You have to take action. You have to show him that you're the one for him."

"I don't know that that's true. But I know that *he's* the one for me."

"Same thing." August gives me a look, like, *I'm waiting*.

"I'll come up with something," I say.

He and Noah look at each other.

"Guess that's good enough. For now, at least," Noah says.

"Hang in there, man. If you want to talk, we're here," August says.

After work, I do something I haven't done since high school. I go to the batting cages and start hitting balls, because I need to work off some energy and figure out how to tell or show Alden how I feel. My usual mode of stress relief—fucking some random guy—isn't an option.

Besides, Alden reminds me of things I used to want. Like a relationship. And like being a baseball player. I got on another track, but I can still chase a few of my old dreams. So: batting practice it is.

Swing.

Hit.

Repeat.

My thoughts are all over the place. Can I be brave enough to show Alden how I feel? My muscles burn. I'm overdoing it. I can see why this is Alden's favorite sport. It requires precision and lends itself to analysis and statistics—except there's still a lot of fun with bats and balls. Maybe I'll join a softball team. I bet we both could.

My phone rings, and I shut the machine off to check it.

It's my mom. "Mijo, ¿cómo estás? When are you going to bring Alden to dinner again?"

I swallow hard. "I don't know."

"What? Why not? He's wonderful!"

"We kind of broke up."

"Oh, Danny. Do you want to talk about it?"

"Not really. That's why I'm at the batting cages."

It's quiet on the line. Then, "You haven't gone there in years. Not since before Brian."

I sigh. "I know. I needed to work out some things."

Another pause. "Do you think you may be scared to love because of what happened with your father?"

I don't answer.

"Because I think you believe some bullshit—"

"Mom! You said a bad word."

"*Bullshit*, mijo. I had your father for years. Not as many as I'd hoped to, but the time we had together was sweet, and I have my memories of him. My life is better because he was in it, no matter what. What's happened since then, that's my choice. By the time I was done grieving, I decided I liked being single. But if I found someone who made me feel the way your dad made me feel— someone who lights me up the way Alden does for you—I'd reconsider."

"How come you never told me any of this?" I ask, rubbing my

chest.

"Because matters of the heart are delicate. And you need to learn them for yourself, not have your mom tell you what to do."

I grin despite myself. "What would my mom tell me to do?"

"I'd tell you to hold on to Alden and not let him go."

When I get home, I'm as antsy as I was before I went to the cages, only now my arms feel like overcooked pasta and my back is threatening a revolt. I shower, and while I'm in there, I realize how I can tell Alden how I feel.

I step out of the shower and don't bother getting dressed. I just wrap a towel around my waist and turn on the camera.

My words pour out in a stream, without conscious thought. "I know not very many people will see this video, because I have barely any followers. I started this channel with the intent to go viral to win a bet with a friend. But that hasn't really gone anywhere. I have something to say, though.

"I started out wanting to teach a coworker—John Doe—who asked me how to be a playboy. How to be good with the guys. Because he was less experienced than me.

"What he's taught me, though, is that I don't want to be a player anymore." I sigh. "I want him. I'm completely and totally in love with him." I pause a moment to collect myself, my emotions getting to me. "Yeah. I'm in love with him. The other night, I told him we needed to take a break because he should experience being with other people, not just me. And I still think that's probably true. I hate the idea of him tying himself to me too soon and eventually regretting it. But ... I hate the idea of being apart from him, too. I've spent years avoiding getting involved, because I was afraid of getting hurt—and right now I'm terrified that one day, he'll realize he can do better than me, and I'll lose him. But despite all that, Alden, I love you. I want to be with you. And if you see this and you want to be with me, I'm yours. For as long as you'll have me. Let's write a new contract."

A tear runs down my face, and I wipe it away.

I grimace, end the video, and upload it before I lose my nerve. Then I set my phone down and throw myself on my bed.

Charlie calls me moments later. "Um, do you have something to share with the class?"

"What are you talking about?"

"I have an alert for your channel."

I rub my face. "Yeah. Okay. So you're saying it was a bad idea for me to post like that."

"No, you asshole. I'm saying you fell in love without telling me."

That makes me chuckle. "I didn't know I had to get your permission."

"You don't have to get anything from me. But this is big news, you have to admit. Also, do you think Alden follows your account? It's kind of pointless to make this big declaration if he's never going to see it."

"I guess I'll go over to his place and tell him." I scrub my face. "Or should I text him first?"

"No. Pretend this is a movie and you're the main character. You'd want to show up on the doorstep, right?"

"I have no idea. I've never been in a movie."

"Go over there and tell him how you feel. I dare you."

"Okay," I say. "Thanks." I hang up and get dressed, feeling the blood coursing through my veins and pounding in my ears.

When I go into court, while I plan carefully beforehand, there's always a certain amount of winging it. I can handle that, because I know my case thoroughly and can think on my feet.

Do I know my own case thoroughly? Do I know how I really feel?

I love Alden Meyer. A thrill runs along my skin and down my spine. Yes, I love him.

That's all there is to it. I can't imagine a life without him. I want him with me. I want to have him however he'll let me.

I grab my keys, wallet, and phone and head for the door.

# CHAPTER 29

*Alden*

I'm lying on my bed when my phone buzzes.

**Mason**: You should check Danny's Ad/VICE account.

**Alden**: As far as I know, he quit posting.

**Mason**: I know. But I randomly checked, and you have to see it. It's trending on other social media, too. Even though he only posted less than a half hour ago. He has like 50,000 shares.

My heart is in my throat. What did he do?

I click on Danny's video and watch. And listen. Really listen.

By the end, I'm shaking.

I find my mom in the living room.

"Alden?" she asks with concern. "What is it?"

Wiping my forearm over my nose, I give her a watery smile. "I think Danny loves me."

A big grin breaks across her face.

"I need to talk to him."

"Then go get him," Mom says. I nod and race back to my room.

Cool kids stay home, right? Cool kids wait for people to come to them.

I've never been a cool kid, and I never will be. Or maybe I've always been cool.

Or maybe ... it doesn't matter. I don't want to be alone. I want to be with Danny.

I can't wait another minute. I tear around my room, looking for clothes to wear, because I can't show up in sweats. Shoving a foot into one leg of my jeans, I hop around trying to pull them up and find a shirt and my keys at the same time.

I catch a glimpse of myself in the mirror. Is that the kind of man who can go and declare love to Danny? Am I worthy of him?

Maybe that's not the right question to ask. Maybe the question is, can I live without him? While technically, yes, I can, I don't want to. I'd feel like part of myself was missing.

That's the answer. I don't have to.

I smooth down my hair and head into the bathroom to brush my teeth. But then I realize my heart is beating so fast I don't know what's going on. I can't delay this any longer.

And that's what I'm doing. I'm delaying.

Because what if there's some mistake? What if he just posted that video to go viral? For the likes. What if I'm the only one of us who's miserable? What if I make a fool of myself by chasing after him?

Fuck it. I'll take that chance.

I race across town to his house and jog up the front steps, raising my hand to knock on the door, but just then it opens. Danny is standing there, keys in hand, looking unbelievably handsome.

I blink at him. He blinks at me.

I let out a stuttering laugh. "Uh, hey. Danny. What are you ...?"

"I was heading to your place," he says. He takes a deep breath, his eyes on me. His lips part, like he can't believe I'm here. He steps back and gestures. "Come in." He looks nervous.

"Did you mean it," I start, but he interrupts me.

"Alden, I have to apologize to you. I wasn't honest with you. Or myself. I wasn't honest about my feelings for you."

My stomach dips and soars, wondering what he's going to say.

CHAPTER 30

## Danny

I cup Alden's face in my hands. "Sweetheart."

He winces, and it makes my heart ache that I caused him pain. I go on, the words pouring out of me in a very unplanned torrent. "I don't know how this is going to work out, or whether I've already screwed things up too badly, but you're worth the risk. If I make a fool of myself, so be it. I'm an adult. I can do this."

"Do what?" he whispers.

"Tell you how much I love you."

He inhales sharply. "For real?"

"So very, very much." My hands are shaking. My voice cracks. "You're the only one I want to be with." I smile, though I think it might be slightly manic. He's looking at me with wide eyes. My heart thunders. "I thought our arrangement was something superficial and just for fun. I thought you were sweet, and so cute and innocent, and I'd help you out. With someone else. But now I can't stand that thought. I don't think I deserve you, but I'm a jealous enough bastard that I don't want anyone else to have a chance with you. I want to be the one who captures all your kisses. I want to be the one in bed with you. I want to be the one to cook you breakfast and have you tell me every baseball statistic you know. You fascinate me, and I don't think that will ever change. Because I get you, and I think you get me."

He doesn't answer, and it's starting to make me queasy. My stomach drops to my ankles.

"Maybe I got it wrong. Shit, I'm sorry. I just wanted you to know that I've fallen in love with you. And if I've misread this—"

"No," Alden finally says. "You've got it right. I love you, too. I just can't believe you're actually saying these things."

"You do?"

"Yes, Danny. I've been in love with you since ... I don't really know when it started. Early on, though. I felt this overwhelming attraction. And then you agreed to kiss me and touch me, and I felt like I didn't deserve it. But it's morphed. You aren't some perfect, fantasy being. You're a man with strengths and weaknesses, and I see them and love them all."

"I don't know what I did to deserve you," I murmur. I pull him to me, kissing the top of his head. Feeling his soft curls and smelling his sunny scent.

"I want us to be together. Can we do that?"

"Yes. Please. I'm sorry I got scared. It wasn't just about Brian. I was worried that what happened to my mom would happen to me. That I'd find the man of my dreams and then lose him." I hold his cheeks with both hands and kiss him. And this kiss feels like it's a seal on a contract. Like I'm officially making him mine. Maybe I already did that when we had sex. Or when I kissed him the first time. Or the first time I listened to him. But no matter what, *he's fucking mine*.

"I love you," I repeat.

His smile transforms his face. He's happy.

I make him happy. We make *each other* happy, because I'm pretty sure my grin matches his.

Back in the day, I'd never smile for pictures, because I thought I was too cool. Now, I want to just be the person I am. I don't care what others think. All that matters is that I'm with Alden.

"You do," he murmurs, "and it's the best thing I've ever experienced. And you're not going to lose me." He closes his eyes.

I grin. Again. "What would you like to do now, babe?"

"I want you to do whatever you want to me, no holds barred. I want to see you take your pleasure."

"I want the same for you. I want to give you pleasure." I could not have said a truer sentence if you paid me.

I want to *live* to give this man pleasure. A man who thought he wasn't worthy. Who denied himself human contact because he was nervous and shy and had been hurt. I want to show him he doesn't have to be afraid anymore.

He leans up and kisses me, and it's like our very first kiss. Fumbling and passionate and we can't get enough of each other.

"You don't have to be so careful with me," he says. "You're always so gentle. You can be a little rough if you want."

"I don't want to be." I want to cherish him. I rake my fingers through his soft hair, tugging it lightly. My hands skim over his torso, enjoying his soft skin. He's lean and doesn't have a lot of body hair, but I like his curves and planes. The little dip above his hip and the way his belly button is kind of lopsided and adorable.

"Let's take this to the bedroom," he says.

"Yes, sir." I grin. I love how assertive he is now.

Once we're both undressed and lying on my bed, I line up our cocks and rub us decadently together.

"Okay," he whispers. "This is good."

I like seeing his arousal rise in the way his eyes get wide, then have to shut because he can't take it anymore. The way he starts to hold his breath and then pants. How he curls his toes and his skin flushes or the small hairs stand on end. I love all of it. I love all of *him*.

It's so simple: we belong together.

"You're mine," I say, needing him to know it.

He snuggles into me, laughing. "I think you're *mine*."

"I am."

He does an expert flip, and now he's straddling me while he looks down at me, his fingers tracing patterns on my chest. Then he boops my nose and kisses me. I laugh and spin us again.

We continue this part make-out session, part wrestling match until I cup his ass and he groans, kissing me more forcefully, and now it's on.

I begin to open him, easing lube into his channel so he can relax and take me.

He flops onto his stomach and rises up on his hands and knees, wiggling his ass in a move that makes my mouth water.

"You are a sight," I whisper, pressing another finger in. I stroke his cock with my other hand and rub my own cock against his leg. He's right here, and he's so sexy and mine.

"You make me feel amazing," he says. "I crave being closer to you than I can be to any other human being."

"You're gonna make me come fast if you keep talking like that," I warn.

"If that happens, we'll just do it again."

"Fair enough." And I realize that's another thing I get to have with Alden. Before, with a one-and-done hookup, I needed to be perfect, because I wasn't going to get a second chance. No, I wasn't going to *allow* myself a second chance.

But with Alden, I can explore him. And it's very, very sexy, because his body has a lot of secrets. While he has the usual erogenous zones, some are all his own. Like the backs of his knees. Or the way he reacts when I suck his cock from the side.

But now, I can tell he's ready for my cock.

I go to grab a condom, and he stiffens. "You don't have to."

"What?"

"I trust you. You got tested. I trust that you've been with no one else but me since then. We don't need condoms."

I make a very unmanly whimper. Because I've never had sex without one. *Never*.

As I line up, ready to fuck him, I realize I'm in even deeper than I'd imagined. I hadn't expected how much I would want to take care of this man—but also how much he'd give me in return. Things I didn't know I wanted or needed. Things I didn't know I was missing.

Like trust.

Like love.

Like valuing my opinion.

Like letting me be intimate with him in more than just a physical way.

"Do it, Danny," he urges. "Fuck me. Please."

And I slip inside.

His warm, lubed heat feels nothing like when there was a condom separating us. I think he can tell the difference, too.

We're skin to skin. Body to body.

A communion of sorts. We are *one*.

I slide all the way in, pressing my pelvis to his ass cheeks, groaning. I huddle over him, reaching for his cock.

"You okay?" I ask.

"I am absolutely not okay." I start to pull out, but he grabs my ass. "'Okay' has nothing to do with this. I think if I were to die during sex, this is when it should happen. Because what a way to go."

"You're talking too much," I growl. "I must not be doing my job."

He laughs, which turns into a moan and then a grunt as I pull back and thrust into him much more forcefully. And again. And again.

Over and over, I slide into him, trying to rub his prostate the right way while his pressure around me makes every part of my dick feel good.

*Fuck*. I increase the speed, fucking him hard now. I can't keep this up, because I'll get caught in an orgasm, but I know Alden likes it when I lose control.

I'm almost there, but I hang on long enough to make sure he's going to be coming first.

As I stroke him and change the angle I'm fucking him at, he erupts, the muscles at his entrance squeezing around my cock. Warm semen spills into my fist and over my fingers and thumb.

Then it's my turn, and I pump into him hard and stay, my dick releasing into him. I feel like a total caveman marking him, and I fucking love it. Because when I pull out—and I eventually do—that's my spend inside him.

Alden is mine.

He collapses onto his stomach, and I crawl to his other side so I can see his face without making him move. His eyes are dazed and contented, and his mouth is red from where he must have bitten his lip.

I kiss him softly.

"Wow," he whispers. "Just, wow."

The feedback is welcome, because no matter how well you think you know your partner, there's always the chance you missed something. I wouldn't want to have missed anything with him.

"I'm glad." I kiss him again. And again. "Is your ass going to be okay?"

"Oh yeah. I'll have to get cleaned up at some point."

"I don't want you to. I want you to have my come in you all night."

He gives me a tiny shove. "Appealing to your baser instincts, am I, Mr. Villaseñor?"

"Completely. All my instincts."

"Danny?"

"Yeah, love."

"We really are boyfriends?"

After all that, he still needs reassurance. I understand. It took us a while to get here, because we both had a lot to work through.

"Yes, love. You're my boyfriend and I'm yours. And ... if you want to be more than that, I'm game."

He startles. "What?"

"I mean—and I don't want to frighten you off—but if in the future you wanted to be more, I'd want that, too."

"Meaning ... what, exactly?"

I expect the words to be scary, but they spill out easily. "Whatever you want. Living together? Marriage?" I shrug. "I closed myself off to the idea, but on some level I think I've always wanted one love. I just never let myself believe I could have it before."

He groans and snuggles into me. "You really are perfect for me, Danny."

We spend the night wrapped up in each other, and my arm doesn't even fall asleep, although I do. Something about Alden's calm breathing makes me relax completely. When we wake up together in the morning, I'm beginning to believe that he's there for me and will be for the rest of my life.

This is going to be good.

# CHAPTER 31

## *Alden*

D anny and I walk into work Friday morning hand in hand, and Shelby looks up from the reception desk and grins at us. "Heyyy," he says. "You two figure things out?"

I look at Danny and smile. "Yeah, I think so. Now we need to make it official."

Shelby startles. "What?"

Letting go of Danny's hand, I lean on Shelby's desk like I'm comfortable with this place. Because I am. "Noah mentioned some paperwork we need to sign."

"Ohh." Shelby's eyes go wide. "You're going to talk to him?"

"We are." Danny nods in agreement.

"That's so awesome! I'm happy for you!"

"Thanks," I say. "And thanks for being there for me."

"Anytime." While I can tell Shelby's genuinely happy for us, I detect a wistfulness in his expression that gets wiped away as soon as he shows it. I hope he finds his own Mr. Right—one who is most definitely *not* straight *or* unavailable.

Danny holds out his elbow like he's escorting me to a ball. "Shall we?"

Laughing, I nod and take his arm.

We head for Noah's office, passing a few coworkers who give us knowing looks. When we get there, August is reclining in one of Noah's client chairs while they chat, but they both look up when we walk in. Noah's expression of surprise morphs into a knowing smirk.

August bursts out laughing. "Do we need to draft up a love contract?"

"Yeah," Danny says, kissing the top of my head. "We do. Twenty million followers seem to like our story."

Because, yeah, his video went viral. No one could get enough of this hot, bare-chested man declaring how in love with me he was.

Least of all, me.

Charlie ended up giving Danny a shout-out on his own channel, which only increased Danny's subscribers. And now Danny and I plan to make some videos of us hanging out, just for fun, and answering viewers' questions.

Danny heads to his office to talk with Johnny Haskell about the next steps in his case. Meanwhile, I burrow into my spreadsheets, content in every area of my life for the first time ever.

* * *

I'm dressed in a rented tuxedo, but I feel pretty good in it. Danny looks amazing in his. We walk hand in hand into his high school reunion, which is taking place at a downtown hotel.

Hip-hop music blares through the open door as we check in, and bad memories of high school come flooding back. The times when I was teased and ostracized. The times when I felt out of place. The times when I was forced to do things I didn't like.

I take a look at Danny and straighten my spine. I've come a long way since then. For the past few months, he and I have been inseparable. But what's most important is that I feel more comfortable in my own skin than I ever have before.

With everything my mom has gone through with her health, I'm all too aware that life is uncertain. She's doing great now, and I hope she and I will both live long, happy lives—but still, the only thing I can be sure of is now. And I am going to take that now and live it to the fullest with the one I love.

I love Danny Villaseñor with all my heart.

I trust him, and I know that underneath that former playboy exterior is a heart of gold. He's one of the most loving people I have ever met. He'd shut himself off because he was scared—but he doesn't have to be scared anymore.

Danny, though, is lifting his chin and puffing out his chest in the way he does when he's feeling a little insecure. I can tell that this setting is bringing back his own difficult high school memories.

We step into the main room, where he's immediately surrounded by a group of girls who all give him hugs and coo over him. I recognize Jessamyn, who's cut my hair several times, and she enfolds me in an embrace.

"I just knew you were going to end up with Danny," she murmurs in my ear. "He's a good one."

The room is huge, and there are quite a few people dancing already, although more are gathered in small groups, talking. I can tell that Danny is nervous about seeing his ex-boyfriend.

He introduces me to person after person but stills when a ginger-haired man walks through the door alone. "Fuck," he mutters.

"Is that him?"

Danny nods.

"Then introduce me." I go on my tiptoes and say in his ear, "I've got you. And you've got this."

He kisses me, takes my hand, and walks over. Some of his normal confidence has returned, and I don't think it's bravado. I think knowing we're together is giving him strength.

"Brian," he says, and the guy startles.

"Danny."

Danny lets go of my hand long enough to give him a bro hug but then clasps it again. "Hey. Good to see you. Um, this is my boyfriend, Alden Meyer."

Brian gives me what looks like a genuine smile. "Nice to meet you." He turns his attention to Danny. "Wow. You look great."

"Thanks." I can feel the tension washing out of Danny. Because this is him facing his personal bogeyman.

Except that Brian's just a man. He's normal. Seems like he's happy enough.

They chat for a few minutes about what they've been doing in recent years, and then Brian digs in his pocket and produces a small box. "I know this is weird, but I found this in my things, and I thought I'd return it. I know I hurt you. But I think things turned out for the best. Don't you?"

Danny takes the box and chuckles, turning it over in his hand. "Yeah," he says. He smiles at me. "Things really did turn out for the best."

* * *

We stay for dinner and dessert, but after a few dances, Danny turns to me and mutters in my ear, "Let's get out of here."

I grin. "One?"

"One," he confirms.

When we get there, both wearing tuxedos and looking sharp, every eye turns to take us in. I feel like, yeah, my boyfriend is hot. You wish you had him.

He gets me a soda, and we dance, laughing and smiling and having a great time. When it's time for a break and we're waiting at the bar for another drink, some guy comes up and taps Danny's shoulder. "Hey, you busy later?"

Old me would be so jealous.

No, old me would be hiding in the corner. Old me would've never come here. Old me wouldn't know I even liked to dance.

But it's a new Danny, too. He slings an arm around my shoulders and kisses my cheek. "Yep, I'm busy with the love of my life." He gives a "What can you do?" sort of shrug, and the guy slinks away.

I lean into Danny, trying not to be smug. I don't want to be smug. I mean, not everyone can find true love the way we have.

Okay, yes. I'm smug. "I'm so happy I have you all to myself," I say into his ear.

He pulls me into his arms and kisses me.

Then the kiss turns deeper.

Then it turns dirty. Tongues sliding against each other and hands caressing bodies until I whisper, "Time to go somewhere more private."

"Your place or mine?" he asks.

"Wherever you are is good enough for me."

We tumble out into the night. It's a warm Los Angeles evening, and people are standing around outside vaping and smoking. We're too engrossed in each other to pay much attention to anything else.

When we get to the Lyft, I have to hold myself back from sitting in Danny's lap. We kiss and kiss and kiss, then barely say goodbye to the driver before spilling into his house. "This really should be your house, too," he says.

"Okay," I agree, and he grins against my mouth.

Since I spend more time here than at my own house anyway, and my mom's feeling so much better, it's the logical choice.

Only logic has nothing to do with it. It's all for love.

Clothes are shed. Kissing continues. We make it to the bed with hard dicks and soft hearts. With love and passion and everything in between.

# *Epilogue—Danny*

*One year later*

Alden and I are sitting behind third base at Dodger Stadium. He's yelling at the ref, and I'm laughing hard because he cracks me up.

He sits back down in a huff. "That call was wrong."

"I know, babe." I kiss his cheek. "They'll get it right the next time."

"Hope so. Peanuts?"

He offers me the bag, and I take some, but I basically spend the game watching him and grinning. Because he's mine. No matter what, no matter who is around, no matter what anyone thinks. This man is mine.

And I trust that he's going to be mine for the rest of my life. He accepts me for who I am, flaws and all. And I accept him for who he is, flaws and all. Alden tells me what he thinks and believes. He tells me when he isn't comfortable with something, and he tells me when he is.

And he tells me that he loves me.

The churro guy comes by, and I buy us two, handing one to

Alden, who grins at me. "I love these things, even though they're gross here," he says.

"I know. It's just expensive bits of long, lukewarm dough. My mom makes better ones."

"We should ask her to," he says. "But the crappy food is part of what makes it a baseball game."

"And the balls."

"I like balls." He winks at me.

"Oh, don't say that. I'll be slinging you over my shoulder and taking you home before the seventh-inning stretch if you're not careful."

"Promises, promises."

I boop him on the nose.

The Dodgers are doing okay, and I'm distracted as usual by all the lights and music and statistics.

But then it's time for the kiss cam. I get a fluttery feeling in my chest as we watch the camera focus on obvious couples.

Until I see my face along with Alden's on the DodgerVision screen.

Alden smiles at me. Before I can move in, he kisses me quickly, and the crowd goes wild.

Little does he know I have a small box in my pocket with a brand-new ring in it.

But I'll get to that after the game.

# Acknowledgments

Goodness. I have a lot of people to thank, and as usual, I don't know what order to do it in because different people help with the multiple parts of writing and publishing a book at various times—but they're all *integral*.

Side note: without the following people's help, I have a 70% chance of getting a comma right. None of them has seen these acknowledgments. Apologies for any errors.

From those who help me develop ideas, to those who proofread it at the end, I'm extremely grateful to the following people for directly helping me with *Studious*:

For development, beta reading, and sensitivity reading: Kristy Lin Billuni, Mary Carr, Megan Dischinger, Melissa Smith Schmidt, and Florence Héroux.

For editing: Alicia Z. Ramos. I feel like I need to emphasize her, because her assistance was and is extraordinary. So, I extra special again thank Alicia Z. Ramos. She'd tell me to delete that second one as repetitive, but she's not here to do it, so too bad.

For proofreading: Virginia Tesi Carey, Jerica MacMillan, and Katy Cuthbertson.

For the cover: Cory Stierley, photographer; Mikey Tarasow, model; Garrett Leigh, designer.

For support, my cohort of MM authors: Rachel Ember, J.E. Birk, Charley Descoteaux, and A.J. Truman.

For promotion: Heather Roberts and Lily Blunt.

For inspiration: LaTina Berkley made a hug book like the one in the book, and I'm using the idea with her permission.

For delivering me mint chip ice cream, Bud Light Lime, and nachos while writing (not at the same time); getting up at dawn to watch Formula 1 races and staying up late for Marvel movies (not at the same time); talking me into zip lining, falconry, and kayaking while on vacation (not at the same time); making me do deadlifts, squats, and bench presses (not at the same time); hanging every rainbow flag Amazon has on our walls (those *are* at the same time); and singing along at every Beck or twenty one pilots concert I can drag you to: my family.

I am sending you, my reader, all the love in my heart and my gratitude for reading this book. Please don't forget to leave a review! I appreciate you more than you know.

# Also by Leslie McAdam

### Sarina Bowen's World of True North (m/m)

*Undone* (audio narrated by Iggy Toma and Tim Paige)

*Unmanageable* (audio narrated by Jacob Morgan and Teddy Hamilton)

### IOU Series (m/m)

*Ambiguous* (audio narrated by Hamish Long and Kirt Graves)

*Studious*

*Oblivious* (coming soon)

### Contemporary Romance (m/f)

### All American Boy Series

*Boy on a Train* (audio narrated by Desiree Ketchum and James Cavenaugh)

### Romantic comedies with Lex Martin

*All About the D* (audio narrated by Stephen Dexter and Ava Erickson)

*Surprise, Baby!* (audio narrated by Jacob Morgan and Muffy Newton)

### The Giving You ... series

*The Sun and the Moon* (audio narrated by Tor Thom and Charley Ongel)

*The Stars in the Sky*

*All the Waters of the Earth*

*The Ground Beneath Our Feet* (audio narrated by Tor Thom and Charley Ongel)

# About the Author

Leslie McAdam is a California girl who loves romance and well-defined abs. She lives in a drafty old farmhouse on a small orange tree farm in Southern California with her husband and two children. Leslie's first published book, *The Sun and the Moon*, won a 2015 Watty, which is the world's largest online writing competition. She's gone on to receive additional literary awards and has been featured in multiple publications, including Cosmopolitan.com. Her books have been Top 100 Bestsellers on both Amazon and Apple Books. Leslie is employed by day but spends her nights writing about the men of your fantasies.

Website: https://www.lesliemcadamauthor.com
M/M-only newsletter: http://eepurl.com/hD9a4r

www.ingramcontent.com/pod-product-compliance
Lightning Source LLC
Chambersburg PA
CBHW071254250626
47159CB00004B/1175